Also by ReShonda Tate Billingsley

The Pastor's Wife

Everybody Say Amen

I Know I've Been Changed

Let the Church Say Amen

My Brother's Keeper

Have a Little Faith

(with Jacquelin Thomas, J. D. Mason, and Sandra Kitt)

And check out ReShonda's Young Adult titles:

Getting Even

With Friends Like These

Blessings in Disguise

Nothing But Drama

can I
get a
witness?

ReShonda Tate Billingsley

POCKET BOOKS

New York   London   Toronto   Sydney

Pocket Books
A Division of Simon & Schuster, Inc.
1230 Avenue of the Americas
New York, NY 10020

Manufactured in the United States of America

ISBN: 978-0-7394-9807-1

To Tanisha
(now please stop harassing me to dedicate a book to you)

Acknowledgments

ac·knowl·edg·ment *noun*

1. an act of acknowledging.
2. an expression of appreciation.
3. a thing done or given in appreciation or gratitude.

—from www.dictionary.reference.com

Here I am . . . embarking on another literary endeavor and facing the hardest part of penning the book—writing the acknowledgments. I felt the need to clarify just what an acknowledgment was for those who called me everything but a child of God for leaving their name off. (Yes, that really happened. I try to tell people it's not that serious, but to some folks, obviously it is.)

As much as I would love to include everyone who has crossed my path in life—my stepbrother's third cousin on my great-granddaddy's side . . . I simply can't. (My editor only gives me so much room.) So, I have to reserve my acknowledgments for those individuals to whom I want to show appreciation for their assistance in **THIS PARTICULAR BOOK**. I am so grateful if you gave me a comment on my first book, but this is thirteen books later . . . so, please don't hold it against me if you're not included here.

Okay . . . coming down off my soapbox. . . .

I am eternally grateful to God that I'm even able to write acknowledgments once again for He has blessed me with the ability to tell stories people want to read. I kid about it, but I'm actually so thankful that I have family, friends, coworkers, classmates, and people who sat next to me on the bus in 1984, who want to be included in my works.

I have to, of course, give my next biggest thanks to my husband, Dr. Miron Billingsley, who pushed me to reach for the stars from the very first moment we met. You supported me, encouraged me, and even carried me when I didn't have the strength to keep going. Thank you for everything.

I would never be able to churn out books the way I do were it not for my wonderful support system. My mother, Nancy Blacknell, who told me for years, "I'm not your friend, I'm your mama." I'm glad to count you now as a friend as well. I know that I can never repay you for all you've done for me (I know you're saying I can at least try). You don't always understand my writing process, but thank you for just patting me on the back and saying, "If you like it, I love it."

My sister, Tanisha Tate. I heard someone tell you that you were lucky to have a sister who is doing all the stuff I do. I want them to know, I'm the lucky one. Thank you for all that you do.

Acknowledgments

To LaWonda "LaShay" Smith, you will never know what a blessing you have been in my life. I can never say it enough—I so appreciate all that you do to keep my life running smoothly. You make me shine; now go do you.

To the woman who proves God does answer prayers, Fay Square. You are a lifesaver. You allow me to do what I do, work like I work, and know that my children are in good hands. Thank you for going above and beyond the call of duty and allowing me to travel and work with peace of mind.

To my self-appointed personal stylist, spiritual advisor, and dear friend, Jaimi Canady (I know I'm a challenge, but thanks for hanging in there with me anyway).

To my friend/therapist/motivator/sister friend and partner in crime, Pat Tucker Wilson, a talented slept-on writer. Shake the haters off and keep doing your thang!

Of course, as always, I show much, much love to my agent, Sara Camilli; my editor, Brigitte Smith; my publicist, Melissa Gramstad; and my publisher, Louise Burke, for giving me the opportunity to shine.

To my good friend, Nina Foxx, who is helping me "elevate myself" . . . thanks for the inspiration. To the other women of the Femme Fantastik—Lori Bryant Woolridge, Carmen Green, Trisha Thomas, Berta Platas, and Wendy Coakley-Thompson—you are absolutely fantastic and I'm honored to be in your ranks.

To Dr. Juanita Bynum, Holly Davis Carter, and Jeff Clanagan at Codeblack Entertainment, thank you soooooo much for making my wildest dreams come true!

Acknowledgments

Special thanks also goes to Sonny Messiah Jiles, Raquelle Lewis, Cale Carter, Candace K., Keith "D-Mars" Davis, Pam Walker, Saki Indakwa, Tamara Davidson, Curtis Bunn, Ken Smickle, and Angela Dotson at Black Issues Book Review.

You know, I've lost count of all the book clubs I've visited with, but I have to tell you I have no doubt that I am where I am in my career because of their support. Thanks to each and every one of you for showing me nothing but love. This go-round I have to give a special shout-out to: Pages Between Sistahs, Go On Girl, Pageturners Too, Cush City (Thanks for continuing to support me despite my hectic schedule!), Supremes, SOW, Cover 2 Cover, MochaReaders, Sistahs (Fayetteville, NC), BSURE, WOW, Black Women Who Read, Conversations (Thanks, Cyrus!), Black Pearls, Keepin' It Real, and all the other book clubs who read my latest two titles and told me you already had this one on the schedule!

Much love to my literary colleagues who provide encouragement and support and are struggling to do this book thing with me: Jihad, Victoria Christopher Murray, Zane, Eric Jerome Dickey, Norma Jarrett, Jacquelin Thomas, Tiffany Warren, and Eric Pete.

As always, much love goes to my wonderful, illustrious sorors, especially Mu Kappa Omega, Chi Omicron Omega, and the Houston Metropolitan Chapters. To all the other Greeks (especially the men of Omega Psi Phi), thanks for showing a sistah mad love and proving we really are all about Unity.

And finally to my family . . . thanks for the inspiration. Let's plan some more family get-togethers . . . I need some new material. . . .

Acknowledgments

Saving the best for last. . . . The biggest thanks of all goes to you, the readers who bought my books, passed the word, and continued to show me support. I am what I am because of you. Until the next book—thanks for the love.

ReShonda

Chapter 1

"Ain't nothing open at two in the morning but legs and liquor stores!" LaShawanna Jenkins wiggled her neck as she thrust a finger up in the air. Her golden braids swung from side to side like they were doing a sultry salsa dance. "And since he didn't come home drunk, you know where he was!"

Darius Jenkins's lip turned up as he fought back a smile.

"See, he thinks it's funny!" LaShawanna snapped. She threw her hands up in exasperation. "Your Honor, he got me messed up 'cuz I ain't the one." She cut her eyes at her husband of six years. "I told him, one mo' time. Just one mo' time and it was over. I guess he don't believe fat meat is greasy."

Judge Vanessa Colton-Kirk sighed as she gazed at the file in front of her. Every day, it was the same thing. Some couple who was once madly in love could no longer stand the sight of each other and came before her seeking a divorce.

Vanessa flipped through the stack of papers. Five kids. No assets. LaShawanna worked at a grocery store. Darius worked as an auto mechanic. Same story, different couple. Vanessa looked up from her papers. "So, Mrs. Jenkins, what is it that you are requesting?"

"I want out. And I want you to make him pay child support and alimony," LaShawanna barked. "And I want him to pay for my statue, which he broke when I put him out. That was my grandma's statue."

"It was a freakin' rooster, Your Honor," Darius said with a smirk.

"So? It was *my* rooster!" LaShawanna screamed.

Vanessa slammed down her gavel. "Please! Both of you, just be quiet." She turned toward LaShawanna. "Mrs. Jenkins, Texas is a non-alimony state, so I can't award your request for alimony. I will, however, order that Mr. Jenkins pay fourteen hundred dollars a month in child support."

"Fourteen hundred dollars!" Darius cried. "I ain't got that kind of money!"

Vanessa looked down at the folder again. "It says here that you bring home roughly twenty-four hundred dollars a month."

"I do, but how am I supposed to live?" he huffed.

Vanessa struggled to maintain her composure. She got so tired of these men who came through her courtroom and didn't want to pay child support. "Mr. Jenkins, if you don't pay to support your five children, who do you suppose will?" she asked, putting her hands underneath her chin.

The smirk was definitely gone from his face now. "Man, this is messed up." He groaned, running his hand over his immaculately braided hair. "I don't even know if Darianna and Demarcus are mine."

"No, you didn't!" LaShawanna shouted. "You know doggone well them your kids!"

Darius folded his arms across his chest. "I don't know nothing."

Vanessa took a deep breath and reminded herself that she had to endure this divorce court craziness in order to climb the ladder of her political career. "Mr. Jenkins, how old are Darianna and Demarcus?"

"Seven and nine."

"And did you not sign the birth certificate?"

"That's beside the point."

"I'm afraid it's not." Vanessa began signing the necessary paperwork to close out this case. "You have taken care of Darianna and Demarcus, along with your other three children, since their births. You have maintained that you were their father since birth." She set her pen down and looked up. "So as far as the courts are concerned, you are the father of each and every one of them. My order stands at fourteen hundred dollars a month."

"Yeah!" LaShawanna sang as she did a victory dance. "That's what you get. Tell your little bimbo that y'all gon' have to make do on a thousand dollars a month. 'Cuz the minute you're late, I'ma have your sorry butt thrown in jail!"

3

"Mrs. Jenkins!" Vanessa snapped.

LaShawanna covered her mouth, though she was still delighted. "I'm sorry, Your Honor."

Vanessa shook her head. "Whatever," she mumbled. "Divorce is granted."

She pounded her gavel one more time as she stood, grabbed her folders, and headed back to her chambers.

Her secretary, Nicole, was waiting right outside her office. She had a folded-up newspaper clutched in her hand. "Judge Colton-Kirk, here's the article I was telling you about." She held the paper out toward Vanessa. "It's an awesome article. Everyone around the courthouse is talking about it."

Vanessa smiled as she took the *Houston Defender*. She had done the interview with the *Defender* reporter two weeks ago, but she had no idea it was going to be an entire five-column profile. " 'Houston Judge Is Heading Places,' " she recited, reading the headline.

"And it even has a quote in there from Judge Malveaux, talking about what a great judge you are and how you have such a promising future," Nicole excitedly said.

Vanessa was shocked. She and Judge Malveaux didn't see eye to eye on a lot of things, so she was surprised that he would go on record as saying something positive about her. She tucked the paper under her arm. "Thanks, Nicole. I'll read it when I get a moment."

Nicole smiled in admiration before making her way back to her desk.

As much as Vanessa loved her job as the judge of Houston's

infamous Divorce Court Number Three, these people could work her nerves. Before the Jenkinses, she'd fielded a couple who had tried a ménage à trois and the wife had ended up falling for the other woman her husband brought in. Yesterday, it was an Anna Nicole wannabe who'd married a man old enough to be her grandfather and divorced him a year later, taking half his money. His family had been furious, but the law was the law, and the law said she was entitled to half.

"Well, I see you've destroyed yet another marriage."

Vanessa walked into her office and threw the folders on her desk, which was covered with a stack of files that all needed her immediate attention. "Hello to you, too, Aunt Ida."

Ida was sitting in the chair in front of Vanessa's large mahogany desk. She wore her usual conservative lace-collared dress and pearls, and her small-framed black glasses were perched on the edge of her nose. Her curly gray hair poked out from under her Sunday-best hat, which she wore proudly even though it was just Thursday. Her Bible, which she never went anywhere without, sat prominently on her lap.

"Don't hello me. You should've made them children go to counseling or something. That's what's wrong with young folks these days, don't want to work at nothing. Just want to throw in the towel at the first sign of trouble." She sighed heavily.

Sweeping the hem of her black robe to one side, Vanessa sat down behind her desk and smiled at her great-aunt. Ida Mae Colton had been like a mother to Vanessa since her own parents died in a fire when she was six years old. Her grandparents had died years before, and Aunt Ida—her grandmother's youngest sister—was the only one who could take in Vanessa and her two sisters, Rosolyn and Dionne.

"Auntie, I've told you before, I don't destroy marriages." Vanessa opened up a drawer and pulled out a small mirror. She gazed at her reflection, taking note of a gray hair that was sprouting at the top of her hairline. Her flawless caramel-colored skin made people think she was a lot younger than her thirty-five years. "I simply preside over their breakups," she continued, plucking the offending hair out.

"Umphh. You the one with all the power. Seems like to me you can make them stay together," Ida grumbled.

"That's absurd." Satisfied, Vanessa placed the mirror back in the drawer. "I can't make anyone stay together."

"I know you can't make them, but you can encourage them. They need Jesus." Aunt Ida reached over and picked up one of the folders to fan her robust frame.

Vanessa laughed as she stuck her hand out for her aunt to give her the folder. "That's your answer to everything, Aunt Ida."

Ida, ignoring the outstretched hand, kept fanning. "It sure is. There ain't no other answer. That's why these marriages today ain't working, 'cuz folks ain't got Jesus at the center of their marriage."

Aunt Ida was the most religious person Vanessa had ever met. But all her years of forcing Vanessa to go to church—not to mention the shady things that went on at some of these churches—had only turned Vanessa off. Now she didn't go unless she was making a personal appearance or it was an election year.

"So, are you ready to go?" Vanessa asked.

Ida stood, finally setting the folder back on the desk. "You can try to shush me all you want, but you know I'm telling you the truth."

"Mmm-hmm," Vanessa said as she stood and slipped out of her robe. She brushed a piece of lint off of her crisp navy Dana Buchman suit. "What time do you have to be at the doctor's office?"

"At four. And I could've gone by myself. I don't need an escort."

"I want to go, because it's the only way I can be sure *you'll* go." Ida had scared everyone after a mild heart attack last year. But she'd pulled through it, and Vanessa and her sisters had vowed to make sure she took care of herself: they took turns taking her to the doctor.

Vanessa glanced at her watch. "Let's get going. I have a reception at six."

"Reception? Isn't today your anniversary?"

Vanessa nodded as she reached for her purse. "Yes, and Thomas has called a hundred times, telling me to make sure I'm home at a decent hour because he has a special night planned."

"Don't sound so excited," Ida mumbled as she walked to the door. "You'd think a woman celebrating her five-year anniversary would be more enthusiastic."

Vanessa swung her crocodile Hermès purse over her shoulder. "It's not that. I just know he's going to start in on me about kids again, and I'm tired of that argument."

"I don't understand why you haven't given that boy any babies yet." Ida shook her head in amazement.

This was a sore point between them, and Vanessa was tired of Ida harping on it, too. "I keep telling you, the time just isn't right."

"The time will never be right, let you tell it."

Vanessa gently pushed her aunt out of the office. "Let's go." She didn't want to have this discussion with Ida—bad enough she knew she was going to hear it from Thomas. He claimed his biological clock was ticking and Vanessa knew he would use their five-year anniversary to hammer home the point that they weren't getting any younger.

Vanessa also knew it was just a matter of time before she was going to have to give in. But in her life plan, she had until forty before she needed to start worrying. And that was five whole years away.

She draped her arm through her aunt's as they walked out to her car. "Stop all that frowning, Auntie. It creates wrinkles," she said, trying to lighten the mood.

"I'm just worried about you, baby girl." Ida sighed heavily.

"Don't be," Vanessa replied. "Thomas and I have a good life. We understand each other, even if he does get upset from time to time."

Ida didn't respond, but Vanessa could tell she was more worried than she was letting on. Vanessa wasn't. She had her husband right in her back pocket.

Chapter 2

Vanessa worriedly checked her watch. Thomas was going to blow a gasket. She handed the valet a five-dollar tip as she jumped into her silver Mercedes S500. She calculated how long it would take her to make it from the Galleria to her home in Missouri City, a suburb of Houston. Even if she sped like a crazy lady all the way, she still had a good twenty minutes before she made it home. That meant she wouldn't get there until well after ten.

Vanessa took her cell phone out of the glove compartment. She had purposefully left it in the car because she knew Thomas would be calling. She flipped open the phone. She was right. Eight missed calls. One from her baby sister, Dionne. The rest were from Thomas.

Vanessa knew Dionne didn't want anything—she never did. And she knew Thomas wasn't doing anything but going off in his messages. "I don't even feel like hearing that drama," Vanessa mumbled as she tossed the phone onto the passenger seat.

Vanessa played out all of the excuses in her mind as she navigated onto the 610 freeway. Maybe she could tell him that Congresswoman Leary wanted her to stick around and meet some very important people. Or maybe she could tell him that the governor was considering her for a Regents spot for a local university and she'd needed to hang around and talk to him about it.

She sighed. For some reason she just didn't see any of those excuses flying with Thomas. All he would say was that she'd stood him up again—and on their anniversary.

"Dang it!" Vanessa slammed her hand on the steering wheel when she realized she hadn't stopped to pick up the Movado watch she'd custom-ordered for Thomas. Now, not only was she late, but she was about to show up without a gift as well.

She banged her head against the back of her seat. Why did she do this? Yes, Thomas was sweet and mild-tempered, and she never wanted to take advantage of that. Yet she found herself doing exactly that time and time again.

"I'll make it up to you, baby," she mumbled as she pressed the gas pedal, trying to hurry home.

Fifteen minutes later, Vanessa pulled into her garage. She climbed out of her car, took a deep breath, and made her way inside their lavishly decorated six-thousand-square-foot home. Ida had blasted them for buying a house so big, but both Vanessa and Thomas had exquisite taste and loved the finer things in life.

She half expected to see Thomas seated glumly at the dining room table, surrounded by the remnants of a romantic dinner. A dwindled, no-longer-lit candle rose in the middle of the long oak table, but nothing more. Vanessa made her way into the kitchen, where she saw all of the food Thomas had no doubt spent all evening cooking. A china plate containing grilled tilapia, asparagus, and roasted new potatoes sat on the granite countertop. Vanessa reached over and touched the fish. It was cold. Another plate was in the sink, the food still on it.

Vanessa inhaled deeply. This was worse than she'd thought. She called for her husband. "Thomas?"

She made her way toward the back staircase. "Sweetie, I'm so sorry, let me explain." Vanessa still hadn't figured out what she would tell her husband but she knew she had to make this up to him.

She saw the light shining under their bedroom door, which was closed. He was probably sitting in there watching TV and ignoring her.

"Baby, please give me a chance to explain." Vanessa eased the door open. "I never intended on staying long, but this was a very important reception. Remember, I told—"

She stopped in her tracks at the sight of her husband leaning over the bed, placing a stack of clothes in a large black suitcase. As always, he was immaculately dressed, wearing a crisp mustard button-down shirt and black linen pants. He had a fresh haircut, making him look like the actor Boris Kodjoe.

"Thomas, what are you doing?"

He didn't respond as he walked over to the dresser and pulled some more clothes out of the open bottom drawer.

"Thomas? I said, what are you doing?"

He stopped briefly, glared at her, then walked over to the bed again without bothering to respond.

Vanessa walked around to the other side of the bed. "Oh, so you're ignoring me now? I asked you what you were doing."

"What does it look like? You're the genius judge," he coolly replied as he dropped the clothes in the overpriced, oversize Cole Haan suitcase. Thomas was a connoisseur of the finer things. That's what she was trying to give him—a better life full of fine things. Granted, he made good money as an architect, but she still made more, not to mention the power and respect she had the potential to bring in. They used to be on the same page, but now he'd become obsessed with having a family and spending time together. Not only were they not on the same page anymore, they weren't even in the same book.

"What are you doing?" she repeated.

"Why do you care?"

Vanessa sighed as she slipped her purse off her shoulder and set it down on the nightstand. "Thomas, you're being unreasonable. I have a perfectly good explanation for missing dinner."

He zipped the suitcase closed. "You always do." His voice was calm as he picked up the suitcase and headed toward the door.

"Are you really leaving?" she asked, feeling a slight prickle of fear.

"Yes, I really am."

She threw up her hands. "I cannot believe you're acting like this over a stupid dinner." As soon as she said it, Vanessa wished she could take the words back.

Thomas spun around and dropped the suitcase. His eyes spat daggers. "That's just it, Vanessa." His voice remained steady. "It wasn't a *stupid* dinner to me. And the fact that it was to you means we have a fundamental problem." He took a deep breath like he was trying his best to stay calm. "I'm tired of this one-sided marriage. I could've gone to the Rockets game with my friends from work tonight. Or I could've taken the two-week assignment in Brazil like my supervisor wanted me to. But you know what? I told my friends, I told my boss, I couldn't do it because it would interfere with my five-year wedding anniversary." His controlled tone was getting louder. "That meant something to me!"

He picked up his suitcase again. "I'm sick of this. I'm sick of giving, only to have you fit me into your schedule when you feel like it. I'm sick of putting my needs on the back burner for you."

"Oh, here we go with this again." Vanessa sighed, exasperated. "Why did I know it would come back to this, having a baby?"

Thomas laughed. "Something else that isn't important to you."

"We've been over this a thousand times, Thomas. We'll have a child when the time is right."

"And when will that be, Vanessa?" He paused and waited for her to answer. When she didn't, he continued, "You know when I think it'll be? Never. Because you will always find something more important to do." He added ominously, "There are women who would love to give me a child."

Vanessa folded her arms across her chest. "What does that mean, Thomas?"

The fire lighting his eyes dimmed again. "It doesn't mean anything, Vanessa. I'm just sick of this. You knew I wanted kids when you agreed to marry me. You told me you wanted them, too."

"I do . . . it's just—"

He cut her off. "Yeah, I know, the timing isn't right. You know, I accepted that you weren't ready for as long as I could. And I'm tired."

She shook her head. "Everything's about you, isn't it, Thomas?"

"Oh, forget it," Thomas muttered. "Why bother?" He headed to the door. "You go on to your political parties. You continue to hobnob with the big dogs. But me, I'm done."

Vanessa left the side of the bed and followed him downstairs. She'd never seen him so determined. Usually she could coax him out of his bad mood. "So, just like that, you're going to walk out?"

"This isn't 'just like' anything. I'm through, Vanessa. It's taken me five years, but I get it. I finally get it. You were born to be by yourself. That's not what I want in a wife."

Vanessa watched as Thomas picked up his keys and headed toward the garage. This was definitely the angriest she had ever seen him. She contemplated following him, but then she stopped and reconsidered. It wasn't so bad. This wasn't the first time he'd gotten so upset that he left. He was probably going over to his best friend Bernard's house to cool off.

Vanessa walked over to the garage door and watched as he pulled out.

He shot her a hostile look and Vanessa fought back a tear. "I'm sorry, baby," she whispered. "I promise I'll make this up to you."

She turned and walked back into the house. She'd convince him how sorry she was tomorrow. For now, she'd give him a minute to cool down. But tomorrow, she promised herself, she was going to show her husband just how sorry she really was.

Chapter 3

Dionne Colton flashed a euphoric smile at the man lying next to her. Roland was definitely *the* one. He was her heart, her soul mate, the man she hoped to spend the rest of her life with. Their relationship was going wonderfully, and Dionne had no doubt that she would meet her goal of being married before thirty after all.

"Good morning, baby," she said as his eyes fluttered open. They were in his king-size bed at his sparsely decorated two-bedroom apartment on the north side of Houston. Even at eight in the morning, he looked like he should be gracing the cover of some men's health magazine. His dark chocolate skin was smooth, and his perfectly cut body was testament to the hours he spent in the gym. His almond-shaped eyes, closely cropped fade, and LL Cool J lips were just the icing on the cake.

Roland greeted her with that warm smile she loved so much. "How is my pretty lady this morning?" he said.

"Awwww." She ran her fingers through her honey-colored mane. She had been told numerous times that she looked like a shorter version of Tyra Banks, so she had no problem in the self-esteem department. But it still made her giddy to hear Roland say it. "You really think I'm pretty this early in the morning?"

"You're pretty no matter what time of day it is." He sat up, stretched, then kissed her lips. "Funky breath and all," he joked.

Dionne swatted his chest with one hand while covering her mouth with the other.

He grabbed her arms. "Oooh, I like my women violent." He pulled her over on top of him as he fell back on the bed. "You're gonna get me worked up all over again." He leaned up and passionately kissed her.

As he covered her neck with kisses, Dionne moaned in delight and muttered, "I love you so much, baby." He planted more kisses. "Tell me you love me, too," she whispered.

"Mmmmm-hmmm," he mumbled.

Dionne pulled back slightly. She was easily irritated and Roland was about to take her there. "Just say it, baby. Why won't you say it?"

Roland stopped kissing her when he saw how serious she was. He quickly pushed her off of him. "There you go with that again," he said as she fell back over on the bed.

Dionne sat up, not letting him get the upper hand. "There I go with what?"

"With that old bratty attitude that I can't stand. Why you always gotta ruin the mood?" He threw back the covers and swung his feet over the edge of his bed.

"I'm ruining the mood because I want you to tell me you love me?" she asked, incredulously. "And what do you mean bratty attitude?" Dionne knew she tended to get an attitude when things weren't going her way. It was a trait she was working on, but stuff like this with Roland didn't make it any easier.

Roland sighed in frustration, then began looking around the floor for his boxer shorts.

"Answer me, Roland. I mean, I'm starting to wonder." She pulled up the sheets so she was fully covered. "You claim you want to be with me. Shoot, you act like you want to be with me. Yet every time I talk about love or marriage, you get all brand-new on me. You know I want to get married." She pouted and waited for him to respond—then fumed as he slipped on his boxer shorts and continued to ignore her.

"So, now you're just gonna act like you don't hear me?" She couldn't stand to be ignored. "Why don't you ever want to talk about love or marriage?"

"Can I at least let the ink get dry on my divorce papers?" he huffed. He was supposed to have his final divorce hearing in a month. He'd been separated from his wife Liz for two years, and Dionne was ecstatic that they were finally about to make it official.

At the thought of him finalizing his divorce, her voice grew softer. "I'm not asking you to marry me right away. I'm just saying, at least let me know you love me." She looked at him with pleading eyes.

Dionne had been with Roland for a year now. She'd been patient and understanding while he went through a bitter divorce with his wife, even enduring the constant harassment from Liz, who tried her best to make Roland's life miserable. They would've been divorced by now if she hadn't fought him on every little issue. It wasn't like Liz even still wanted him. She just wanted to make him pay for cheating on her, which was why they were getting a divorce in the first place.

Or so Dionne thought. She also thought she would have long been married by now, but Roland had been the closest thing to a prospect she'd had in a while. He had a good job, made good money, and treated her like a queen. She was desperate for them to move forward.

Roland stopped just as he was slipping his T-shirt on and spun toward her. "You know, Dionne. I'm so sick of this conversation. Every time things are going good, you want to mess—"

The sound of someone banging on the door caused him to stop talking in mid-sentence.

Roland was grateful for the distraction, and hurried out of the bedroom. Dionne threw on her baby-doll T-shirt and Daisy Duke shorts and followed him out. She was about to go make some coffee when she saw the horrified expression that crossed his face after he looked out the peephole.

"Oh, no!" He groaned.

"What?" Dionne asked.

"Shhhh," he replied, holding a finger up to his lips.

"Open this door, Roland!" the voice on the other side screamed. "I saw your ol' nasty eyeball in the peephole, so don't act like you ain't there!"

Roland muttered curse words as he looked around frantically.

"Who is that?" Dionne asked, surprised. She'd never seen him like this.

"Awww, naw!" the woman screamed. "Is that a female's voice I hear?" She started kicking the door, landing solid thumps. "I know you don't have another woman in there!"

"Oh, no. Oh, no," Roland muttered as he paced back and forth across the living room floor.

"Roland, who is that?" Dionne asked again, this time more forcefully.

"That's my girlfriend," he growled, wringing his hands.

"Your *what*?"

"My girlfriend, Tasha. And she is crazy." Roland regarded Dionne with a look of panic. "Look, I'm gonna need you to hide."

Dionne couldn't believe what he was saying. "Have you lost your mind? I'm not *hiding* anywhere. And what the hell do you mean, your girlfriend? Since when did you get a girlfriend?"

Roland was distracted as he said, "Since '99. Off and on."

"Since 1999?" she said, shocked.

He nodded helplessly.

"B-but you've been married five years."

"I was with her before I got married." He ran his hands over his closely shaven head. He looked at the door, then back at Dionne.

"But you said you got married in 2002."

"I did." He squeezed his eyes closed like he was in pain. "I don't believe this. She is going to kill us both."

"Open this door, Roland! I ain't playin' with you!"

Tasha kicked the door so hard it seemed like the hinges would come off, and Dionne jumped. "So you mean to tell me the woman on the other side of the door has been your girlfriend the whole time you were married?" she asked in disbelief.

"Something like that," Roland admitted.

"I do not believe this." It was Dionne's turn to start pacing. What had she done wrong in her life? Why was God punishing her so when it came to men? Her last boyfriend had turned out to swing both ways, and the boyfriend before that dumped her to "focus on his rap career." All she wanted to do was find a decent man and settle down.

Suddenly a sour memory came to her. Roland had explained to Dionne how Liz had caught him with another woman, which was why she was so bitter toward him. But he'd definitely left out the part about the other woman being a long-term girlfriend. "Is that who Liz caught you with?"

Roland nervously bit his lip. "That's her."

Dionne was astonished. "But we spend almost every night together." This wasn't making sense. How could Roland have a girlfriend?

"She lives in Dallas," Roland said, as if he were reading her mind. "Sh-she hung in there because she thought we'd get married. She put up with my wife, but she's gonna go ballistic if she sees you here." Roland grabbed Dionne's hand. "Go hide just until I can get rid of her. Please?"

Dionne snatched her hand away, then crossed her arms defiantly to let him know she wasn't about to hide anywhere. She jumped when another crash came from the door. Roland looked like he wanted to curse her out before he turned and sprinted down the hallway into his bedroom.

"Open this door, Roland!" Tasha screamed again. "I'm not goin' anywhere, so you might as well open the door!"

Dionne shook her head in disgust. This was ridiculous. She was not about to fight some woman over a two-timing dog. She felt a headache coming on. She wasn't in the mood for a confrontation, but she wasn't about to hide out in Roland's house either.

Dionne stomped to the door and unlocked it.

The woman burst in before she could even get the door open. "Roland, get your sorry behind out here!" She spun toward Dionne like she was just noticing her presence. She didn't look as ghetto as she sounded. Her fiery red hair sat in a bushy ponytail on top of her head. She was very pretty and had to be a good five nine, her thick frame towering over Dionne. "I knew I heard a woman in here. Who are you?" Tasha snapped, one of her hands going to her hip.

"I'm the *other* girlfriend—the one who didn't know you existed," Dionne said, shaking her head.

"Oh, really?" Tasha responded, looking around the room. "Where is Roland?"

"Cowering in the bedroom, I suppose." Dionne pointed, hard, toward the back. It was taking everything in her power to contain her anger.

Tasha ran her eyes up and down Dionne before taking off to the bedroom. "Oh, it's about to be on," she spat.

Dionne quickly followed her down the hall. They both stopped in the doorway to Roland's bedroom, which was empty. The flimsy gold curtain was flapping through the open window. Dionne and Tasha both raced over to the window just in time to see Roland reach the fence in the back of the apartment building and begin to climb.

"Oh, you wanna run like a little punk, huh?" Tasha screamed out the window after him.

Roland looked back just as he made it over the fence.

"You forget I ran track in high school!" Tasha kicked off her shoes and swung one leg over the windowsill. She stopped with her body halfway out and turned to Dionne. "And if you know what's good for you, you'd better be gone when I get back."

The next thing Dionne knew, Tasha had climbed out of the second-story window and taken off after Roland.

The whole thing was like a scene out of a bad movie. She didn't know exactly what, if anything, Tasha would do to her when she returned. But she did know one thing—she wasn't about to stick around and find out.

She and Roland were through.

Chapter 4

"So let me get this straight," Ida said as she leaned back in Rosolyn's recliner. "Not only was the man two-timing you, but he took off like a little pansy and left you in his apartment with his girlfriend?"

Dionne let out a disgusted sigh and took another sip of her wine. "And I haven't heard from him since."

Ida shook her head. "And this happened when?"

"Day before yesterday," Dionne replied.

"I told you there was something sneaky about that boy," Ida replied, shaking her Bible at Dionne. She'd only met Roland a couple of times, but like the rest of the family, she didn't particularly care for him.

Vanessa watched her aunt and sister go around and around.

Can I Get a Witness?

She hadn't really felt like visiting tonight, but it was her older sister Rosolyn's birthday, and Vanessa knew she couldn't bail on her birthday dinner, which they had been planning for months. They were all at Rosolyn's house, a three-thousand-square-foot cookie-cutter home that Rosolyn had decorated to look like something out of *Better Homes and Gardens*.

They'd just finished dinner and were now sitting around the living room talking, eating cake, and drinking tea, except for Dionne, who was on her third glass of wine.

"I thought we were going to get married," Dionne whined. "I can't believe he was playing me all along."

"I can. Shoot, the boy didn't make nothing but booty calls."

"Aunt Ida!" Vanessa admonished.

"What?" She flashed a stare at her grandniece. "It's the truth and you know it's the truth. In my day, if a man couldn't call me before six, he didn't need to call me at all." She turned toward Dionne. "You let that boy come over whenever he felt like it. Hmmph. He was probably coming over your house so late because he was at her house at a decent hour."

"She doesn't even live here. She lives in Dallas," Dionne said defensively.

"Well, maybe he has yet another girlfriend because he sure wasn't giving you his time," Ida muttered. "Except after hours."

"I knew I shouldn't have told you all that."

Just last week Dionne had shared with them that she didn't get to spend as much time with Roland as she would like because he was always working. In fact, she'd said the only real time they spent together was late at night.

"You had to talk to somebody," Vanessa said. She was actually worried about her little sister. Both she and Rosolyn had a protective nature when it came to Dionne, the baby of the family.

"Yeah, but I didn't expect y'all to throw it back in my face." She pouted like a little girl.

"Don't nobody care about you sticking your lips out," Ida continued. "It's bad enough that you get with him before his divorce was even final. But a man's only gonna do what you allow him to do, and you allowed him to play you, as you young folks like to say."

Vanessa contemplated telling her aunt to chill since it was obvious she was getting to Dionne. The last thing Vanessa needed when she was feeling blue was a big family argument.

Dionne sank in her seat. "Gee, thanks, Aunt Ida. You sure do have a way of making me feel better," she said sarcastically.

"I'm just trying to tell you. Then you want to talk about how y'all were supposed to be getting married," Ida said, shaking her head. "*You* probably were the *only* one talking about getting married. You know how desperate you are."

At this mean comment Dionne grabbed the wine and poured herself another glass. She stopped when she noticed Ida eyeing the bottle.

"And I surely hope you don't think you're going to find the answer to your troubles in there." She pointed toward the wine.

Dionne obeyed, putting the bottle back down. "What's so wrong with wanting to be married?"

"Nothing when you allow it to be done in God's time. Not your time," Ida responded.

"Well, God needs to come on because I'm ready."

"Maybe God wants you to get yourself together before He sends you a man," Ida said, wagging her finger.

Dionne rolled her eyes and Vanessa chuckled. Her aunt might as well be talking to a brick wall. Dionne had been obsessed with finding a husband since she was twenty-three. The funny thing was, she couldn't keep a decent boyfriend for more than six months, let alone find somebody to marry. She'd been needy all of her life and her men only exacerbated the problem, catering to her temper tantrums and childish demands. Since Dionne was just a baby when their parents died, everyone tried to overcompensate for her.

"Don't get Aunt Ida started on God," Vanessa warned.

Aunt Ida peered over her wide-rimmed glasses at Vanessa.

"What?" Vanessa asked, not really wanting an answer.

"I didn't say a word," Ida said, smiling thinly.

"You didn't have to," Vanessa responded, glancing toward the kitchen. "And what's taking Rosolyn so long to make some tea?" She turned back to see her aunt staring at her. "Why are you looking at me crazy?"

"Sounds like to me somebody else needs to be turning their relationship over to God as well."

Vanessa held up her hands to block off the onslaught. "Don't start with me. My relationship is fine."

"Mmmm-hmmm. How was your anniversary?" Ida pointed out.

It was Vanessa's turn to roll her eyes. "Of course, Thomas was upset. He left the house." She shuddered slightly, remembering the look of hatred he flashed before he left. "But he's just overreacting, being his usual childish self. I apologized for missing dinner, but it wasn't enough." She frowned, knowing she didn't deserve to be shut out like this. "He knows this is an election year."

"Ummph." Ida tsked. "Wonder if them polls keep you warm at night?" She turned toward Rosolyn, who had just walked out of the kitchen back into the living room. She was carrying another tray of tea and looked like the all-American housewife in a peach floral cotton dress that tied around the waist.

"You think them polls can take her to the hospital when she ain't feeling well? You think them voters gon' sit by her side as she lies on her deathbed, waiting to meet her Maker?"

Rosolyn smiled, displaying her deep dimples. A sea of curls framed her pear-shaped face. As usual, she wore only a hint of lip gloss. Vanessa was always after her to wear more makeup to bring out her natural beauty. "Uh-uh. Don't put me in the middle of that." She set the tray down and poured each of them some more hot tea. Dionne declined, instead raising her glass for more wine.

"You better tell your sister," Ida said as she eased up in her seat, picked up the bottle of wine, and firmly moved it next to her on the table.

"Auntie, you know Vanessa isn't tryin' to hear anything anybody says," Rosolyn said. "Her or Dionne."

Vanessa groaned. Dionne was the hothead of the family and Vanessa herself was so ambitious that she could be stubborn sometimes as well. But Rosolyn was the perfect one. The one who went to church, married the right man, had a child, and lived the life that would make a mother or great-aunt proud. She was even the director of The Mason House, an agency where the state sent kids who had been abused or abandoned.

"They need to be listening to you," Ida chastised. "You been married to a wonderful man for twelve years. You got a beautiful little boy. They could learn a thing or two from you."

"Hel-lo." Vanessa waved her hand, thrusting out her chin. "We can hear you guys, you know?"

Ida turned up her nose. "That would be the purpose of the conversation."

Vanessa sucked her teeth and picked up her teacup. As if she'd want her sister's boring life. Vanessa loved her older sister, but Rosolyn was content being a mother and a preacher's wife. No, thanks. Settling for the domestic life simply wasn't in the cards for her. Thomas knew that when he married her. So why he was all of a sudden trippin' was beyond her.

"Your husband done up and left you, and instead of going after him, begging him to forgive you, what are you doing? Sitting up here sippin' tea. Lord, have mercy." Ida shook her head like she was amazed at Vanessa's stupidity. "To be so smart, you sure can be dumb."

"Auntie!" Rosolyn cried, coming to her sister's defense.

Dionne giggled, grateful that her aunt had gotten off her case.

Vanessa wanted to tell her aunt a thing or two, but since Ida was prone to throwing whatever was near her at whoever was near her, she kept her mouth closed.

"All I'm saying is the man ain't asking for nothing no other husband would want. No other man would want," Ida declared.

"Auntie, Thomas will be fine. He's just mad right now," Vanessa said, growing exasperated. "He didn't leave me. He just probably spent the last two nights over at one of his friends' house or at his sister's place."

Ida bolted upright in her chair, shock registering on her face. "He's been gone for two days? And you don't know where he's staying?"

Vanessa shook her head. Although she was trying to act nonchalant, the uneasy feeling in her stomach was intensifying. She'd tried to call Thomas when he didn't come home last night, but he hadn't answered his phone.

"And you're not out looking for him?" Ida looked at Vanessa like she'd lost her mind.

"Aunt Ida, it's not even like that. Thomas just likes to go off and clear his head when he gets upset."

Ida leaned back in her seat. "If you say so. But you mark my words, what you won't do, another woman will."

Rosolyn cleared her throat as she shifted uncomfortably. "Well, I wasn't going to say anything, but . . ."

Everyone turned to her. "But what?" Dionne asked when Rosolyn didn't continue.

Rosolyn nervously sipped her tea. "Well, Henry said he saw Thomas pulling out of the gas station by the Galleria this morning. And . . ." She fumbled with her teacup.

"And what?" Dionne asked, getting irritated.

"And there was a woman in the car with him. A pretty young

woman." Rosolyn rushed the words out. "Henry tried to get his attention, but Thomas didn't see him." She forced a smile. "I'm sure it was nothing. Just one of his assistants or something."

Vanessa's eyebrows rose. Thomas didn't have any young female assistants.

"An assistant, huh?" Dionne mumbled, obviously not buying that theory.

"Yes, I'm sure that's what it was," Rosolyn said with a little more force in her voice.

"Umph. I told you, what one woman treats like trash, another woman will treasure," Ida said.

Vanessa was getting tired of the homespun wisdom. "What is that supposed to mean?"

"It means what it means," Ida responded matter-of-factly.

Vanessa rolled her eyes. That had to have been a client Henry saw Thomas with. His assistant was an elderly woman, but he did meet with clients from time to time. "Whatever. If I don't know anything else, I know Thomas is faithful to me. Just like I'm faithful to him."

"You know this, huh?" Ida said. "Unless you got your man's woody in your pocket, you don't *know* nothing."

Vanessa and her sisters all frowned up. "You're gross, Auntie," Dionne said.

"I'm just speaking the truth," she replied.

"Well, I know Thomas is faithful to me," Vanessa replied, even though she was feeling less and less confident.

"Yeah, just like I thought Roland was faithful to me," Dionne muttered as she downed the rest of her drink.

31

Vanessa smiled at her man-hunting little sister. "Yeah, right. As if you can even compare Thomas to him."

Dionne was coming right back with a retort when suddenly she grabbed her stomach. "I gotta throw up," she said, getting up and rushing off to the bathroom.

"That's all that wine you sat here and guzzled," Ida called out after her. "Lush!"

"Can you all please not go at each other's throats on my birthday?" Rosolyn finally asked. "I didn't get rid of my husband and son to sit up here and listen to you guys fuss."

Vanessa was glad her aunt let the conversation drop, although Ida and Dionne had now stirred up some doubt in her mind. *Thomas wouldn't cheat, would he?* No, they'd been married five years and although they'd experienced their share of problems, outside women had never been one of them.

She stood up. "Well, I have to get going. I have some work to do." She leaned over and kissed Rosolyn on the cheek. "Happy birthday. Let me know when you want to use your gift certificate to The Root of You Salon and Day Spa and I'll go with you." She moved over to the next chair and kissed her aunt also. "Talk to you later, Aunt Ida. Tell Dionne I'll catch up with her later."

As she headed to the door, Vanessa heard Ida mumble, "She ain't foolin' nobody. She's goin' to find her man."

She didn't look back, but her aunt was right. That uneasy feeling was creating knots now, and Vanessa wouldn't rest until she found her husband.

Chapter 5

"Henry said she was young and pretty." Rosolyn's words rang in her head. Vanessa had never doubted Thomas's fidelity. But the fact that he hadn't come home again and still wasn't answering his cell phone was causing her mind to work overtime.

Finally, after driving by Bernard's house and seeing that Thomas's truck wasn't there, Vanessa decided to try a tactic she'd learned from one of the women who had come through her divorce court. She returned home, logged onto the computer, went to the American Express website and entered Thomas's credit card information.

"Old, predictable Thomas," she noted in satisfaction as she successfully entered the same password he used for everything, LOVEJUST, after two of the founders of his fraternity. Vanessa liked to think he partly made it up because of her, too. She'd asked him once, and he said, "Of course," which didn't mean anything, but it made her feel better anyway.

Vanessa navigated the page until she reached the "pending charges" box of the account section and saw the charge for the Lansing Hotel. Her heart sank when she realized it was across the street from the Galleria Mall, where Henry had seen Thomas with the other woman. Was that where he was taking her?

Vanessa quickly logged off and shut down her computer. Then she jumped into her car and raced across town to the Lansing Hotel. She didn't know how she would find Thomas's room, but she had a bad feeling in the pit of her stomach and she couldn't just sit around and let it fester. She thought about their anniversary. The great lengths Thomas had gone to cook her a nice meal. The fact that he'd turned down a trip to Brazil so he wouldn't miss their anniversary. And she'd totally blown him off. She inhaled sharply as she fought back tears. Had she gone too far this time?

It took her less than twenty minutes to reach the hotel. Vanessa wanted to die when she saw Thomas's black Range Rover parked prominently in the valet section.

Vanessa valet-parked and made her way inside the lavishly decorated hotel. Expensive artwork adorned the walls and the furniture was definitely first-class. Leave it to Thomas to pick the nicest hotel in town.

Vanessa headed toward the front desk, then lingered back when she saw the tall white man wearing a manager's tag. She pulled out her cell phone and acted like she was on it until she saw the man walk to the back. Then she hurried over to the front desk.

Can I Get a Witness?

"Hello," she told the young, perky girl working behind the counter. "I'm Judge Vanessa Colton-Kirk. My husband and I are staying here, and I locked myself out of my room." Vanessa flashed a smile at the clerk and then spoke into the cell phone. "Yes, honey. I'm on my way. I'm going to grab your tie and I'll be right over. I just have to get a key from the front desk." Vanessa pretended to listen, then continued. "What? Hold on, baby."

The clerk smiled at the domestic scene. "Yes, Mrs. Kirk, what room are you in? And do you have any ID?"

Vanessa fumbled in her purse for her driver's license. She pulled it out while she continued to pretend she was on the phone. "Yes, I'll get that, too." She leaned in toward the clerk. "I don't remember what the room number is."

"Ma'am, I really need to know the room number since your name isn't listed specifically on the room."

"Hold on, sweetheart," Vanessa said, adding a touch of wifely exasperation. "Look, I'm a judge. My home is being re-modeled and we just checked in, so I don't remember the room number. I come here all the time, just look in your system. Mr. Thomas Kirk, that's who the room is registered under. 5312 Canyon Creek Drive. You see the same address right there on my driver's license." She pointed at the laminated card. "We are heading to the governor's private reception and really, I don't have time for this," Vanessa said, though adding a smile. "Thomas, do you remember what the room number is?" she said into the phone. "Thomas? Thomas?" She huffed, then snapped her phone shut. "His battery went dead. This is ridiculous. Where's your manager? Better yet, please get my personal friend, Arthur Lansing, the owner of the hotel, on the phone."

The girl looked like a deer caught in the headlights. "I'm sorry. I was just following our company policy." She quickly pulled out a key card, activated it, and handed it to Vanessa.

"What's the room number?" Vanessa snapped, trying to act irritated.

"It's 1213," the clerk said.

"Thank you." Vanessa snatched the key and headed across the elegant lobby. She couldn't believe she had stooped to that level. But that queasy feeling in her gut was getting worse as she thought of her husband lying up in a hotel room with another, younger woman.

Vanessa caught the elevator up to the twelfth floor. Storming down the hall, she stopped in front of 1213. She was just about to use the key and go inside when she stopped.

"What are you doing?" she asked herself. *What if he's in there with another woman?* She quickly shook off that thought. Thomas wouldn't do that, would he?

Vanessa was still contemplating what she should do when the door to Room 1213 swung open, startling her. Thomas was laughing, an ice bucket in his hand. His smile instantly faded when he saw his wife.

Vanessa crossed her arms and glared at her husband. Yet her heart felt like it was about to jump out of her chest. She was deathly afraid of what she'd see inside.

"What are you doing here?" Thomas asked, stepping out into the hallway and letting the door close behind him.

"I could ask you the same thing."

"This is where I'm staying."

Vanessa looked toward the door. "By yourself?"

Thomas rolled his eyes. "Don't even go there, Vanessa. As a matter of fact, just go home. Or to one of your political receptions. Go woo some voters." He stepped around her and began walking down the hall.

Vanessa followed right after him. "Is there a woman in there with you, Thomas?" she demanded. "You better tell me the truth."

Thomas spun around, a smirk across his face. "I didn't know you cared."

"Don't play with me. Are you lying up in that hotel room with some tramp?"

"You're a trip." He shook his head and walked into the small ice room.

No he wasn't trying to blow her off! She was not about to let him or some two-bit tramp make a fool out of her. Vanessa stomped back down the hall and inserted her key into the door. She braced herself for the bimbo she was sure was lying across the bed in a skimpy negligee. She just needed to see it for herself. She had to see that her husband was indeed a cheating dog.

"What are you doing?" Thomas called out as he saw her unlocking the door.

Vanessa ignored him and swung the door open. She stormed inside. ESPN blared from the twenty-seven-inch TV. The bed was completely made up, with Thomas's *Architectural Digest* open on the spread. But other than that, the room was empty.

Vanessa marched to the bathroom. "Don't try to hide, you

home wrecker!" She pushed the door open. It was deserted. The almond tiles sparkled to let her know that the bathroom hadn't been touched.

When she came out of the bathroom, she bumped into Thomas. He looked at her with disgust. "Did you find what you were looking for?"

He turned and loudly set the ice bucket down on the dresser.

Vanessa glanced at the window to see if there was any way someone could have made a run for it. There wasn't, unless they were willing to jump twelve floors. It finally dawned on her that Thomas truly was alone. She instantly felt like crap.

"Thomas . . ."

He held up his hand. "Save it, Vanessa. You see I'm alone. Just like I've been the entire five years I've been married to you. Now please, just go home."

Vanessa wanted to stay and beg her husband for his forgiveness, to tell him she was sorry and that she would be a better wife. But she was so embarrassed by the way she had acted, she couldn't find the words to say what she felt.

"Thomas, I'm sorry."

She looked up at him, trying to find a hint of sympathy. The full force of how low her suspicions were hit her like a blow.

She turned and headed out the door, too ashamed to face him a moment longer.

Chapter 6

Vanessa felt like crap. And Aunt Ida's constant nagging wasn't making things any better.

"Umm-hmmm. You ought to be ashamed of yourself." Ida shook her head, her pink hair rollers close to falling out. "I'm sure you looked like a plumb idiot."

Vanessa rubbed her temple. "Auntie, please. You're the one got me all hyped up in the first place, telling me to go find Thomas." She was so stressed out, she'd headed straight to Rosolyn's, hoping to talk to her sister about her marriage. Vanessa had completely forgotten that her aunt was staying there while her kitchen was being remodeled.

Rosolyn sat at the kitchen table, looking sad for her sister, who was pacing back and forth across the room. Although Rosolyn was the quiet one of the family, as the oldest, she always felt protective about her sisters. Vanessa could tell Rosolyn wanted their aunt to go back to bed so the two of them could talk, but like Vanessa, she knew it would be pointless to try.

Ida pulled the belt around her robe tighter. "I was just telling you to get your man to come home, not go out there like you Nancy Drew or somebody." She sighed heavily. "And why are you back here anyway? Didn't you tell him you're sorry?"

Vanessa didn't respond as she plopped down in a chair across from her sister. Ida walked over in front of her, her hands planted firmly on her hips. "Well, didn't you?"

Vanessa glared at her aunt. "No, I just left, okay?"

"No, it's not okay." Ida threw up her hands in amazement. "I just don't know what's wrong with you young folks!"

"Everybody ain't you and Uncle Louis," Vanessa retorted.

"Do you think me and Louis didn't have our problems? Your uncle loved him some booze, but you know what? I'm a praying woman." She patted her heart lightly. "I knew Louis would give it up. Not on my time, but God's time. And guess what? He did just that. And I was right there when he did." She leaned over the table, emphasizing her point. "I prayed my man through his storm. I didn't give up and run away. That's what you and all them people that come through your court do. Lord have mercy. Whatever happened to the sanctity of marriage?"

"I'm not running away," Vanessa protested. "I'm just . . . just . . ."

"Just not facing the fact that you messed up. How long did

you think Thomas was gonna play second fiddle to your career? How long you think a man is gonna take not feeling like a man?"

Vanessa felt tears welling up in her eyes.

"I know you don't want to hear this," Rosolyn added, covering Vanessa's hands with her own, "but I agree with Aunt Ida. You think I'm too submissive to Henry, but a man needs to feel like he's a man—even if you're just making him *think* that he is."

"I know it's late, but you march right back to that hotel and fetch your husband," Ida demanded. "Matter of fact, y'all just stay in that room and do nasty thangs all night long."

Vanessa smiled for the first time that evening, though her sight was sparkly with tears. "Auntie, you are so nasty," she said, wiping her eyes.

"Ain't nothing nasty about getting some good lovin'—as long as it's from your husband."

Rosolyn gave Vanessa a reassuring hand squeeze. "Girl, go get your man."

Vanessa squeezed her sister's hand back, then stood and kissed Ida on the cheek. "Thank you, Aunt Ida, for helping me realize what's important."

"Any time, baby. Any time."

Vanessa grabbed her keys and headed out the door.

Twenty minutes later she was back at the Lansing Hotel, standing outside of Room 1213. Vanessa ran her fingers through her wavy honey-brown hair and took a deep breath. She fluffed out her gray floor-length knit skirt and pulled down her sweater over her hips. She was casually dressed, but the way the sweater stopped right at her cleavage made her look sexy. Vanessa hesitated, then knocked three times. *I've got to get him to forgive me,* she thought.

Vanessa heard the lock on the door turn, and she mustered up a smile. But her smile quickly faded when the door swung open and a pretty, young, petite, chocolate-colored woman opened the door. She looked like she was in her early twenties. Her jet-black hair was hanging to her shoulders. She was a little on the heavy side but otherwise looked like she belonged on someone's runway.

"Yes?" the woman said, pulling the hotel's oversize bathrobe tightly around her body.

Vanessa leaned back and looked at the room number again. "I'm sorry. I must have the wrong room."

"Alana, is that room service? Hurry up. I'm starving."

Vanessa's heart dropped to the pit of her stomach at the sound of her husband's voice. The woman's eyes widened and she quickly attempted to close the door, but Vanessa put her arm up to stop her, then almost knocked the woman over as she walked in. She was amazed at her own strength, but right about now she was probably capable of anything.

Thomas jumped up off the bed as Vanessa entered. He was fully clothed, but the small pink duffel bag resting at the foot of the bed told her he wouldn't be clothed for long.

"Vanessa!" Thomas exclaimed. "Wh-what are you doing here?"

"You bastard!" Vanessa felt her chest heaving up and down

as she tried to keep her anger from boiling over. "I don't believe you could be such a liar!"

"L-let me explain," Thomas said as he dove across the bed away from her.

"Explain what? You cheating, low-down—"

The woman was standing there with her hands on her cheeks. "I'm sorry, Thomas. I wouldn't have opened the door, but I thought it was room service."

Her high-pitched, squeaky voice set Vanessa off even more. "You tramp!" The woman jumped out of the way just as Vanessa lunged at her. Vanessa caught the belt on the woman's robe as she scurried out of the way.

"Vanessa, calm down! It's not what it looks like." Thomas grabbed Vanessa from behind as the woman's robe fell open, revealing a huge stomach.

Vanessa felt as if time were standing still. Her eyes took in the woman's belly, its full roundness. She wasn't heavy, she was pregnant, at least seven or eight months.

"Let. Me. Go," Vanessa said. She never took her eyes off the woman as she closed her robe back up.

"If I let you go, you need to be rational," Thomas pleaded.

Rational? This fool must be on drugs. What woman could possibly be rational in a situation like this?

"Fine, Thomas, just let me go before I scream at the top of my lungs." Vanessa's breathing was still heavy and tears were streaming down her face, but she had calmed down.

Thomas slowly released her. "We need to talk about this," he said gently.

Vanessa turned around to face her husband, then reached back with all her might and slapped him across the face. "You're cheating on me with a pregnant woman? How low can you get? You are disgusting, you sick piece of sh—" She caught herself. She was not going to let this two-bit skank see her act a fool any more than she already had. "And you," she said in disdain. "In here with my husband, while you're pregnant."

Thomas rubbed his cheek, bright red from her smack. "Vanessa, stop."

She spun toward him. "No, *you* stop. You made me feel so bad earlier. How could I suspect my loving husband? But my hunch was right all along. You're up in here, boning some trick."

"Just stop it, Vanessa," Thomas snapped. "I'm not boning anyone. And Alana—Alana is not some trick. She . . . she's about to be the mother of my child."

It felt like someone had taken a baseball bat and hit a grand slam into Vanessa's stomach. She stared at Thomas in disbelief. Then she looked over at Alana, who diverted her gaze to the floor.

Vanessa opened her mouth but no words would come out, so she did the only thing she could: she ran from the room before she threw up.

Vanessa frantically punched the elevator buttons, hoping it would come before Thomas followed her out. She glanced down the hallway, waiting on the door to his room to open. Of course he was going to come after her, try to explain how he could do this to her.

Can I Get a Witness?

The ding of the elevator door opening snapped Vanessa out of her daze. She stood staring into the elevator. The young couple inside shot her a funny look. "Umm, are you getting on?" the girl asked.

Vanessa eyed the room again. "Oh, umm, no, go ahead." She took a step back. The girl huffed and punched the button to close the elevator doors.

Vanessa felt a wave of tears overtaking her. The door to Room 1213 still didn't open. He wasn't coming after her. She weakly punched the down button again. Her hand was trembling. Thomas had betrayed her and was now twisting the knife even harder by not bothering to come after her.

Chapter 7

Vanessa cringed as the morning sun shot through the blinds and hit her in the face. She sat up, groggy, her head feeling like she'd been partying with Jack Daniel's all night long.

But Vanessa hadn't taken a drink. The last thing she remembered was coming home and trashing her room. She looked around the large master bedroom at the evidence of her rage. All of the dresser drawers were hanging out. Clothes were flung all over the room. And every single picture of Thomas was ripped into a million pieces.

Vanessa felt the tears trying to build again as the sinking feeling returned to her gut. The reality of what had happened last night set in again. Dionne had called just as Vanessa was returning home, and she'd told her everything because she just wanted to vent to someone. That hadn't helped, though, because Dionne was more fired up than she was. So Vanessa had unplugged her phone and tried her best to calm down.

Vanessa was about to plop back down in bed and throw the covers over her face when she heard the chime signaling the alarm was being deactivated.

Vanessa threw back the gold down comforter and raced down the stairs. "I know Thomas does not have the nerve to show his face here," she hissed. She caught a glimpse of herself as she passed the beveled mirror in the hallway. She looked a hot mess. Her hair was matted to one side of her head. Her eyes were puffy and swollen. Vanessa took a moment to brush her hair down before turning the corner to find Thomas fumbling in the hall closet.

"You must have a death wish," Vanessa snarled.

He turned toward her, sadness etched across his face. "Vanessa, I don't know what to say, except I'm so sorry."

"*Sorry?* Is that the best you can do? You're sorry you screwed another woman? You're sorry you got her pregnant? Or are you just sorry you got caught?" She folded her arms across her chest and rapidly tapped her right foot. It was taking everything in her power to keep from going off.

"I'm sorry for everything. I never meant for it to happen like this." He took two steps toward her, then stopped as if he was too scared to come any closer.

"You never meant for this to happen?" Vanessa replied. "Obviously when you had sex with her with no protection, you meant for something to happen!"

Thomas hung his head. "Vanessa, please. You're not making this any easier."

Vanessa looked down at the hall table, where a pair of African statues sat. It was a good thing they were originals from Gambia, or else she would've taken one of them and smashed it upside Thomas's head.

"Am I supposed to make this easy for you?" She cocked her head. "I'm sorry, I missed that chapter in the wives-whose-husbands-cheat manual. Tell me, Thomas, what can I do to make this easier for you?"

Vanessa's pain had been replaced with pure anger now. Granted, she hadn't been the perfect wife, but that didn't give him the right to break her heart.

Thomas shook his head. "I'm sorry."

Vanessa said tensely, "Yeah, I know. You said that. Next."

He started to get annoyed. "I told you, it's not as bad as it seems."

"Is that so? Because it seems pretty bad to me," she spat as tears started flowing down her cheeks. She was angry with herself because she didn't want him to see her shed another tear.

"What do you want me to say?" Thomas finally asked.

Vanessa could no longer stand it. How could he be so rational about this? She stepped up to him and pounded his chest. "Say something!" She pushed him forcefully. "Tell me why you forgot you were married and went to another woman."

Thomas took his blows, keeping a hand up to protect his face. He finally stepped back as she paused to catch her breath.

"Vanessa, you're the one who forgot we were married. A long time ago," he said flatly.

She looked up at him through tear-filled eyes. "Oh, so now this is my fault? I didn't give you the child you wanted, so you went and found a woman who would?"

At last Thomas looked just as emotionally drained as she was.

"It's not like that at all. Me and Alana . . . it just sort of happened."

Vanessa slumped to the floor and suddenly burst into laughter. "It just happened." She laughed nonstop for a long time. Thomas stared at her like she was losing her mind. She actually felt like she was.

"You bastard," she said, finally calming down. "You think you can get another woman pregnant, then waltz back in here and I'm supposed to pretend everything is all right?"

"I know everything isn't all right," he stoically said.

"You damn right," she snapped, pulling herself up to her feet. As she stood, she eyed the closet floor and saw what Thomas had been trying to get. The rest of his suitcases.

"Oh, so you're leaving for good?" she said, slowly nodding her head.

"Would I have been able to stay?"

Vanessa shot him a "you know the answer to that" look. He sighed heavily, then went back to pulling out the suitcase.

Vanessa watched uncertainly. She couldn't believe it: a small part of her didn't want to see him go.

"How do you even know the baby is yours?" She didn't

know why she was asking the questions, but she desperately needed answers.

Thomas shrugged slightly like he really didn't want to respond.

"Answer me. You owe me that much!"

"I just know." He found the last of his suitcases, then pulled it out. He didn't say anything as he rolled them upstairs to the bedroom.

Vanessa followed him, not saying anything until they were in the bedroom.

"Why, Thomas?" she sternly asked.

"I don't know, Vanessa."

"So, you don't know why you messed with her?" she huffed.

He shook his head as he opened his closet and removed some clothing.

"Where'd you meet her?" Vanessa asked.

Thomas pulled up short and stared at her. "Why are you doing this?"

"Where. Did. You. Meet. Her?"

He lowered his head. "At one of your political receptions. The one for Senator Johnson."

Vanessa's mouth dropped open.

"I'm sorry. I don't want to lie to you."

She glared at him as the tears threatened to build up again. "You don't want to lie to me *anymore*?"

"Vanessa—"

She cut him off, outraged by how sneaky he'd been. "So, while you're at a function with me, you're off picking up other women?"

"If you recall," Thomas said slowly, "you left me sitting at a table by myself for well over an hour and a half. Alana was there with a friend and she sat down. We just started talking."

Vanessa was stunned. He'd done this right under her nose. "I don't believe this." She paced back and forth before spinning around. "So let me get this straight. While I'm working the room, trying to solidify our future, you're picking up women?"

He snorted as he tossed the stack of clothes into his suitcase. "First of all, you were working on *your* future, not ours. And I didn't pick her up. I bumped into her at the grocery store about a week later and that's when we exchanged numbers." Thomas paused in his packing. The words came harder now. "We started out as just friends, occasionally talking on the phone. Pretty soon I found myself confiding in her. And she listened."

"I bet she did," Vanessa said, upset.

"She listened. You never listen to me," he said, flaring with anger. "If we're not talking about you or what you want, or your future in politics, you never listen."

She crossed her arms over her chest. "So we're back to this is my fault?"

He shook his head. "No, it's mine. I'm responsible for my own actions."

"So you've been sleeping with her all this time?" She watched him intently, trying to see if he was going to lie to her.

"I know you won't believe this, but it was only one time."

"Yeah, right," Vanessa scoffed. "Did you forget I saw her naked in your room?"

"She was just taking a shower. We weren't doing anything."

Thomas seemed to have turned into a different person overnight. Where had this lying dog come from?

"You expect me to believe that bull?"

Thomas shrugged bitterly. "I can't control what you believe. I love you, Vanessa. I really do. But we have some major issues. And Alana, she's . . . she's more like my best friend."

That cut Vanessa deep, but she was determined not to let it show.

"A best friend that you're screwing." She plastered on a fake smile. "How sweet, a new best friend and a new baby. Who cares if that baby wasn't with your wife!"

Thomas started toward her with a pleading look on his face. Vanessa stepped back in disgust. "Vanessa, you've got to know that I wanted a child with you more than anything in the world. I never intended for anything like this to happen. I just . . . after a while, I started to tell myself God does everything for a reason. And maybe this was His way—"

Vanessa cut him off. "Don't you dare bring God into this, you sick son of a—ughhh! I can't believe you!" She walked to the window and looked out into the backyard, a yard she really and truly had hoped to one day run around in with her husband and kids. "Get out! Just get out of my house. Get out of my life! I hate you!"

Thomas knew it was best that he leave and come back later for his things; he retreated out the door. Vanessa followed behind him down the stairs. "I'm sorry again. I hope that one day you can find it in your heart to forgive me," he said, stopping to turn and face her.

"You must be out of your mind. If anything, Mr. Kirk, I'm going to make you regret the day you ever met me!"

Thomas stood in the door, a pitiful look on his face. "As much as I love you, Vanessa, I already regret it." He let the door slam before Vanessa could utter another word.

Screw Gambia, Vanessa thought as she picked up one of the statues and hurled it at the door with all her might before she collapsed to the floor in tears.

Chapter 8

The sounds of thunder boomed through Dionne's small two-bedroom apartment just as she slammed the phone down on its cradle. She closed her eyes and took a deep breath, trying her best not to get worked up. She had been trying unsuccessfully to get in touch with Roland for the past week. She'd given him a year of her life and the least he could do was give her some type of explanation for what he'd done. But so far he hadn't bothered. Shoot, he hadn't even bothered to call.

"Ugggh!" she screamed as she picked up a throw pillow off her bed and flung it across her bedroom. So much for trying not to get worked up. Dionne still couldn't believe that Roland had cheated on her, then been so low as to not even call and apologize.

She reached for the phone again, thinking she'd call him back, only she would block her number this time. She was just about to pick it up when it rang.

"Hello," she said, her voice full of anticipation.

"Are you still in a funk?" her friend Melanie asked. Dionne had filled Melanie in on what had happened with Roland the same day it had happened. But right about now, she wished she hadn't said anything to anybody.

Melanie, her former college roommate at Prairie View A & M University, had been calling every day, trying to get Dionne to go out, get her mind off Roland. Dionne wasn't the least bit interested in the club scene. She preferred to stay home and mope. She'd all but cursed Melanie out the last time they'd talked.

"Nah, girl. I'm sorry about going off the other day," Dionne said, flopping back on her bed. "I'm a little stressed."

"That's why I keep tellin' you, we need to go out," Melanie said. "I'm headed out now to Maxwell's."

Dionne could picture Melanie clear as day, in the mirror, music blaring, as she put the finishing touches on her makeup. She lived with her boyfriend, but Dionne knew he was out of town on business. That meant her friend would be in rare form tonight.

"Trust me, the club scene is not the answer to my problems." Dionne groaned. In school, they'd both been party animals, but that was seven years ago. Dionne had grown up. Unfortunately, Melanie had not.

Melanie smacked her lips. "Well, goin' clubbin' beats sitting up there all depressed over some dude."

"Roland is not just '*some* dude,' " Dionne said defensively. "He was going to be my husband."

"Oh, here we go with this mess," Melanie huffed. "Last time I checked, he already had a wife *and* a girlfriend, and he hadn't made any moves toward putting a ring on your finger."

Dionne moved the phone away from her ear as she contemplated hanging up. Then she said, "Look, can we just change the subject, okay?" She knew there was no sense debating with Melanie. Even though she lived with Marcus, her boyfriend, neither of them wanted to get married. Dionne had decided long ago that Melanie was one of those women who was destined to be single forever, so it wasn't like she could even understand anyway.

"Fine, mope all you want." Melanie's tone immediately changed. "Let's talk about your sister Vanessa," she said excitedly. "I read on the Houston Buzz that your sister was divorcing her husband."

For Dionne, this new subject wasn't any better. Granted, Vanessa was always trashing her boyfriends and Thomas had turned out to be no better than them. Still, she didn't want to see her sister getting hurt. "Why do you insist on reading that trashy tabloid blog?"

"You read the Insite blog, by that reporter from Fox."

"That's because it has legitimate information, not gossip like The Buzz."

"Whatever, The Buzz is the only way I can find stuff out. And since I don't hear you denying it, it must be true."

Dionne sighed, but remained silent.

"Come on, tell me the scoop. The Buzz said she's getting a divorce because her husband got a woman pregnant with triplets."

Dionne shook her head vigorously, as if Melanie could see her. "That's a lie."

"Well, is she getting a divorce? I mean, that's a trip if she is, since she's this big-shot divorce court judge and all." Melanie laughed. "What, is she going to preside over her own divorce?"

Dionne sat up in her bed. Melanie was her girl and all, but Vanessa was her blood. She wasn't going to have Melanie going around spreading a bunch of gossip.

"Look, Mel," Dionne said, "my sister *is* getting a divorce, but her husband did *not* get somebody pregnant with triplets." *It was just one kid,* she wanted to say, but why give Melanie anything to run with? "So I would appreciate it if you didn't go around spreading her business."

"Girl, it's on The Buzz. I ain't gotta spread it." She laughed again. "Nah, Dionne, you know I got love for your sister. I'm not going to spread anything. But this does prove my point that marriage should be outlawed. Shoot, if a dang divorce court judge can't stay married, who can?"

Dionne bit back her immediate reply. This was all Melanie needed—something to bolster her belief that marriage was for the birds.

"Seriously, Melanie, I'm really bummed about my sister. Her and Thomas made a really cute couple. I thought they'd be married forever." Dionne had always been a little jealous of her sister's marriage, mainly because she thought it was perfect.

Rosolyn and Henry had a great marriage, too, but since he was a preacher, they were supposed to have a good marriage. Vanessa's was different, though. Thomas doted on Vanessa all the time. It was something Dionne had longed for herself.

Dionne's mind shifted back to Roland and how her dreams had been shattered. "Do you know anyone who is happily married?"

Melanie was quiet a minute like she was thinking. "Nope," she finally replied. "And the people who tell you they are happily married are lying."

Dionne shuddered and pushed down the lump in her throat. That was not the answer she wanted to hear.

After declining Melanie's request to go out one more time, Dionne said her good-byes. She hung up the phone, then said a silent prayer that her friend couldn't possibly be right. But between what happened with her and Roland and with Thomas and Vanessa, Dionne was starting to wonder if maybe Melanie was right. Maybe marriage was really for the birds.

Chapter 9

Love wasn't no joke. Dionne closed her eyes and tossed her Eric Jerome Dickey novel to the side. As lonely as she was, she didn't need to be reading any steamy love scenes, even if he was her favorite author. But she had tried watching television and that didn't work. No matter what she did, she couldn't stop thinking about Roland, or the news she'd received this morning, which still had her stomach in knots.

Dionne took a deep breath, dialed *67 to block out her phone number, and called Roland yet again. She was expecting to get his answering machine, as she had gotten the last fifteen times she'd called him over the past two days. She was surprised, however, when he picked up.

"Hello?" he said.

Dionne didn't respond. She'd rehearsed the one hundred and one ways she was going to curse him out when she finally got in touch with him. But the sound of his voice had rendered her speechless.

"Hello?" Roland repeated.

She kept her voice even. That was what Vanessa would do in this situation. "You know it's really sad that you're the one who cheats on me, yet I'm the one who has to track you down for an explanation."

Roland was silent for a minute. Then he replied, "Dionne, I'm sorry. I don't know what to say."

She could feel the heaviness in his voice. He really did sound sorry he had hurt her.

"I just need you to help me understand. I thought we had something special," Dionne said, her eyes misting up. People thought she was crazy, but she saw a side of Roland that no one else did. Her family didn't care for him because he only had time for her at night. They wouldn't accept that Roland worked so much, that his job as an insurance claims adjuster kept him on the road a lot. Her friends didn't like him for that same reason. But she'd known all along that he was the man for her. That was why his betrayal had cut her so deep.

"We did have something special, D," he replied. "I just . . . I don't even know how to explain it."

"Try," she said with a little more of an edge.

He let out a groan. "That's why I haven't called. I really didn't know what to say. I never meant to hurt you."

"That's what they all say." Dionne rolled her eyes, recalling her last boyfriend, Greg, whom she'd also caught cheating. But she'd known all along that Greg was no good. Roland, on the other hand, had her completely fooled. Sure, he wouldn't fully commit, but he'd never given her any indication that he was seeing someone else—or that he even wanted to, for that matter. He was passionate in bed with her. He was happy when they went out. Why the hell did he need this Tasha?

Dionne was getting frustrated. She didn't know what she wanted Roland to say, but she expected more.

"I just can't believe you played me like this," she said. "And what's with the whole wuss routine? Jumping out a window? The Roland I know would never punk out like that."

He let out a small chuckle. "That *was* pretty jacked up, wasn't it?" he replied. "Look, Tasha is crazy and I just wanted to get away. I didn't want to deal with her drama."

She wanted to ask him why he would even mess with someone like her. Instead, she asked the question that had been eating away at her. "So I guess this means things are over for us?"

"I guess so," he softly replied.

Dionne bit down on her lip as tears began trickling down her cheeks. That was not what she wanted to hear. "Just like that. It's that easy for you to just let us go?"

Roland sighed. She could picture him running his hand over the back of his head, what he did whenever he was stressed out. "Ain't nothing easy about this, D."

She struggled to keep from crying. "Maybe we should get together and talk. Maybe we can work through this." Dionne couldn't believe she was begging him after what he'd done. Her friends would have a fit, and she knew she was above begging a man to be with her. But right now nothing mattered, not her friends, not her pride. She just wanted to get Roland back. She *needed* to get him back.

"I'm sorry. I just need some time to get my head together."

Dionne swallowed the lump in her throat. She picked up what had made her call Roland in the first place. "So, you're staying with Tasha, huh?"

"It's not like that at all. I just need some me time right now."

She hesitated, before saying, "Okay, cool."

"Please understand. Don't be mad."

"I'm not mad. It's all good," she lied.

"Can we be friends?"

"Yeah, I can always use another friend," she said wryly. Then she remembered something she'd planned to say to get back at him. "I was thinking I should get out and date anyway."

Roland was silent. Dionne knew that would sting. The thought of her with another man would eat him alive. That idea actually empowered her. If only for a minute.

"Well, I gotta run. You take care of yourself. Friend." She hung up the phone before he could reply and before she broke down in tears.

Dionne sat on her sofa, the phone in one hand, the little white stick in the other. The plus sign blared brightly at her. She was all cried out. But she couldn't help but wonder what she was going to do now. How in the world was she going to raise a child by herself?

Chapter 10

"Good Lord, you look like a crackhead." Ida stood in the doorway of Vanessa's home, her eyes roaming up and down her niece's body.

"Aunt Ida, don't start."

Vanessa left the door open and walked back into the house. She knew she looked a mess. Her curly hair was matted and in need of a good wash and condition. She was still in her bathrobe, which she hadn't taken off since Thomas walked out.

Ida followed her in, shutting the door behind her.

"So this is how you deal with your problems, huh?" Ida surveyed the living room. "I have been calling you for the last two days. I left messages and you haven't returned my calls. I even called you at work. They told me you were sick and somebody else was taking your caseload. What's going on with you?"

"Thanks for caring." Vanessa plopped down on the sofa and turned her attention back to the Lifetime movie she'd been watching. She'd gotten all of Ida's messages. And Rosolyn's. And Dionne's. But she wasn't in the mood to talk to anyone.

She'd stumbled across her wedding video this morning, and like a fool, she'd watched it. She and Thomas were so happy then. They were so in love, they'd gotten married after only seven months of dating. She was in her last year of law school when they met. He'd already been working as an architect for three years, and his company had been commissioned to redesign the law library. They'd struck up a conversation one night while she was studying, then went out to dinner and had immediately clicked. She loved his sense of humor and his outlook on life. He admired her physical beauty, her intelligence, and her ambitious nature. The same ambitious nature that seemed to be such a problem for him now.

Ida stared at the pizza box and the empty Häagen-Dazs container on the coffee table. "Since when do you eat junk food?" Her condescending tone snapped Vanessa out of her thoughts.

Vanessa picked up a piece of cold pizza and took a huge bite. Her usual health-conscious eating habits had gone out the window these past two days. "Since I found out my cheating husband got another woman pregnant."

Ida gasped in disbelief. "Oh, my Lord."

"Yep. Your perfect Thomas is no better than all the rest of the dogs in this world." Distressed by the thought, Vanessa flung the half-eaten piece back in the box. She still couldn't believe that she had trusted him so blindly. Thomas had convinced her that he was a one-woman man.

"Oh, my." Ida sat down in the love seat across from Vanessa.

"What you have to say now?"

"Oh, my," Aunt Ida repeated, in a state of shock.

"Stop saying that."

Ida started to recover herself. "I told you you needed to take care of home or someone else would."

Vanessa drew back in surprise. "I can't believe you're defending him," she said incredulously.

"I'm not defending what he did," Ida protested. "I'm just saying, I don't know how long you expected that man to settle for being second-best in your marriage. A husband ain't supposed to be second to nobody but God."

Vanessa didn't feel like having an old-timey discussion with her aunt. She refused to take the blame for Thomas being a two-timing dog.

"Aunt Ida," she said firmly, "I'm tired and need to get some rest. I go back to work tomorrow." She stood and drew her robe tighter around her body.

Ida stood as well, picking up the pizza box. "Well, you just go on up to bed. I'm gonna clean this pigsty up. I'll lock the door on my way out."

Vanessa was too tired to argue. Instead she headed upstairs to take a shower.

"And make sure you do something with your hair!" her aunt called out after her.

Vanessa let out a small chuckle as she stopped in front of her dresser to look at her hair. It was horrible. She had picked up the comb to begin trying to detangle it when she glimpsed a blue gift box hidden behind the mirror. She set the brush down and pulled the box out. Her heart dropped when she saw it was from Tiffany's. Vanessa untied the ribbon and opened the box. Tears filled her eyes as she removed the diamond and platinum Tiffany Legacy Pagoda pendant. She took out the card as well. " 'I want a lifetime with you. Love Thomas,' " she read.

Vanessa wiped away a tear. The day she'd graduated from college, they'd seen this necklace in the mall. He'd told her if she would marry him, he would one day get it for her. Vanessa held the necklace to her chest and sobbed.

The next morning, Vanessa felt somewhat better, but she definitely could've used another day in bed. She'd fallen into a deep sleep and had dreamt of happier times with Thomas. This morning, though, she'd pulled herself together. She placed the Tiffany necklace back in the box and put it in the drawer. Maybe Thomas still had the receipt and could take it back. Then she'd driven to the courthouse, the look on her face daring anyone to mention her own marital problems. No one did.

"Oh well, time to face the world," Vanessa muttered as she walked out into her courtroom.

"All rise," the bailiff announced.

Vanessa nodded at him as she took her seat behind the

bench. The court clerk had set a stack of folders in front of her. Vanessa opened the top folder, the start of a long day.

"Reginald Dumas versus Cara Dumas. Are the parties present?"

"We are, Your Honor," the couple said at the same time as they stood.

Vanessa looked up at both of them. They were a beautiful couple. She was a brown-skinned beauty with bright eyes and a warm smile. He was a shade darker with smooth skin and a muscular physique.

"Do you have representation?" Vanessa asked.

Both of them shook their heads. Vanessa was amazed at the number of people who came into her court without an attorney, although she knew most of them couldn't afford one. She herself was going to hire the best divorce attorney in the business when she took Thomas's no-good behind to divorce court.

The thought suddenly filled Vanessa with sadness. After years of presiding over family courts, she was about to appear in somebody's divorce court herself. She shook off the thoughts and turned her attention back to the Dumases.

"So, Mrs. Dumas, you're seeking a divorce on the grounds of infidelity?"

Cara nodded, as her eyes watered up. "Your Honor, I gave him everything. I gave up my career because he wanted me to be a stay-at-home mom. I had three children because it was what he wanted. I tried to be the perfect wife and then I found out he was keeping another woman, right in the apartment below us."

Vanessa couldn't contain the scowl that crossed her face. Reginald was just like Thomas. A low-down dirty dog.

"Mrs. Dumas, what is it you're seeking?" Vanessa asked.

"Custody of the kids, child support of one thousand dollars a month, and the car," she said softly.

Vanessa studied the folder for several minutes before looking up. She couldn't help but scowl at Reginald, standing there like he was Mr. Playboy Extraordinaire, with his curly hair and hazel eyes. One look and Vanessa could tell he was a snake. "Request granted." She banged her gavel.

"What?" Reginald shouted. "Don't I get a chance to say something?"

Vanessa glared at him again. "Mr. Dumas, did you or did you not cheat on your wife?"

"Well, yes, but—"

"Then there's nothing you need to say. Request granted." Vanessa pounded the gavel again. She motioned for the bailiff to remove Reginald, who had started screaming and cursing, from the courtroom.

Vanessa couldn't remember how she made it through the rest of the day. All she did know was that by the end of the day, she'd granted nineteen divorces, a record in her courtroom.

"Ummm, Judge Colton-Kirk?" Vanessa's secretary, Nicole, stuck her head in the door. "Are you okay? You seemed . . . ummm . . . rather harsh today."

"I'm fine. Just tired of sorry, trifling men coming through my courtroom," Vanessa snapped as she removed her robe.

Vanessa could tell her longtime secretary wanted to say

more. But she must've decided against it because she simply said, "Okay, if you need anything, anything at all, please give me a call."

Vanessa nodded. "I need someone to murder my husband," she muttered as Nicole closed her office door. "You think you can handle that?"

Chapter 11

Murder was still on her mind. Vanessa could see the headlines now: "Famous Judge Slices Husband's Throat." That thought was about the only thing that was keeping her from going off right about now. How dare Thomas show up at her front door, looking like he hadn't done anything wrong?

"What do you want?" she snapped.

Thomas's eyes scanned her body. She knew he was probably shocked at her appearance. She'd come straight home from work and changed into frumpy gray sweats and an oversize Texas Longhorns T-shirt.

"Are you deaf? I said, what do you want?"

"I . . . I was hoping I could pick up some more of my things," Thomas stammered.

Vanessa contemplated telling him to get all of his things, but honestly, she was too tired to fight.

"Whatever, Thomas, just hurry up," she replied as she made her way back over to the sofa, where she'd been watching reruns of *The Cosby Show.*

After twenty minutes, Thomas eased up behind her. She could feel his presence as he stood in silence. "Vanessa, can we talk?" he finally said.

"We don't have anything to talk about." Vanessa didn't take her eyes off the TV.

"I just want us to end this amicably."

"End it amicably?" She turned to him and laughed harshly. "Amicably. Ha! I didn't know you were going into the comedy business."

Thomas gingerly sat down on the love seat across from her. She was glad to see he was suffering, too. He looked worn out. There were bags under his eyes and stress had dug crevices in his forehead. "Vanessa, I never meant to hurt you. I can't say that enough."

Vanessa couldn't believe his gall. "I hate to see what damage you could do if you really tried to hurt me."

"Let's be real. Our marriage was over a long time ago. I used to think we were on the same page, that we wanted the same things out of life—"

"Oh, here we go again," she said, fed up. "How about we talk about the only thing we need to be talking about—our divorce."

Thomas released a defeated sigh. "Vanessa . . ."

"Thomas, get your stuff and get out."

Vanessa was picking up the remote when Thomas's next remark stopped her in mid-click. "What are we going to do about the house?"

Vanessa looked at him like he'd lost his mind. "What are you talking about?"

Thomas glanced down at the floor as he fidgeted with his hands. "I mean, are we going to sell the house or what?"

"*We* ain't doing nothin'," she said, wagging the remote back and forth between the two of them. "*I'm* staying right here in *my* house. You go design your own damn house with your mistress and your kid."

"Vanessa," he said, shaking his head adamantly, "I put a lot of time and money into this house."

"*And?* You should've thought about that before you went out and had a baby with another woman."

"This house is worth half a million dollars."

"Six hundred and fifty thousand, to be exact," she informed him. "And you forfeited the right to one penny of it when you decided to have a baby with another woman."

He ran his hands over his forehead, squeezing his eyes shut in frustration. "I know I was wrong," he said, his voice drawn, "but that doesn't mean I lose my rights. I was hoping we could just sell it and split the profits."

No, this fool wasn't talking about her selling her house because of his infidelity.

Vanessa leaned forward, her brow furrowing. "You look here, you ungrateful bastard. If you even think about trying to take my house, I will make you wish you'd never been born."

Thomas wasn't backing down on this issue, though. "I can see you're not going to make this easy," he said as he rubbed his hands on his pants legs. "But I'm letting you know now, I'm not walking away from this marriage with nothing." He stood up and walked out of the room.

Vanessa jumped up and was close on his heels. "Bring it on, Thomas. You forget, I know every trick in the book," she snarled.

He stopped just as he opened the front door. He looked back at her and said, "My attorney will be in touch." He let the door slam behind him.

Vanessa quickly glanced over at the remaining Gambian statue on the table. "You and your attorney can go to hell!" She hurled the statue at the door and watched as it shattered.

Chapter 12

Dionne hadn't hung out with her girls for months and now she was remembering why.

"Honestly, Dionne, I don't know why you are in such a big hurry to get married," her friend Trina said. Dionne, Trina, Melanie, and another girlfriend named Kyla were sitting on the patio, enjoying appetizers at Pappadeaux's Seafood Restaurant. They'd met at Melanie's insistence in an effort to cheer Dionne up.

Dionne had just finished filling in Trina and Kyla on what had happened with Roland. Trina had been unhappily married for four years and, like Melanie, was not a proponent of marriage at all.

"Girl, take it from me, it ain't nothing but a big headache,"

Trina huffed. "It's like having a second job with no benefits that you don't get paid for."

Dionne exhaled in frustration. She was so tired of hearing that. "If married life is so miserable, then why are you still married?" she asked Trina.

"'Cause he won't leave!" Trina exclaimed. "And I haven't figured out how to kill him yet and get away with it." She leaned in, whispering heavily. "But I tell you, I'll look at him while he's sleep at night, thinking, 'Just stop breathin', just stop breathin'.'"

They all laughed at Trina, who was the comedian of the group. She talked about how much she couldn't stand her husband, yet she made no moves to ever leave him. Every time Dionne saw them together, they looked very loving.

"Kyla, will you tell this girl she does not want to be married?" Melanie said, turning to Kyla, who was on her third husband, even though she wasn't but twenty-nine years old.

"Why do we have this conversation every time we get together?" Kyla said as she looked over the menu. She openly admitted that the third time she'd married for money, not love. After the first two marriages, which she'd done in the name of love, had ended terribly, she found her a sixty-year-old rich man, and was happy as all get-out being his trophy wife. "Besides, I thought we had talked you out of this marriage nonsense the last time we went out," she added. "Girl, I keep trying to tell you, you had better enjoy being single while you can."

"Yeah," Trina chimed in. "If I could turn back the clock, believe me, I would."

"You guys are just like my sisters. You don't get it," Dionne said wearily. She was even more passionate about getting a husband now that she was pregnant. Of course, she couldn't tell her friends that. "All of you have someone at home," she pointed out. "Now, whether or not you want them there is a different story. But when we leave here tonight, you will go home and climb up in the bed next to a warm, cozy body. What do I have waiting on me at home? A freakin' teddy bear I've had for fifteen years."

"First of all," Melanie replied, "I am not married and don't want to be. Second of all, I don't even want to know what you been doing with that teddy bear that has him hanging around for fifteen years."

Trina laughed and added, "Melanie, you may as well be married. You've been with Marcus for almost eight years and living together for three, so what's the difference?"

"The difference," Melanie stressed, "is when that fool gets on my nerves, I can pack my crap and leave with no strings attached."

Dionne was truly frustrated with her friends. They were supposed to be comforting her about Roland. Instead, they were harping on their usual topic: marriage bashing.

"See, that's what I'm talking about. I don't want to feel that way about my husband, boyfriend, or whatever," Dionne said. "You all have such a negative attitude toward being married, but I bet not one of you would survive being single for more than a month."

"Wanna bet?" Kyla laughed.

"I'm serious," Dionne continued. "It is not easy dating nowadays. Men today are either gay, taken, or got four baby mamas. I swear I'm gon' make me a T-shirt that says 'Gay? Married? Playa? Check one!' " Everyone at the table cracked up laughing.

"It can't be that bad." Kyla chuckled.

Dionne looked at her archly. "Oh really. What about that clown Chris? You remember him?"

Melanie and Trina burst out laughing.

"Who is Chris?" Kyla asked. She'd only become their friend over the last few years, so she'd missed out on some of their dating horror stories.

"Well," Dionne began, "Chris was this guy I went out with twice, which was two times too many. The only reason I went out with him that second time was because on the first date he had taken me out to my favorite restaurant for my birthday and had been the perfect gentleman. On our second date, he wanted to cook dinner for me at his place and I agreed."

Melanie giggled before Dionne could even get the rest of the story out.

"First of all," Dionne continued, ignoring Melanie, "the smell of weed hit me in the face the second he opened the door. Two of his friends, with their eyes bloodshot red, were walking out when I walked in. That should have been my first clue to get up out of there, but I decided to give him the benefit of the doubt. All during dinner his phone kept vibrating, and finally after dinner, we heard keys jingling in the lock from outside. Before he had a chance to move, his mama walks in and smooth goes off! She wanted to know why her house smelled like weed, and who was the hoochie he had up in her house while she was at work. She told him that since he didn't pay any rent, he didn't have any business bringing company up in her house when she wasn't home. I grabbed my purse and walked out just as she was saying something about we better not have been doing the nasty on the clean sheets on her bed."

Melanie was laughing like it was her first time hearing the story.

"Did she mention that Chris was thirty-seven?" Trina threw in, fighting back laughter herself.

"Dang." Kyla laughed. "Did you talk to him after that?"

"Girl, I haven't heard from Chris since that night, and it's a good thing, too, because I'd probably have a few choice words for him," Dionne responded. That memory alone was reason enough why she didn't want to return to the dating scene.

Kyla put her drink down and said, "All jokes aside, have you ever thought about whose fault is it that you always seem to choose the losers?"

Dionne narrowed her eyes. Leave it to Kyla to get all philosophical. She thought maybe she just might tell them about the baby. According to her doctor's visit this morning, she was eight weeks along. But then she decided that she wasn't ready to share her news. Not because she hadn't decided if she was going to keep it—abortion simply wasn't an option for her. Rather, she wasn't in the mood to hear anyone's mouth about how she could let herself get knocked up.

"My pastor always says that if you keep choosing the same

type of man, then you are in a cycle and you need to change cycles," Kyla continued.

Dionne thought about that as the waitress brought them another round of drinks. "All I ask for is an honest Christian man who has good morals. Someone I can trust completely, who I can count on no matter what, and who has a good sense of humor and knows how to communicate," Dionne finally said as she took a sip of her cranberry spritzer.

Trina flashed a smile. "Girl, you just described Jesus. You better lower your standards a little and work with what you get."

"That would be a no!" Dionne exclaimed. "I lowered my standards and it got me all the busters I've dealt with up until this point. I'm through lowering my standards. Roland has opened my eyes. I'm prepared to wait on my prince." Dionne didn't know who she was trying to convince more—her friends or herself.

Trina tapped on her glass, making it ding. "You're waiting on a prince?" she asked. "Then prepare to grow old alone."

Everyone laughed, except Dionne.

Chapter 13

Dionne stared at the kiwi green BCBG warm-up suit that hugged the mannequin's body. It was similar to the no-name gear she had on right now, except it looked expensive. Dionne fingered the knit material, debating whether to shell out the money, even though she really didn't have it.

She decided against the idea. Usually she loved shopping, and being broke had never stopped her before. But right now she didn't even feel like making the effort. Dionne knew she had to be down in the dumps if a trip to the mall wasn't cheering her up. But it wasn't just depression over the breakup with Roland. A bout of morning (or, rather, afternoon) sickness was kicking her butt.

"I think that would look so cute on you," Rosolyn said as

she walked up to her sister. They were inside the new Neiman Marcus, which had just been built at Memorial City Mall. Rosolyn was dressed in a tracksuit, too; but with that elastic at the ankles, hers looked like something Aunt Ida would wear.

"Yeah, Auntie Di, that's tight," Bryson said.

Dionne tousled his curly hair. She always loved being around her adorable little nephew. Bryson was spoiled rotten since he was the only child in their family. But he was still basically a good kid. "What do you know about something being tight?" she said, a smile finally crossing her face. "You ain't but seven."

"Seven and a half," he replied. "And I know when somethin' is tight."

"What did I tell you about that language?" Rosolyn chastised.

Bryson poked out his lips, then turned his attention back to his Game Boy. He'd begged to come to the mall with them and Dionne could tell by the look on his face that it was a decision he now regretted.

Rosolyn shot him a stern look before turning back to Dionne. "Seriously, though. That outfit is cute. Why don't you get it?"

"Please," Dionne responded, fingering the outfit again. "You know I can't afford anything in this store. I thought about getting it, but then I wouldn't have any electricity to see how good I looked in it because I wouldn't have the money to pay my light bill." The meager salary she was paid as a receptionist at a travel agency would never bring her the lifestyle she desired.

She found herself once again regretting dropping out of Prairie View her junior year. She'd kept promising herself that she'd go back, but so far that had been nothing more than talk. The one time she'd gotten serious about going back, Roland had come along. And since he always had a thick roll of money, her education once again took the back burner.

Roland hadn't been big on dating, but he did shower Dionne with fine things. He worked as an insurance claims adjuster, but Dionne knew he was dabbling in something shady because he always had a pocketful of cash. One night when she was at his place, some well-dressed man named Link had dropped by. Dionne had excused herself but watched from the other room as the man had slid Roland a wad of money and told him to pad the damage claim for his company, Casper Dealings. At first Dionne was shocked, but then Roland had given her money to go shopping so she didn't say anything about it. She should have known then, she told herself. A man who could cheat at his business could cheat at home.

"You know what? Can we go? I'm really not in the mood to shop," Dionne told her sister. Thinking about Roland had gotten her depressed all over again.

"Let's go to Marble Slab Creamery," Rosolyn announced. She draped her arm through Dionne's and led her out of the store. "I bet some strawberry and banana ice cream could cheer you up."

Dionne decided against protesting and followed her sister out. She knew nothing, not even her favorite ice cream, could bring her out of this slump.

Dionne had broken down and called Roland again yesterday. He'd started talking that mess about "me time" again and all but told her he thought it would be best if she didn't call him anymore.

They made their way to the food court and walked up to Marble Slab. Bryson immediately began eyeing the play area.

"Mommy, can I go play?" he begged.

"What about your ice cream?" she asked.

"I'll get it later. Please." He clasped his hands together and batted his big puppy dog eyes.

Rosolyn smiled. "Fine, since I can see you from here. We'll be sitting right there." She pointed at a small table near the play area. "You only have about ten minutes before—" Bryson dashed off before she could finish her sentence. Rosolyn shook her head as she walked up to the counter and ordered for both herself and Dionne, who was already heading for the table.

"How long are you going to be in a foul mood?" Rosolyn asked after handing the cup to her sister.

"You just don't understand," Dionne said as she took a nibble of her ice cream. "Your life is so perfect."

Rosolyn sat down and chuckled as she played with her ice cream. "Nobody's life is perfect, little sister."

Dionne put her spoon down and massaged her temples. Her head had been pounding ever since her conversation with Roland yesterday. "I just don't get it. What's so wrong with me? Why can't I find a husband?"

Rosolyn spent a few seconds weighing her words before she said, "Honestly, you seem to be in love with the idea of marriage and not the idea of love."

Dionne cut her eyes at her sister. "What the heck does that mean?"

"Just what I said. How about you look for love and just let marriage come."

"I have been looking for love," Dionne protested. "Shoot, I loved Roland. And I loved Greg before that. And Mike before that."

Rosolyn shook her head. "Let's see: Greg told you before you started dating that he couldn't be monogamous. But you thought you could change him. And Mike, the only date you ever went on with Mike was to Costco to pick up free samples of food. You let him convince you that that foolishness was romantic. And you found out just how much he really loved you when he wiped out your checking account." She held up a finger, thinking. "And the only time you saw Roland was at three in the morning when he was calling to say he was on his way over. You've never met his family. Yet you think you two were in love?" Dionne wouldn't meet her eye. She hated when Rosolyn acted like the know-it-all big sister. "Let me see, what else?" Rosolyn went on. "Oh yeah, he was cheating on you *and* his wife! That's some kind of love."

Dionne didn't respond. Her sister was right, but she did love Roland. She didn't care what anyone said.

"And I keep trying to tell you the grass is not always greener on the other side," Rosolyn continued. "Look at Vanessa. She was married and look what happened to her."

"That's because Vanessa doesn't know how to take care of her man. I took good care of Roland."

"Yeah, so did his wife and his other girlfriend."

Tears welled up in Dionne's eyes. Rosolyn relaxed her harsh look as she noticed Bryson walking back over to their table. "I'm sorry, I shouldn't have said that, but you've got to shake yourself out of this slump. It's been two weeks." Rosolyn repeated some words of advice she'd given her baby sister before. "Get to know Dionne. Fall in love with Dionne. Then maybe you won't have a problem getting someone else to love you as well." She smiled just as Bryson came bouncing toward her.

"I'm ready for my ice cream now," he announced.

Rosolyn stood up, transforming easily into a mother. "I'll be right back."

Dionne sat for a few minutes, letting her sister's words sink in. Rosolyn was right, she thought. Rosolyn was so balanced. Rosolyn had love for herself. She had just resolved to listen to Rosolyn's advice when her eyes suddenly grew wide. She recognized the wild red bushy hair immediately. Even better, she recognized the tall, muscular man sitting across from her. He was playfully feeding the woman french fries.

"What are you looking at?" Rosolyn asked as she and Bryson returned to the table. When Dionne didn't respond, she turned and scanned the room. "Uh-oh . . ."

"That low-down—" Dionne stood up.

"Dionne, wait!" Rosolyn said, reaching for her sister's arm. But she wasn't fast enough. Dionne had already begun stomping over to their table.

"What happened to some 'me' time?" Dionne snapped as she approached.

Roland looked up in shock. "Dionne, wha . . ."

"What's the matter, cat got your tongue?"

The woman chuckled as recognition set in. "Well, well, well. If it isn't the *other* woman. Excuse me," she said, taking a french fry from Roland's outstretched hand, "but me and my man aren't in the mood for company."

"I don't think I was talking to you," Dionne growled, holding her palm up toward Tasha's face.

Tasha stood up, ready to do battle. "No, you didn't. I knew I should've kicked your butt the other day."

Dionne didn't back down from anyone. "What day would that be?" she said sweetly. "Would that be the day me and Roland spent making love to each other? Or the day that this coward here"—she pointed at Roland—"scaled a fence to get away from you?"

"Dionne, chill," Roland said as he nervously looked around the food court. He never had been one for scenes.

Right about now, Dionne couldn't care less. "Don't tell me to chill," she spat. Personally, she didn't like scenes either, but she could not believe Roland would show off this tramp in public. "You just told me you wasn't messing with her."

"Well, then he lied." The woman folded her arms across her chest and rolled her neck.

"I didn't tell you I wasn't seeing her. I said it's not like that." Roland tried pleading. "Dionne, look, please don't come up in here starting nothing."

By that point Rosolyn was standing shoulder to shoulder

with her sister. "Yeah, Dionne," she whispered, "let's get out of here. You can deal with this later. In private."

Dionne snatched her arm away. "Don't start nothing?" she exclaimed. She knew she was getting emotional, but the pain she felt in her heart was unbearable. "I think you started something when you lied to me."

Tasha leaned in to Roland. "See, baby, I told you when you mess around in the gutter, you can't help but pick up trash."

No, she didn't have the nerve to call me gutter trash. "Oh, I got your trash," Dionne said, grabbing Tasha's bushy ponytail. She was surprised when it came off in her hand, leaving a stub of natural hair sticking straight out.

"Owwww!" Tasha screamed, grabbing her head. Before she could say another word, Dionne pounced on her. She wasn't a fighter, but something in her just snapped.

"Dionne, no!" Rosolyn screamed as the people seated around them scattered out of the way.

"Y'all stop," Roland said, stepping off to one side. "C'mon, you two." He had the nerve to be laughing like it was funny.

Rosolyn grabbed Dionne's arm again and pulled her back. "Have you lost your mind?"

"Yeah, she must have!" Tasha screamed from the floor. "And I'm about to kill her!"

Dionne lunged at Tasha again just as she pulled herself up off the floor. This time, though, Tasha managed to grab Dionne's hair and push her face down on the table. "Girl, you don't know who you're messin' with!" Tasha shouted as she picked up

Dionne's head and slammed it onto the table. Dionne cried out in pain.

Two security guards finally showed up and managed to pull Tasha away. Set loose, Dionne scrambled away. Her chest was heaving as she tried to calm herself down. Luckily, Tasha was as wild as a banshee, so Security focused completely on her.

"Why y'all on me?" Tasha screamed, struggling to free herself from their grip. "She started it!"

"You see what you have me doing?" Dionne shouted at Roland. "You got me up in here fighting!"

Rosolyn took Dionne's hand, firmly this time. "Come on, Dionne. Let's get out of here."

"You'd better chill out before I have you arrested," one of the guards said to Dionne.

"Ain't nobody got you doing nothing," Roland said, still laughing.

Rosolyn squeezed Dionne's arm again. At that moment Dionne hated him with every bone in her body. Her eyes filled with tears as she said, "You make me sick," before breaking free from her sister's grip and stomping off.

Rosolyn didn't catch up with Dionne until they were outside in the parking lot. Bryson stood next to her, a look of terror on his face. "Auntie, are you okay?" he softly asked.

Rosolyn took his hand and marched him toward the car. "Auntie's fine, baby. She just got a little mad." She cut her eyes at Dionne, who opened her mouth in protest.

"It wasn't my fault. I—"

"Unh-unh." Rosolyn cut her off. "Don't say a word. Don't

say a word to me until we get home and I can get my son away from this foolishness."

No one spoke until they were back out on the freeway. "You know you were out of order, right?" Rosolyn finally asked.

Dionne leaned her head back on the headrest. "Just let it go, Ros."

"I can't do that." She continued driving, fingers rigid on the steering wheel, then sighed heavily. "You know, maybe you need to find you another man. That will help you get Roland out of your system."

Dionne gazed out the window. "I don't want another man."

"Just somebody to help you take your mind off Roland." Rosolyn's eyes grew bright, like an idea was just popping into her head. "And I know just the person."

"Please," Dionne groaned. "I am not trying to meet any of those busters from your church."

Rosolyn grinned. "No, I think you'll like this one. Give me a minute to find some things out. If he's single, then I definitely think he's the one."

"Whatever," Dionne mumbled. She wasn't paying her sister any attention. There was only one man she wanted, and she'd just seen him at the mall with another woman.

Chapter 14

Dionne couldn't take the look of disgust written all over her sisters' faces. Rosolyn had dropped Bryson off at a playmate's house and she and Dionne were now sitting in the living room at Rosolyn's house. Dionne just wanted to go home and cry herself to sleep. She wasn't in the mood to be lectured. It didn't help that Vanessa was waiting outside Rosolyn's place when they pulled up. Rosolyn had called her from the car and told her that it was "imperative" that she come in for a "crisis intervention."

Now both of them were towering over Dionne like she was a child being scolded.

"I can't believe you were up in the mall fighting some woman over a man." Rosolyn shook her head like a schoolteacher. "Where are your standards? You don't think more of yourself than that?"

"Yeah, Dionne," Vanessa added. "What is that about? I can't believe you stooped to that level. Aunt Ida would die if she knew you were out there fighting like some hood rat."

Dionne tried to tune them out, but the way they both were dumping on her, she could tell that it was going to be virtually impossible. They would never understand. The thought of being a single mother was eating her alive. That was not her life's plan. She was supposed to marry Roland, then they'd have kids a year later. She wasn't supposed to be pregnant *and* manless. That was what was sending her into an unimaginable depression and had her doing things she knew she didn't have any business doing— like fighting in malls—while she was pregnant.

"I don't know why we women do that," Rosolyn said, pacing back and forth across her living room. "You should be getting mad at your man. That woman doesn't owe you anything. We get mad at our man cheating and want to jump the woman." She looked snidely over at Vanessa.

"What?" Vanessa frowned up. "Don't look at me, Rosolyn This is about Dionne."

Dionne nursed her left cheek, which was still sore from when Tasha smashed her face into the table. She should've known better than to go toe to toe with Tasha, since Roland had already told her Tasha grew up in the Fifth Ward, the rough part of town. But when she saw them together, a tide of rage had overtaken her. "Please, you guys. I'm not in the mood for a lecture, okay?"

"Somebody needs to lecture you because you are getting out of control," Rosolyn chastised, sounding like somebody's mama.

Dionne finally decided to speak up for herself. "You two just don't understand. If everything you ever wanted was coming to an end, you'd be upset, too."

"Everything I ever wanted *is* coming to an end," Vanessa said glumly.

Rosolyn took a deep breath. "Both of you need to get yourselves together." She glared at Dionne again. "And you should be ashamed of yourself. Bryson had to witness all of this nonsense. How could you act like that?"

"Look, Mrs. Perfect," Dionne snapped, "everybody can't have the fairy-tale life. You wouldn't understand why I reacted the way I did. You have the perfect husband, the perfect child, the perfect Martha Stewart home with your flowered couches and doilies all over the coffee table."

Rosolyn was silent for a few minutes before she said, "You're right. I'm in no position to judge you."

Dionne ignored her and continued her rant. "Some of us have problems in our lives, you know. We're not perfect like you."

Rosolyn told Dionne sadly, "I said I was sorry, okay? And I keep telling you all that my life is not perfect."

"Whatever," Dionne shot back. "Big Sis is as close to perfect as I'll ever get."

"I'd have to agree, Ros," Vanessa chimed in. "You couldn't possibly understand what either of us is going through. I mean—"

"Stop it. Stop saying that now," Rosolyn loudly snapped, cutting her off.

Both Vanessa and Dionne stared at her, their eyes wide. Rosolyn never had outbursts, so this one caught both of them by surprise.

"I am so sick and tired of people talking about how perfect my life is," she said, her voice cracking. She sank into the recliner and started crying so hard that it scared her sisters. Both of them stood up and went over to her. Rosolyn was their rock. She wasn't supposed to break down.

"Rosolyn, what's wrong?" Vanessa asked.

"I'm just tired of trying to put on this happy face when my life feels like one big lie," Rosolyn wept.

"Okay," Vanessa said, "something is going on and you need to talk to us."

"Yeah, Ros. What's up?" Dionne asked, her voice laced with concern.

Rosolyn took a deep breath like she was trying to gather up her strength. "Henry is not . . ." She stopped short and shook her head.

"What?" Dionne demanded.

"Are you guys having financial troubles?" Vanessa asked.

Rosolyn shook her head again but didn't say anything.

"Don't tell me he's cheating?" Dionne interjected, bridling at the thought. "'Cuz if ol' holier-than-thou Pastor Henry is cheating, then there's no hope for the rest of us!"

Rosolyn had dated Henry since they were in high school. He was a little bit anal but, other than that, as close to perfect as a man could get. He was handsome, intelligent, and loved Rosolyn to death.

"Henry's not cheating," Rosolyn said somberly.

"Well, are you cheating?" Dionne laughed. Could all three sisters have messes at the same time? The smile quickly left her face as she narrowed her eyes at her sister. "Oh, my God. You *are* cheating."

Rosolyn began fiddling with her hands but kept looking at the floor. "Not anymore." She wiped her tears. "But I did. A long time ago."

Vanessa and Dionne relaxed a bit. "Well, maybe you just had to get your freak on a minute. I mean, you have been with Henry since you were sixteen," Dionne said. "I understand that. And what Henry doesn't know won't hurt him."

"Henry knows," Rosolyn said mournfully.

"What?" Vanessa exclaimed. "Did you tell him?"

"Ooooh, did you get busted?" Dionne asked.

"No, I told him."

Vanessa and Dionne exchanged glances over Rosolyn's head. "So, what did you go and do a dumb thing like that for?" Dionne asked. They both knew their big sister was an honest person, but this was something you took to your grave.

"I didn't have a choice." Rosolyn got up and walked over to the living room window.

"What does that mean?" Vanessa said, following behind her.

Rosolyn took another deep breath as she kept her back to her sisters. "I had to tell him." She fought back more tears. "My affair happened seven years ago."

"Well, that is a long time ago," Vanessa said. Now she didn't see what all the fuss was about. "You two seem to have rebounded well."

Rosolyn turned and looked Vanessa dead in the eye. "Bryson is seven."

Vanessa's mouth immediately dropped open and Dionne's eyes widened in horror.

"Are you saying what I think you're saying?" Vanessa whispered, shocked. Rosolyn slowly nodded.

"Oh, my God. You are lying!" Dionne gasped.

"I wish I was."

Rosolyn picked up a family photo from the mantel. They looked like the picture-perfect family, all of them dressed in their navy suits. "Have either of you ever wondered why my son is so light-skinned and his daddy is so dark?" She lovingly returned the picture to its right place.

"Shoot, I thought it just reached back some generations," Dionne said. "You know Grandma was half white. I never in a million years would've imagined it was because you were creepin'."

Vanessa shot Dionne an admonishing look. Rosolyn didn't seem bothered by her sister's crass remark as she continued. "Naturally, Henry was devastated when I told him. And I had to tell him," she emphasized, glancing toward Dionne. "You know I don't believe in abortions, and I couldn't have lived with the lie of trying to pass off another man's baby. I just prayed that Henry wouldn't leave me. It was hard, but he eventually forgave me and took Bryson in as his own."

"Wh-who is Bryson's father?" Vanessa stammered. She was having a hard time digesting everything.

Rosolyn let out a pained chuckled. "A man I met at a church conference before Henry became a minister. I thought Henry had cheated on me with another woman. She called me to tell me about her and Henry's affair. He denied it, but I didn't believe him. He was gone all the time at seminary school, so I just assumed the worst. I was angry and slept with Damon to get revenge. He's the only other man I've ever been with," she said, making the point clear. "We met up a couple of times, but Damon wasn't the one-woman type, so he quickly grew bored and moved on." She let out a long sigh. "Yep, I was trying to pay Henry back for hurting me. And as it turns out, the other woman was playing me, trying to cause problems in my marriage."

"What?" Vanessa and Dionne exclaimed at the same time.

Rosolyn slowly nodded. "I found out that she wanted Henry, but the feeling wasn't reciprocated. She didn't take rejection very well and set out to cause problems between us."

"Dang, so you had unprotected sex with another man? Several times?" Dionne asked, still amazed. "You? The first lady?"

"I wasn't the first lady then, and we did use protection."

"Well, then, how do you know Bryson isn't Henry's child?" Vanessa wanted to know.

Rosolyn pursed her lips, then admitted, "Henry is sterile. He can't have any children." Her sisters jerked back slightly, never having suspected it. "But just in case there had been some kind of miracle, we had a DNA test. Bryson is Damon's child.

And since Damon already had two kids out of wedlock, he was very happy to let Henry officially adopt Bryson. He signed over his rights without batting an eyelash and we haven't spoken of it since. But it's never stopped eating me alive."

"I am so sorry. I didn't know," Vanessa said gently.

"I was a great actress," Rosolyn said bitterly. "I lied to everyone, always playing the happy-go-lucky pastor's wife, and inside I was dying." She looked at Dionne. "So see, my life isn't perfect. I carry my guilt every day. I know what I'm talking about when I say you have to let that anger go. It's not healthy and it can lead to you doing something you regret."

Dionne contemplated her words. "Or I can look at your story as a sign that maybe me and Roland will work out after all," she said.

Vanessa and Rosolyn looked at each other in amazement. "How did she come up with that?" Rosolyn sniffed, finally forcing a small smile.

"She got that because that's what she wanted to get," Vanessa said, letting out a small laugh herself.

Dionne massaged her temple. A big part of her knew she needed to leave Roland alone, especially after the way that he'd just humiliated her at the mall. But the other part of her felt like they should at least try to work things out for the baby's sake.

"Uh-uh," Vanessa said, eyeing Dionne closely. "I know you're not thinking of giving Roland another chance."

Vanessa and Rosolyn continued to stare at their baby sister. She hated their judgmental looks.

"Okay, I'm going to nip this in the bud right now." Rosolyn stood up and marched over to the phone.

"What are you doing?" Vanessa asked.

"Calling Bruce."

"Who is Bruce?" Vanessa asked.

Rosolyn punched a number into the cordless phone. "The guy who fixes our computers at work. I told him I wanted him to meet my sister."

Dionne's mouth dropped open. "Rosolyn, I told you I wasn't trying to meet anyone."

Rosolyn ignored her sister as she put the phone to her ear. Dionne stood and walked over in front of her sister. "Hang that phone up," she demanded.

"Hey, Bruce," Rosolyn said, edging away from Dionne, "this is Rosolyn Frazier from The Mason House. Can you give me a call when you get a chance? I told my sister all about you and she's anxious to meet you. Talk to you soon. 'Bye."

Vanessa exchanged smiles with Rosolyn. "Way to go, sis. Nothing like one man to make you forget about another. Got anybody for me?"

Dionne huffed as she put her hands on her hips. "That was foul, Rosolyn. When that computer nerd calls back, you just tell him you were lying because I'm not trying to meet anyone else."

Rosolyn set the phone back in its cradle. "He's not a nerd." She gave Dionne a patient smile. "Seriously, just go out with him once. He loves to read, just like you do. He's funny, charming, and he makes good money."

"And he's probably butt-ugly," Dionne responded.

"Actually, he's kinda cute," Rosolyn replied. "He looks like a shorter version of Tiger Woods."

"If he's not ugly, then he's gay," Dionne retorted.

The look on Rosolyn's face turned serious. "Dionne, please do this—for me. Just one date. If you don't like him, I won't pressure you anymore."

Dionne walked back over to the table, defiantly shaking her head.

Vanessa tried another tactic with her sister. "You know, you said the thought of you with another man would drive Roland crazy. You should go out with this Bruce just so you have something to throw up in Roland's face."

As Vanessa guessed, Dionne's eyes brightened at that idea.

"You gotta speak her language," Vanessa whispered to Rosolyn.

"Okay, I can get with that," Dionne said, nodding like she was warming to the idea.

Rosolyn sighed. "Dionne—"

Vanessa held up a hand. "Shhhh. Whatever works."

Rosolyn shrugged in defeat. Dionne was beaming now. "Yeah. I will make sure Roland knows I went out with someone else."

"Dionne, Bruce is a nice guy," Rosolyn protested. "I don't want you using him."

"It's just a date, isn't that what you said?" Dionne's mood had done a three-sixty. "When Bruce calls you back, give him my number. Tell him I can't wait to talk to him."

Rosolyn tsked. "I'm only going through with this because he really is a nice guy and I think you'll like him when you get to know him."

Dionne nodded. "Yeah, yeah, yeah." She definitely wasn't feeling another man. But making Roland jealous? Now that was something she could get with.

Chapter 15

Vanessa watched Rosolyn's husband, Henry Frazier, in the pulpit. You could tell that man had been called to preach. He didn't shout every word like some preachers. Rather, he reminded Vanessa of that mega-preacher Joel Osteen, the way he calmly delivered the Word.

Henry was an average-looking man with skin the color of coffee. He had a strong, muscular physique and graying hair, but he always seemed to practice what he preached. For that reason he'd always been all right in Vanessa's book, and usually she halfway liked what he was saying whenever she did hear him preach. Today, however, he was talking sheer nonsense.

"Church, do you know the devil has been assigned to your marriage?" Henry proclaimed. "He's assigned to destroy the family structure. He doesn't want you to be happy. And he's the happiest when he's wreaking havoc in your family. That's right, the devil stirs up lies, causes cheating and anything else he can do to break those bonds of love."

Vanessa couldn't go along with that. *The devil didn't make Thomas screw another woman. His libido did.*

Ida, who was sitting to Vanessa's left, reached over and patted her niece's thigh. "Let it go, baby. Let that anger go. It can't bring you no good," she whispered.

I'll let it go when I've taught Thomas a lesson, Vanessa thought. Over the last few days, she had been consumed with thoughts of revenge. Aunt Ida must have known what was on her mind because she opened her King James Bible to Romans 12:19 and thrust the book toward Vanessa.

Dearly beloved, avenge not yourselves, but rather give place unto wrath: for it is written, Vengeance is mine; I will repay, saith the Lord. Vanessa read the passage, plastered on a smile, and handed the Bible back to her aunt.

All that was fine and dandy, but the Lord surely couldn't expect Vanessa to just sit idly by and let Thomas hurt her the way he had. The Lord definitely had to understand Vanessa's anger.

Ida kept her attention focused on Henry as she took the Bible back. After he started talking about how more and more people weren't honoring their vows made before God, Vanessa tuned him out completely. Instead, she focused on coming up with a plan. Despite what anyone might say, she *was* coming up with a plan to make Thomas sorry he had ever wronged her.

Thirty minutes later, Vanessa was happy to see the service

wrapped up. She'd devised a good idea to make Thomas pay and was anxious to get home and put her plan in motion.

Vanessa was waiting in the church lobby as Ida said hello to some friends when she heard the James Earl Jones–sounding voice.

"Well, hello, Judge Kirk."

Vanessa turned toward Senator Lee Johnson, the man who had been courting her to run for a seat in the Texas Senate.

"Senator." She reached out and gently hugged him. "So nice to see you. How's the family?"

The tall, handsome man not only sounded like James Earl Jones, but he resembled him as well. He flashed that smile that made him a favorite among voters. "Lauren is wonderful and the kids are great. I'm still the luckiest man alive. And how is Thomas?"

Vanessa immediately tensed up. She didn't want the senator to know her personal business because he was big on family values. She kept her expression perfectly neutral. "Thomas is fine. Working hard."

Senator Johnson looked around, then leaned in and softly said, "Have you found a charitable cause to align yourself with?"

Vanessa winced. The last time she'd talked with the senator, she assured him that she would find a charitable organization to throw her support behind. He'd told her that she needed that to make herself more favorable in her run for political office.

"Vanessa," he began when she didn't reply, "how am I supposed to help you if you won't even take my advice into consideration? I know you do some work with your sorority, but you've got to get some major charitable experience." Disappointment was spread all across his face.

"No, no, Lee," Vanessa replied, racking her brain to come up with something. "I'm on top of things. I . . . I have begun working with The Mason House." Rosolyn's job was the only thing that could come to mind. "My sister runs it and it's just a wonderful agency."

A bright smile replaced his disappointment. "Wonderful. I've heard great things about them." He looked around again, then said in an undertone, "Make sure and get some photos of you hanging around with some of the kids. And find the crappiest-looking ones you can. Nothing like a sad-faced, scrappy-looking kid to woo the voters." He winked as he walked off.

"So, if you hate Thomas so much, why are you acting like everything is fine?" Ida said, walking up as Senator Johnson left.

Vanessa was flustered. "Oh, that," she said, feigning indifference. "I just don't want people all up in my business."

"Umphh," Ida said, leading the way out to the parking lot, "whatever you say. And since when did you start working with The Mason House?"

"Did you eavesdrop on my whole conversation?" Vanessa snapped.

"I sure did," Ida said stiffly. "Y'all didn't look like you were up to any good. And you know I like to know what's going on."

Vanessa shook her head, deciding to let the subject drop before her aunt asked any more questions.

"Rosolyn said she'll catch up with us later. She has some stuff to do around the church," Ida said as they headed out the double doors. She got to the bottom of the steps, hesitated, then said, "You know it's a shame the way you just tuned out God's word today."

"Aunt Ida, please. I don't know why I let you drag me to church today anyway," Vanessa replied, passing her aunt on the sidewalk.

"I'm trying to save your soul, get you to go to church and pray on a regular basis," Ida said reprovingly.

"Auntie, you know I'm busy." They reached her car, and she hit the remote, unlocking the doors.

Ida climbed in. "Yeah, I know. Too busy for church. Too busy for your husband. Too busy for the feeble old woman who raised you." She raised a warning finger. "You'd better watch yourself. You're gon' get to Heaven, ask the Lord to come open the Pearly Gates and let you in, and He's gon' say, 'I can't do it right now. I'm too busy.'"

Vanessa smiled at her aunt, who was sitting there looking like she was preaching the Word of God herself. She decided to just let the conversation drop. She'd never get her aunt to see her point of view anyway.

R. Kelly's song "When a Woman's Fed Up" began playing on the radio as they pulled out of the church parking lot. Vanessa turned up the volume and began singing along, at least to the chorus, which was all she knew.

"When a woman's fed up, it ain't nothing you can do about it," she sang.

Ida cut her eyes at Vanessa, then reached over and pushed the tune button until it hit 92.1. "Shake the Devil Off" by Dorothy Norwood began blaring through the car. "Now, that's what you need to be listening to," Ida said matter-of-factly.

Vanessa groaned but left the radio alone. Both that song and another after it had wrapped up before Ida started on her again. "You know, I ain't no psychologist or nothing. But what you're feeling ain't healthy. I know Thomas wronged you, but you have to forgive the wrongdoing, the wrongdoer, and move on."

"Ha!" Vanessa laughed. "Not gonna happen. I won't be able to move on until Thomas gets his."

Ida shook her head as Vanessa pulled up in front of Rosolyn's house. She turned to Vanessa just as she was about to step out of the car. "Seeking revenge only deepens the hole in your heart. It prevents you from moving forward. I'm gonna pray for you, baby girl."

Vanessa didn't respond as her aunt headed up the walkway. She knew her aunt's intentions were good, but nobody could understand the pain she was feeling. The only thing that could make this pain go away was revenge.

Chapter 16

Nothing about this man looked like Tiger Woods. Dionne stood unnoticed back in a corner at Boudreaux's Restaurant. She had arrived late on purpose so that she could check Bruce out before she committed to spending an evening with him.

He was standing over at the crowded bar, watching ESPN as he waited for her. Dionne ran her eyes up and down his body. He was the same color as Tiger and that was about it. He wasn't ugly, but he definitely wasn't as cute as Rosolyn made him out to be. He wore brown slacks, and a cream sweater vest with a T-shirt underneath; his small-framed glasses did give him a nerdy look. Dionne liked her men tough, and Bruce didn't look like he could stand up to a fly.

Dionne contemplated leaving, but then she glanced over at

the bar and saw Quentin wiping down a glass. Her heart fluttered. Quentin was one of Roland's best friends, which was why she'd chosen this restaurant to meet Bruce.

Bruce had called her shortly after she left Rosolyn's yesterday, and Dionne had agreed to meet him this evening so they could get to know each other. Although she had actually enjoyed their hour-long conversation—in which they had talked about their mutual love of books, music, and reality TV—she didn't want him to get his hopes up thinking they had a real chance at being together. She'd told him as much, but he still wanted to meet. She'd told him she would be wearing a camel-colored jacket and Baby Phat jeans.

"May I help you?" the hostess finally asked.

"No, I see the person I'm looking for," Dionne replied, removing the black shawl she had wrapped around her jacket in the event she decided to duck out.

Dionne strutted over to the bar area. She moved slow and sexy, trying to give Quentin time to notice her. When she saw his eyes light up in recognition, she pretended not to see him and tapped Bruce on the shoulder. "Hello."

He turned around, a huge smile across his face. That stupid grin made him look like an even bigger nerd. He was lucky he had captured her with his conversation, because he dang sure couldn't do it with his looks.

"Dionne. You're just as beautiful as your sister said you were." He leaned in and planted a gentle kiss on her cheek. "I'm so glad you could make it."

"Sorry I'm late."

"No problem. I was just catching up on my sports news for the day." He pointed toward a booth. "You want to take a seat?"

Dionne led the way to the booth, sliding in while trying her best not to glance toward the bar.

"I really enjoyed talking to you last night," Bruce said. He'd told her all about his computer software company. He was an engineer, more on the designing side. But he repaired the computers at The Mason House as a way to give back. He was twenty-seven and single. He'd told Dionne it was not by choice. He just had yet to find the perfect woman for him.

"I enjoyed talking to you, too," Dionne genuinely responded. They made small talk after placing their order. For a while Dionne got lost in their conversation and forgot about Quentin. That is, until she looked up to see him standing over their table.

"What's up, D?" he said, his tone grim.

"Hey, Quentin, what are you doing here?" Dionne asked innocently.

He motioned toward his apron. "I work here, remember?"

"Oh, yeah. I forgot about that." She motioned toward Bruce. "Quentin, this is Br—"

"So, where's Roland?" he asked, ignoring Bruce.

"Nice to meet you, too, man," Bruce chuckled. He didn't seem at all fazed by the snub.

Dionne raised an eyebrow. "I guess Roland is at home with his woman. As I'm sure you know, I don't keep tabs on him anymore."

"That's just temporary," Quentin snarled. "You know you and my boy are meant to be."

Dionne was a little offended by Quentin's blatant disrespect for Bruce. She had wanted Quentin to see her, but she didn't appreciate the way he was acting toward her date.

"Right now," Bruce said, leaning forward on the table, "she's meant to have dinner with me. So, if you don't mind . . ."

Quentin flexed his thick muscles. "Was anybody talking to you?"

"Am I supposed to be scared, Hulk Hogan?" Bruce asked, standing up.

Dionne stood also, putting her arm in between the two men. "Quentin, if you'll excuse me, I'm trying to enjoy dinner with my friend."

Quentin kept his eyes fixed on Bruce. "Umph, your friend, huh?"

"For now," he said with confidence.

"'Bye, Quentin," Dionne said forcefully. "Don't you need to get back to work?"

Quentin kept his eyes glued to Bruce before finally walking away.

"Say, dude, can you bring me a Heineken?" Bruce called out after him.

Dionne fought back a laugh as Quentin threw them both disgusted looks.

"I guess that means no," Bruce said, sitting back down.

"Sorry about that," she said, smiling. "That's my ex's best friend."

"Awww, don't sweat it. He didn't faze me."

"I see that," Dionne said, impressed by the way he'd handled himself. Bruce had surprised her. Maybe he wasn't such a nerd after all. She sat back down, relaxed, and enjoyed the rest of her date.

Chapter 17

Dionne sat in front of her computer and stared at the email. *Just press Send,* the little voice in her head kept telling her.

Dionne was still fuming. She'd called Roland this morning, planning to drop hints about her date with Bruce, if Quentin hadn't already filled him in. But she never got the chance because when she'd called Roland's house, Tasha answered the phone.

"Roland's busy," she'd said after Dionne had asked to speak to him. "And if you know what's good for you, you won't call our house again, tramp!" She'd slammed the phone down in Dionne's ear.

Our house. The words kept ringing in Dionne's head. Not only had Roland totally disregarded her feelings, he hadn't even

112

called to check on her after the fight at the mall. So he deserved whatever happened to him.

Dionne read the email out loud for the twentieth time.

"Dear Mrs. Lewis. You don't know me, but I know you're in the middle of an ugly divorce. I just thought I'd let you know that your soon to be ex, Roland, has two hidden bank accounts: one at Washington Mutual, where he has at least sixty thousand dollars, and the other with the Bank of Texas, where he has another forty-five. It is my understanding that you have no knowledge of either of those accounts, but you really should check this information out. You also may want to have the authorities and Roland's employer look into Casper Dealings, LLC. I know for a fact that your husband has taken under-the-table money from a man known as Link, the owner of Casper Dealings, in exchange for inflating insurance claims on their various properties. I'm sure this will help bolster your case and assist you in getting what's rightfully yours. Hope this helps, signed a concerned sister friend."

Dionne pressed the Send button before she lost her nerve. "There. That'll teach Roland that he can't just go around playing with people's feelings."

Getting Roland's wife's email address was easy. Dionne had simply asked to use Roland's computer and made a note of it, back when she and Roland had first gotten together and Liz had been harassing her. They'd never met face-to-face, but somehow Liz had gotten Dionne's home number and had left several menacing messages.

When the Message Sent icon popped up, Dionne sat back and smiled. She'd give anything to be a fly on the wall when Mrs.

Lewis opened her email. Dionne didn't too much like helping Liz out, but she didn't mind sticking it to Roland one bit. She knew hitting Roland in his pocket would hurt him the most.

The ringing of her telephone brought Dionne out of her vindictive thoughts. She scouted around the bedroom for her cordless phone, finally finding it under her bed, where she had flung it after talking to Tasha.

"Hello," Dionne said.

"Goodness, what took you so long?" Rosolyn replied.

"I couldn't find my phone." Dionne glanced at the computer screen, smiled one more time, then lay down across her bed. "What's up?"

"You know why I'm calling," Rosolyn excitedly said. "How'd the date go?"

"Hold on." Dionne moved the phone away from her mouth. "Ummm, Bruce, you made me pancakes," she said huskily. "After last night, I should be the one making you breakfast in bed." Dionne held in her laugh as she put the phone back to her ear. "What were you saying, sis?"

Silence filled the phone.

"Hello? Ros? Are you there?"

"I know you did not sleep with that man on the first date." Rosolyn's words were slow and steady.

Dionne couldn't hold it in any longer. "No, girl," she said, bursting out laughing. "I'm just messing with you. Whoo, I needed that."

Rosolyn released a sigh of relief. "Girl, don't play."

"Naw, it was cool. He actually is a nice guy."

"Well, I'm happy to hear that you liked him. When are you two going out again?"

"We're not," she replied, recalling his remark about them being friends *for now*. She liked him and really didn't want to lead him on. "Another time, another place, he might've actually had a shot, but I got other things on my mind right now."

"Dionne," Rosolyn said, being encouraging, "maybe Bruce can help you forget about Roland. You know, I'm not into rebound guys, but I really think he'd be good for you."

"Naw, I can't forget about Roland. Not yet, anyway. Not after the way he played me," she said, her mood souring again. "But don't worry, I'm about to cross the river of no return with Roland. I already—" She let her words hang.

"You already what?" Rosolyn asked.

Dionne was itching to tell her sister what she'd just done. But at the same time, she really didn't feel like being judged.

"Okay," Dionne said, deciding she couldn't hold it in. Plus, after what she'd just learned about her sister, Rosolyn definitely was in no position to judge anyone. "Do you want to know what I was doing on the computer?"

Uneasiness filled Rosolyn's voice. "Why do I have the feeling this isn't something good?"

Dionne smiled wickedly as she flipped over on her back. "I sent Roland's wife an email."

"An email? For what? And just what was in this email?" Rosolyn asked.

Dionne shook off the melancholy mood creeping up on her.

"Skeletons, which will help her win her case against her no-good husband. They go to court in three weeks."

A strict tone came into Rosolyn's voice. "Dionne, what did you do?"

Dionne didn't sound guilty in the slightest as she said, "I just let her know some things that she didn't know. I wanted to give her something that she could use in court. Man, I wish I could be in the back of the courtroom and see the look on his face when she drops this bomb on him."

Rosolyn sighed. "I hope you know what you're doing, little sister."

"What's that supposed to mean?" Dionne said, annoyed. She knew she shouldn't have said anything. Yeah, Rosolyn might have slipped up and gotten pregnant by another man, but she was still a Goody Two-shoes, which was evident by the fact that she'd come clean. Guilt or not, Dionne would've never admitted Bryson wasn't Henry's child.

"All I'm saying, Dionne, is you should have left well enough alone," Rosolyn admonished. "I told you revenge doesn't do anyone any good. Roland would've gotten his." She might as well have been Ida, as she added, "God don't like ugly."

"And neither do I. That's why Roland had to pay. He messed with the wrong chick."

"I just hope you know what you're doing. I'll leave it at that."

"Thank you for your two cents. Now, I need to run. I'll talk to you later." She didn't give Rosolyn a chance to say good-bye as she hung up the phone. She silently cursed as she fell back on the pillow. Rosolyn had spoiled her good mood.

Chapter 18

Vanessa glanced around the cramped facility. It saddened her to see how bare and dilapidated the inside of the building was. The paint was chipping off the bright yellow walls so badly you could barely make out the mural. The five tables positioned throughout the room all looked like they had been donated from the Civil Rights era. Still, from the looks of the young people sitting around laughing and playing various games, you wouldn't know how run-down the place was.

"You don't have to look so disgusted, you know," Rosolyn said, nudging Vanessa toward her office.

Vanessa smiled at her sister, whose arms were filled with files. "I'm sorry. I just, well, I didn't know things were this bad here."

"What? You thought I was exaggerating? I told you times are hard, and with state funding getting cut back, it's only going to get harder."

"I know, but dang. It doesn't make any sense for these kids to have to live in a place like this."

"Who are you telling?" Rosolyn asked. "That's why I'm so glad that you're going to become an advocate for the center. I've only been trying to get you to come down for the last year."

Vanessa flashed an apologetic look. "If I had known it was this bad, I would've come down here the first time you asked."

"Well, I'm just glad you're here now." Rosolyn smiled. "Even if you are just using us."

"Uh, I am not using you guys," Vanessa protested.

"Please. This is your big sister you're talking to. Aunt Ida told me all about your conversation with the senator. But don't sweat it. Use us. As long as we can get some money in the process, use us up." Rosolyn pushed open her office door and motioned for Vanessa to follow her in.

"Shelly, what have I told you about being in my office?" Rosolyn asked the pretty, brown-skinned young girl who was sitting at Rosolyn's desk, writing. She had big puppy dog eyes that said she'd seen too much, too soon. She wore her hair in a ponytail on top of her head. She looked like she couldn't be any more than twelve.

Shelly looked up from her paper but didn't crack a smile. "Sorry. But it's the only place I can write in peace."

"You tell me that every time I catch you in here. But I still don't want you in my office when I'm not around," Rosolyn chastised.

"Okay, okay," Shelly said, gathering up her stuff. "I'm leaving."

Rosolyn waved her hand. "No, you're here now. You might as well stay. What are you working on? Another poem?"

For the first time Shelly smiled. She nodded eagerly and announced, "This one is called 'Black Butterfly.' "

"Shelly writes awesome poetry," Rosolyn said, turning to Vanessa. "She's only eleven, but as Aunt Ida would say, she has an old soul."

"Wow, poetry, huh?" Vanessa said.

"This is my sister, Vanessa." Rosolyn motioned toward her.

"I love poetry." Vanessa came over and glanced down at Shelly's paper. "My sister writes it all the time. She used to make us listen to it when we were little and I always have loved it."

Rosolyn chuckled. "I forgot about Dionne and those 'Roses are red, violets are blue, I got my man and I'ma take yours, too' poems."

Shelly looked offended as she closed her tablet. "I don't write about no lame boys."

Rosolyn stroked her hair. "I know you don't, baby." She turned back to Vanessa. "Shelly writes about deep stuff. Too deep, if you ask me."

Shelly headed toward the door. "I just write what I know," she said matter-of-factly.

"That's the sad part," Rosolyn replied.

Shelly shrugged. "I'm gonna go. Maybe I can get a shower before everybody starts bombarding the bathroom."

"'Bye, Shelly. Nice to meet you," Vanessa called out as the little girl left.

Shelly flashed a meek wave, but didn't turn around.

"What's her story?" Vanessa asked as soon as she was gone.

Rosolyn placed the papers down on her desk.

"Dad shot her mom, then himself, with her sitting at the kitchen table watching." Rosolyn shook her head. "I just for the life of me can't understand how these parents can be so selfish. Not once did he ever think about what this would do to his only child."

Vanessa cringed at the story. "Wow. How long has she been here?"

"Four years. No one wants to adopt a preteen."

"She's been here for four years?"

Rosolyn nodded. "Yep. Her parents did leave a small life insurance policy. She went to live with her father's family and so they got the money. But then the mother's side acted such a fool that the state intervened and took custody of her. The sad part is, after a few months here the money ran out; nobody wanted her. She's been here ever since." Rosolyn shook her head, discouraged. "She really is a sweet girl. She's just a loner, that's all."

Vanessa glanced toward the door. Shelly's story tore at her heart. "That is so sad." She brightened up as a new idea came to her. "Maybe she could be the face of the center. You know, kind of give people a reason to support you guys."

Rosolyn shot Vanessa a chastising look. "My sister, always

the businesswoman. Nope. You can use me. You can use the center, but I can't let you use the kids."

"But—"

"No buts. That's not even an option."

Rosolyn sat down before her computer, intending to start work. Yet when she tried to turn it on, nothing happened. She pounded it in frustration. "This dang computer is about to drive me crazy. It's so old that you have to do a Fred Sanford on it just to get it to come on." She tapped the side twice, then hit the top once. The machine sputtered, but the screen didn't light up. "I guess you just don't feel like working today," Rosolyn hissed at the computer. She reached for the phone. "Let me call Bruce and ask him to come fix this thing again."

Vanessa stood up. "Well, I need to be going. Thanks for letting me come take a tour." Her mind returned to Shelly. "Putting faces with your plight here at the center really hammers home how much you guys need help."

"Thank you so much, Vanessa," Rosolyn replied as she punched the numbers on the telephone.

Vanessa blew her sister a kiss as she headed back toward her car. She looked around, hoping to catch a glimpse of Shelly, but the girl was nowhere to be found. Vanessa took one last glance around and felt more charged than ever. She had come to the center hoping to get enough political ammunition to bolster her run for office. She had a feeling, though, that helping the center was going to be good for her in more ways than she could ever imagine.

Chapter 19

Dionne groaned inwardly. Something told her not to answer the phone when she saw Aunt Ida's number pop up. It was, after all, seven in the morning. Her aunt knew better than to call that early. And on Dionne's day off at that. But it was obvious Ida didn't care, the way she was going on and on.

". . . and you know my dreams be coming true and I saw fish clear as day," Ida rambled. "It was a whole slew of them swimming in a bathtub."

Dionne tried to sound fed up, but she was actually shocked. "Auntie, I assure you, I'm not pregnant, so it ain't me." She didn't like lying to her aunt, but she wasn't ready to share her news until she figured out what she was going to do. Now that Roland was out of the picture for good, she needed to snap out of her funk and pull herself together. Lots of women had babies by themselves. Or better yet, maybe she needed to look at giving Bruce a real chance, since he seemed like he could definitely provide for her.

Naw, she thought. She was a lot of things, but she wasn't into using men, especially nice guys like Bruce. She told herself she just needed to find a better-paying job. That way, when she broke the news of her pregnancy to family and friends, no one would trip with her about being a single mother.

"Well, maybe it's Rosolyn," Ida continued. "Or, Lord willing, it's Vanessa, and maybe she and Thomas will work things out."

"Or maybe it's Alana, the chick Thomas got pregnant. Or better yet, maybe you're just crazy," Dionne tried to joke.

Her stomach was in knots. She'd been tossing and turning all night as thoughts of Roland filled her head. Initially, they had been hate-filled thoughts. Then they had turned to happier times, like the time he'd surprised her at work with barbecue for the whole staff to celebrate her birthday. Or the time he'd moved mountains to get her front-row tickets to the Prince concert, even though he hated concerts. People didn't see all of that. But she knew—in her heart she knew—she and Roland were good for each other. And even though he'd never said it, he loved her, despite what he did to her.

"Ummph, you talk about me all you want." Ida's raspy voice snapped Dionne back to her phone conversation. "But you know my intuition doesn't lie. Remember that time my palm was itching and I hit that Cash Five lotto?"

Dionne grinned at the memory. "Yeah, that six thousand dollars that you won gambling, but you claimed God was okay with it because you gave fifteen percent to the church."

"That's right," Ida replied, very pleased with herself. "And I told you— Wait, are you trying to be funny?"

Dionne was about to respond when she heard pounding on her front door. "Auntie, I gotta go. Someone's at my door. Check with Rosolyn or Vanessa and see if they are the ones pregnant. I'll call you later. Love you."

Dionne hung the phone up, raced downstairs, and flung open the door. She'd been expecting a delivery from UPS for something she ordered off eBay.

Her mouth dropped in disbelief as she stared at the fine chocolate specimen leaned against her door frame.

"Hey, baby," Roland said, with a huge grin.

No, this fool didn't have the audacity to come show up on my doorstep like nothing is wrong.

Dionne folded her arms across her chest. "Roland, what do you want?"

He pulled a bouquet of white roses from behind his back and held them out toward her. "I want you. I'm here to tell you that I'm sorry."

"Go tell someone who cares," she replied, starting to push the door closed.

He put his hand out to stop her. "Awww, come on, baby. Don't be like that. Let me talk to you. I miss you, girl."

"Roland, go to hell, or back home to Tasha, which is probably the same as hell anyway."

"I'm not with Tasha anymore."

"Yeah, right. Then why was she just at your house answering your phone yesterday?"

He held up his hands in innocence. "She came over to get the last of her stuff. She answered my phone when I went to the bathroom." He paused, letting her see he was on the level. "We're done. I'm for real. That's history."

She eyed him suspiciously. "Like I believe that. You've already shown me how much of a liar you are."

"It's the truth." He licked his lips in that LL Cool J way that turned her on. He knew that because she'd told him. "I messed up, D. I've been sick without you."

I've been sick without you, too, she thought. "Whatever, Roland. You are so full of it."

"Tell me you don't want to see me and I'll leave." He held the flowers up again.

She glared at him. "I don't want to see you."

He dropped the flowers down by his waist and nodded, trying to keep his voice controlled. "This wouldn't happen to have anything to do with the dude you went out with the other day, would it?"

Dionne was momentarily speechless.

"Yeah, you went to Boudreaux's, so you knew my boy was gonna come back and tell me."

"I thought Quentin was just supposed to serve drinks, not spy on the customers," Dionne said, trying to contain her elation.

"Whatever, D. You knew what you were doing." His frown dropped away. "But it worked. I was sick when he told me."

Dionne folded her arms across her chest. "So, you're only here because you don't want me with anybody else."

His voice became earnest. "No, I'm here because I don't want to be without you. And yes, I didn't know how much I wanted you until you were gone."

"Roland, you are so full of it. Just leave."

"You don't mean that," he responded.

Dang, he looked good. The bad part was she *didn't* mean it. Her heart was filling with joy at the sight of him standing there, saying the words she'd prayed to hear him say. She wanted him so bad it hurt.

Dionne let out a long breath as she leaned against the door. "Roland, I'll ask you again. What do you want?"

"I just need to talk to you. I miss you so much."

Dionne sighed as she opened her door and motioned for him to come in. She knew she shouldn't, but she wanted to hear him explain how he could've hurt her like he did. Roland walked in, letting the door slam behind him. "You have five minutes," she said.

As she brushed past, he grabbed her arm and pulled her back to him. Before she knew anything, he was planting a deep, wet kiss on her lips. She loved his kisses. "Ooooh, baby. I've missed you so much," he moaned as he slowly kissed her neck.

Dionne felt her body weakening at his touch. She wanted to curse him out, go off on him. But it was like her body wasn't getting the message her brain was trying to send.

"Girl, I can't get you out of my mind," he whispered

hoarsely. He ran his hand up under her T-shirt. "I'm so sorry. I messed up, bad. Please forgive me."

She was fighting her feelings but both his words and his touch were melting her defenses. "Roland, stop."

"Baby, I'm sorry. Let me make it right," he pleaded.

"What happened to your 'me' time?"

He nuzzled her neck. "There's no me without you."

That sounded too rehearsed. She pushed him away again. "Please. Go run that game somewhere else."

He grabbed her, not enough to hurt her, but enough to catch her by surprise and get her attention. "D, you got my head messed up. I mean, I didn't know how bad I had it for you until I didn't have you anymore. I need you in my life. I'm begging you to give me another chance."

Dionne couldn't help it. Her hand immediately went to her stomach. She thought about her baby. *Their* baby.

"You hurt me," she said softly. A single tear began to trickle down her cheek.

"I know. And I'm so sorry." He took her face in his palms and gently kissed away the tear. "I love you, Dionne."

She froze. A month ago, she would've given anything to hear him say that. But hearing it now tore at her heart even more.

Dionne closed her eyes and let out a soft moan, but then shook her head and pulled herself together. "No, get off of me," she said, snapping out of the trance he was luring her into. She pulled away from him completely. "You have a lot of nerve. You were cheating on me and dumped me for some old girlfriend I knew nothing about. And I'm supposed to just welcome you back with open arms?"

"I made a mistake. I came here to tell you that and let you know how much I love you."

"Whatever, Roland," she said as she flicked him off and walked into the kitchen. She pulled out a bottle of Dasani water and took a sip. She had to cool off the heat building in her body.

"You're not going to offer me any?" Roland asked, appearing in the kitchen doorway.

"No, I'm not, because you won't be here long," she said pointedly.

Roland sat down at the kitchen table. "Can I ask you a question?" He waited for her to say something and when she didn't, he asked, "Have you ever made a mistake?"

She looked at him, confused. "What?"

"Have you ever in your life made a mistake?" he repeated.

"Of course I have," she retorted. "What kind of question is that?"

"Well, I made a mistake by letting you go."

He looked so sincere, he was making her sick. "Sell that crap to someone who's buying," she sarcastically replied, glad that she was cooling off and coming back to her senses.

"I'm serious," he cried. "I can't be with Tasha, or anyone else for that matter, because I can't stop thinking about you."

Dionne tried not to smile. Roland always did know what to say to get to her.

Seeing her soften, he said, "Dionne, sit down." He pointed to the chair across from him. Dionne didn't move.

"Babe," he continued anyway, "I know I was wrong to keep seeing Tasha when I was with you. But she's been around for so long, she was like an old security blanket. You know you should get rid of it, but it just feels safe." Dionne wasn't convinced, and he poured it on. "Besides, she just rolled with the punches, took whatever I gave her. So she was low maintenance—until she started trippin'. The closer I got to the divorce, the more she talked about us being together exclusively." He scowled at the pressure he'd felt, and that did seem real. "By that point, I had met you, and before I knew it, I was falling hard for you. After the disaster of a marriage I had, I promised myself that I would never allow myself to fall in love again, but I did. And losing you made me realize that I can't live without you."

Dionne could hear her girls calling her all kinds of names right now, but they didn't know Roland like she did. Love might be blind, but she could see very clearly that Roland loved her. And she loved him just as much. That was reason enough to give him another chance. But throw in the baby and she knew she had to forgive him.

He must have sensed that he was getting to her because he stood up and walked toward her. "Please, D. Give me another chance. I tell you what. I'll call Tasha with you right here. You can hear me tell her I want to be with you." He glanced at the wall phone, showing how serious he was. "I've been miserable without you. I didn't realize how much I needed you. How much I wanted you until you were gone."

He took her in his arms. She pulled back reluctantly and he lifted her chin. "Just one more chance, baby? I promise you won't regret it." A new idea came to him, and he quickly added, "Let's go to Vegas. I want to spend the whole weekend with you and make up for hurting you."

Dionne was getting lost in Roland's light brown eyes. As much as her brain wanted her to say no, her heart wouldn't let her. Instead she said, "You'd better not hurt me again."

He breathed a sigh of relief as he hugged her tightly. "I won't, baby. I promise you I won't."

Chapter 20

"I'll take a Grande Caffè Mocha, no whip." Vanessa rattled her order off to the Starbucks cashier, then began digging in her purse for the money to pay for her coffee.

After she paid the cashier, Vanessa stepped to the side and waited for her drink to be prepared. The Starbucks employee handed it to her, and as she turned to walk off, she bumped right into another patron.

"Oh, I'm so sorry," Vanessa said, gazing down at the hot liquid as it spilled onto the floor. "Did it . . ." She stopped mid-sentence as her eyes made their way up and met Alana's.

Vanessa was breathing fire as she took in Alana's appearance. Pregnancy definitely agreed with her. Her young, smooth skin seemed to be almost glistening. Her shoulder-length hair was pushed back off her forehead with a pair of sunglasses, the soft unruly strands hanging loosely. But it was the pink T-shirt that had Vanessa's heart on pause. The arrow leading from the words "Baby on Board" across her chest down to her stomach, letting the world know that she was pregnant.

"Oh, hello, Miss Vanessa," Alana said. The way she said it made Vanessa feel old.

"Excuse me," Vanessa said abruptly as she walked around Alana and headed out the door. She couldn't believe that little twit was getting her frazzled. In court she could handle mountain-size men. Vanessa almost dropped her coffee again as she fumbled for her car keys.

"Miss Vanessa, can I talk to you for a minute?" Alana had followed her out.

Vanessa tried her best to regain her composure. "Don't call me Miss Vanessa," she said sharply. "As a matter of fact, don't call me anything at all."

"I'm sorry. I was just taught to always respect my elders."

Vanessa glared at her, but instead of responding, pulled out her keys.

"Wait, I just need to talk to you," Alana said.

"I don't think we have anything to talk about." She hit the remote, unlocking the car.

"It doesn't feel good, does it?" Alana sneered. The change in the tone of her voice made Vanessa stop short. The innocent look Alana had worn earlier was gone, replaced by a satisfied smirk.

"Excuse me? What are you talking about?"

"It doesn't feel good, does it? You know, watching your marriage fall apart?" She lovingly rubbed her belly, which looked like it was about to pop at any moment. "All the marriages you destroy. It doesn't feel good to have someone destroy yours, does it?"

Enraged, Vanessa stepped toward her. "Why, you little . . ."

Alana didn't budge. "Lay a finger on me and it will be on the front page of every newspaper in Houston tomorrow morning. Pregnant woman beaten up by judge," she scoffed. "Then, after the press rips you apart, I will sue you for every dime you have." Vanessa drew back at the pure hatred in Alana's eyes. She had a lot of nerve. If anything, Vanessa thought, she was the one who should've been hating Alana. She was so glad Alana brought up suing. This little girl was trying to make her act a fool. She'd lost her marriage behind her, she wasn't about to lose her career as well.

"Sweetheart, don't get it twisted," Vanessa hissed, leaning in to whisper in her ear. "I will beat your ass now and think about the consequences later." She straightened up and looked Alana directly in the eye. "However, I'm gonna pass right now, since I'm not in the mood to get my nails dirty. But just so you know, I don't have to lay a hand on you. I can ruin your life with the stroke of a pen."

"What is that supposed to mean?" Alana said, placing her hands on her hips.

Vanessa smiled as she opened the door to her Mercedes. She wasn't about to let this dime-store trick push her around. "I can show you better than I can tell you."

Vanessa got in her car and pulled off. She was boiling mad, but she kept a smile plastered on her face. It was on. Alana had messed with the wrong woman. Before it was all over, that home wrecker was going to wish she'd never laid eyes on Thomas.

Chapter 21

Alana's face was still front and center in Vanessa's mind. Since their run-in yesterday, she had been unable to think of anything else. Even now, as she took her spot on the bench, images of Alana clouded her thoughts.

"You may be seated," Vanessa said to the people in the courtroom who had just been ordered by the bailiff to stand. Shaking off her thoughts of Alana, she grabbed her stack of folders and inwardly groaned as she glanced at the first couple on the agenda.

"Nina Lawson versus Jeffrey Lawson," she said. "Are both parties ready?"

The couple stood and nodded, each standing on opposite sides of the room.

"Mrs. Lawson, you're seeking a divorce from your husband of ten years on the grounds of infidelity?" Vanessa fought back the anger building in her stomach. Did every man on the face of the earth cheat?

The woman, dressed in a conservative hunter green suit, nodded. "Mr. Lawson," Vanessa began, "let's talk about your infidelity."

The court clerk loudly cleared her throat. Although no one knew for sure, rumors were running rampant around the courthouse about her divorce with Thomas. Vanessa knew her clerk was trying to remind her not to let her personal feelings overcome her. Vanessa continued, "Did you not care at all about making a vow to your wife? Are you just that low-down that you said screw the commitment I made before God, I'm gonna get mine!"

"Huh?" Jeffrey replied, startled.

"You heard me. You promised to love, honor, cherish, her and only her, then you go out and cheat."

"Yep, you tell him, Judge!" Nina shouted.

Vanessa ignored Nina's outburst and continued talking to Jeffrey. "And you want me to have some sympathy for you?"

"But I never cheated," Jeffrey protested. "She just thinks I did because she's a paranoid psycho."

"Yeah, that's what they all say." She glanced down at her folder again. "And you have the audacity, the unmitigated gall, to ask that *she* pay *you* spousal support?"

Jeffrey looked flabbergasted. "But, Your Honor, we've been married ten years and that makes me eligible for support since she's the one that makes all the money. She's a celebrity hairstylist, and because she's on the road so much, I'm the one with the kids all the time. That's why I think they should stay with me, and she should pay child and spousal support."

"Oh, because your trifling behind wouldn't work you want her to provide for you?" Vanessa spat.

"But she wanted me to quit!" Jeffrey insisted. "She said the kids needed a familiar face at home with them. I didn't want to but since she made more money, it made the most sense."

"Shut up!" Vanessa ordered. "None of that excuses, or justifies, you going out and cheating on her. If anything, that makes it worse. While she's out working her behind off, trying to take care of her family, you're out cheating."

"But, Your Honor, I did not cheat! And she even started a website called girl don't dare date him. She has my picture plastered all over the Web."

"Hmph. Good, maybe it'll keep another woman from falling victim to your wiles."

He was ready to say something else, but Vanessa held her hand up to silence him. She then turned to the wife. "Mrs. Lawson, I am sorry that you have had to endure the pain and humiliation caused by your husband. Your divorce is granted. You will retain custody of the children and there will be no order of spousal support. Mr. Mom here needs to get a job within four weeks, at which time I will determine the amount of child support he will need to pay." She slammed her gavel. "Next case, please."

Vanessa went through the day granting every divorce that

came before her. She knew she was losing a little objectivity, but if she could help these women right the wrongs that had been done to them, she was going to do it.

Still, she was grateful when the day wrapped up. She knew she was letting her emotions get in the way of her judgment. The clerk didn't even look at her at the end of the afternoon session.

Back in her chambers, she had just removed her robe and was about to relax when her door swung open to reveal Judge Robert Malveaux, the senior judge in the Harris County court system.

"What in the world is wrong with you?"

"Excuse me?" Vanessa said.

He stomped into her office. "The courthouse is abuzz about what's been going on in your courtroom lately. I ignored the gossip at first, but then decided to peek in on your last case." He fixed her with a stern look. "Have you gone mad?"

Vanessa recalled her last case. A woman with a violent temper had stabbed her husband when she caught him in bed with her sister. She'd tried to act evenhandedly. "I don't understand what the big deal was. It was a clear-cut case."

"What's clear about attempted murder?"

"It was a crime of passion." She could tell that he was outraged. In a quieter voice she said, "Besides, I wasn't hearing an attempted murder case. I was handling the divorce."

Malveaux, a fifty-something black man with salt-and-pepper hair, huffed at that excuse. "You are not being objective in hearing these cases. You are automatically siding with every woman, regardless of the circumstances. Even the cases where the woman was at fault. You're granting divorces without any second thought." He raised his arms, made wide by his black robe. "Are you on some kind of drugs? I can't believe what I'm hearing, or what I saw with my very own eyes." He came closer and leaned over her desk. "It's bad enough that you have always been such a proponent of divorce, but now you're taking things to a whole new level. You're granting divorces with such callousness, it is not reflective of your commitment to uphold and adhere to the law!"

Vanessa rested her knuckles on her desk and leaned right back at him. "The people elected me. That means I only answer to *the people*."

"I'm sure the people would not appreciate you not upholding your responsibility and following the law—"

"But the people can appreciate men who cheat on their wives?"

Malveaux took a deep breath, trying to calm himself down. When he began again, his tone was more reasonable. "Vanessa, I understand that you are going through a hard time. It's no secret what's happening between you and your husband. That is why I think it's best that you take a leave of absence."

Still angry at his accusations, Vanessa began straightening files on her desk. "Nobody asked you to think on my behalf. Of course you're going to side with these no-good men. I heard you cheat on your wife, too."

He slapped the desktop loudly, his nostrils flaring. "Number one, my personal business is none of your concern, because unlike you, I don't let it interfere with any of my work. And number two, I have been happily and faithfully married for nineteen years. I will continue to be faithful," he thundered. "And if we did have some kind of problem, we would take it to God, not divorce court."

She'd never seen him so upset, but she also thought he was protesting too much. "Yeah, yeah, yeah. Is there anything else I can help you with?" she said dismissively.

Judge Malveaux stared at her, his eyes hard. "I want you to know that I am filing a formal complaint, and I will recommend that you be forced to take a leave of absence until you get yourself together."

"Whatever," Vanessa said.

He shook his head, then left out the room. Only then did Vanessa realize that her hatred for Thomas had made her blind to plain old common sense. She rubbed her lower abdomen, which had started cramping on a regular basis. The stress was truly getting to her.

Maybe Judge Malveaux was right. Maybe she did need a break.

Chapter 22

V anessa forced a smile to fill her face. After her day at work yesterday, she wasn't in the mood for the pomp and circumstance surrounding the kickoff for the "Revitalize The Mason House" campaign. If she hadn't already had her office send media releases, she probably would've canceled today's reception. Besides, the kids seemed to really be enjoying the event.

Vanessa's smile turned genuine as she watched Shelly do the bump with Ronald McDonald. She was giggling and her eyes were filled with joy. It was the first time Vanessa had seen the little girl act like a child. She'd dropped by the center twice since her initial visit, and both times Shelly had sat in a corner quietly writing poetry. They'd talked a little, but Shelly never had much to say.

"Miss Vanessa, did you see Ronald tryin' to do the Soulja

Boy?" Shelly asked, racing over to where Vanessa stood at the back of the room.

"I did," Vanessa replied, gingerly moving a strand of hair out of Shelly's eye. "But he didn't have anything on you. Girl, where'd you learn to dance like that?"

Shelly blushed, but didn't answer.

"Shelly! Shelly!" Another little girl raced over and pulled Shelly's arm. "Come on, they just brought Krispy Kreme doughnuts!"

Shelly's eyes danced with excitement. "Ooooh, my favorite. 'Bye, Miss Vanessa." She took off with the little girl before Vanessa could say another word.

"Hey, you," Rosolyn said, walking up to her sister. She looked great in a fitted navy knit suit, her thin braids pulled back into a bun.

"Hey, yourself." Vanessa ran her eyes up and down her sister's outfit. "Look at you."

Rosolyn did a small twist as she spun around. "You like?" Then she became her usual pragmatic self. "It's not often I get all this media attention. I need to look together. People won't want to donate their money to a place being run by a run-down-looking old hag."

Vanessa lightly pushed her sister. "You are not a hag. Old, maybe. Hag, no."

Rosolyn laughed. "Okay, funny lady. I see you're hitting it off with Shelly."

Vanessa looked over at Shelly stuffing a jelly doughnut into her mouth. "She's sweet. It's something about her that just gets to me."

"Yeah, she has that effect on a lot of people. Just not enough for anyone to permanently take her home." Rosolyn looked around the room with a questioning look. "What time did you tell the press to get here?"

"Ten," Vanessa said, glancing at her watch, "which is in about fifteen minutes. We'll have the kids sitting in the first row. I'll welcome everyone, introduce you. You tell them about The Mason House and then I'll come back up to talk about our fund-raising efforts. I've already gotten Windsor Village United Methodist Church to donate ten thousand dollars. So I'll use that to jump-start the donations."

Rosolyn stared at Vanessa, her eyes watering.

"What? Why are you getting all teary-eyed?"

Rosolyn hugged her. "I'm just so thankful. I prayed for a way that we wouldn't have to shut our doors. I didn't know God was going to send an answer in the form of my own sister."

Vanessa squirmed to get away. "Stop it."

Rosolyn stepped back and dabbed at her eyes. "No, seriously. I know you started this just as a campaign strategy, but I know your heart. You're really into it now."

"I am." Vanessa smiled appreciatively. She saw a motion out of the corner of her eye, and glanced toward the door. "Oh, here's Channel 26. Let's get this show on the road. Where's Dionne? I thought she was coming."

"She said she was," Rosolyn replied. "But Roland is taking her to Las Vegas next week, so she said she was going out shopping."

"Roland?" Vanessa exclaimed. "Are they back together?"

"It looks that way," Rosolyn groaned.

"I thought she went out with Bruce." Vanessa sighed as she threw her hands up. "Whatever. It's her life," she said, waving at the cameraman. "We have more important things to deal with. Come on." Vanessa draped her arm through Rosolyn's. "Let's go get some people to throw their money your way."

Chapter 23

"Hell hath no fury like a woman scorned." Vanessa chuckled as she read the blurb of the novel on her secretary's desk. "Ain't that the truth?" she said, tossing the novel back down on the desk and making her way into her office. They could've interviewed her for that book. It would have definitely been a bestseller then.

Vanessa had pulled herself together to come to work today. She had made it through the reception with no problem, and by day's end, The Mason House had gotten pledges of almost fifty thousand dollars. By the time she'd made it home, she was exhausted and just wanted to crawl into her bed.

The stress with Thomas was now making her physically sick. Vanessa had started cramping again right after her conversation with him this morning. Before that call she'd actually thought maybe she should chill and just let Thomas and Alana go on about their business. But his call had changed all of that. Vanessa felt her anger rebuilding as she replayed their conversation.

She'd answered the phone even though the caller ID said "private call."

The line was silent for a few seconds before Thomas said, "Hi. How are you?"

Vanessa huffed. "What do you want, Thomas?" She wasn't in the mood for niceties. No sense in being fake.

"I just wanted to let you know that my uncle Walter is in the hospital. He had a mild stroke."

Vanessa felt badly. She liked Thomas's carefree uncle and hated to hear that something had happened to him. "Is he going to be all right?"

"Yeah, he's going to be fine." He coughed to clear his throat. "You know, it used to make his day to see us together. I just thought, you know, maybe you'd like to go by and see him with me."

"And why would I do that?" She let out a disgusted sigh. "Thanks for the update. Now, let us just say good-bye." She'd find out where Walter was on her own. But there was no way she'd go smiling in Walter's face, pretending everything was okay.

"Look, Vanessa, things don't have to be ugly between us," Thomas said. "We can still be friends."

"Thomas, you made things ugly the day you cheated on me

and got another woman pregnant," she reminded him. "And for the record, I have enough friends. I don't need any more, especially lying, cheating, low-down dogs."

Thomas let out a long groan as if he didn't want to go down that road again.

"By the way," Vanessa added, "do you mind telling your little pop-tart to stay the hell away from me?"

"What are you talking about?"

"Her taunting me about 'taking my man' is going to get her into a whole lot of trouble," Vanessa snapped.

He tsked and adopted his totally rational attitude. The one intended to make her feel irrational. "Vanessa, let's just keep this professional. This is between you and me. You don't have to make up stuff about Alana. That's not even her personality."

Vanessa gripped the phone tightly in her hands. *No, he wasn't taking up for her.* "Excuse me?"

"Don't take this out on Alana," Thomas continued. "Keep your issues with me. There is no need to make up stories or dog out Alana."

"Fool, I don't need to make up stories," Vanessa said. "Your mistress accosted me at Starbucks and all but threw in my face the fact that she had stolen my husband."

Thomas let out another groan. "Alana told me all about the incident at Starbucks. From what she told me, it was you who were doing the accosting—and judging by your attitude right now, I believe her."

Vanessa had to hold her hand up and inhale deeply. Good

thing that he wasn't standing next to her because there was no telling what she would've done if he had been within striking distance.

"Let me explain something to you, Thomas Edward Kirk," she began, struggling to keep her voice down so she didn't get even more stressed out. "I don't need to lie. I'm sure she has you fooled with this young and innocent act, but the girl is a conniving wench and your dumb ass is so blinded by what you think you weren't getting from me to see it."

"Okay," he announced. "I can see this conversation is going nowhere."

"You're right about that." Vanessa slammed the phone down. "Uggh!" she screamed. She hurled her coffee cup in the sink so hard, it cracked the handle off. Why did she let that man get to her? She didn't even love him anymore.

That had been less than two hours ago. She'd driven to work, blinded by fury. Now she was back to her original plan of seeking revenge.

Vanessa opened her computer and punched in her password. She checked her personal email. "Yes," she said, when she noticed the email from misterpi@yahoo.com.

She clicked it open and smiled as everything she ever wanted to know about Alana Irving filled the screen. Vanessa started perusing the file. "Age, twenty-five. Driver's license number, Social Security number. Parents, Leslie and Mark Irving." Vanessa paused. Those names sounded familiar for some reason. She shrugged it off and continued reading. Alana was a kindergarten teacher at the exclusive Baines Academy Montessori School.

Vanessa scrolled down to look at whether Alana had any criminal records.

"Well, well, well," Vanessa said, settling in on the third line in Alana's criminal file. "A drug conviction and a theft by check conviction in California. Hmmm, I wonder if Baines Academy knows about this?" She Googled the school, then got the address and the principal's name. "We'll just have to make sure that they do know." She copied the conviction record onto a blank page, printed it, then addressed the envelope to the principal. After placing the printout into the envelope, Vanessa tossed it in her outgoing-mail box. "Little girl, you picked the wrong woman to mess with."

She had just returned to reviewing her cases when she heard a knock at her office door.

Her secretary, Nicole, stuck her head in the door. "Judge Colton-Kirk, I'm sorry to disturb you, b-but there are some men out here to see you."

"Well, who are they?" Vanessa asked.

Before Nicole could answer, Judge Malveaux pushed his way into the office. Standing behind him were two courthouse security guards.

"Judge Vanessa Colton-Kirk," Judge Malveaux intoned, "on behalf of the Texas Judicial Commission, I am here to deliver papers declaring a forced leave of absence."

Vanessa was speechless as the guards moved closer to her desk.

"According to this letter, approved by the commission, you are hereby ordered to take leave for eight weeks, at which time the commission will reexamine your work practices and conduct a personal evaluation to determine if you are capable and competent to reassume your position."

"Are you out of your mind?" Vanessa exclaimed, standing up.

"No, but you clearly are. And as a representative of the people and the state of Texas, you have left me no choice." He dropped a document on her desk. "You will see that those papers are in accordance with your contract. Now, you can leave of your own accord, or these nice gentlemen"—he motioned toward the security guards—"can escort you out."

Vanessa picked up the letter and quickly read it. "You can't do this."

"Watch me." Judge Malveaux stared at her with disdain.

Vanessa glared at the burly security guards, who stood on either side of the desk, their arms folded.

Nicole was still in the doorway, shock written all over her face.

Vanessa didn't want a scene, so she grabbed her purse. "Fine. I can use some time off anyway." She stomped toward the door. "Nicole, please lock up my office." She turned an arched eyebrow at Judge Malveaux. "Unless, of course, Judge Malveaux plans to kick you out of here as well."

She shot him an evil look, then walked out of the office with her head held high. Vanessa knew she was well-respected around the courthouse and she didn't want anyone here to see her crumble. But inside, she felt like she was falling apart. First her marriage, now her job. How much more could she be expected to endure?

Chapter 24

"Hey, you seem out of it." Rosolyn waved her hand in Vanessa's face.

Vanessa shook herself out of her trance. She was lost in thought, beating herself up for letting her personal life interfere with her career. She *had* been unusually harsh. What was she thinking? Now her job was in jeopardy.

"Oh, I'm sorry," Vanessa said. "I'm just trying to process this whole forced leave-of-absence thing."

"Well, I can go over this paperwork myself. You don't have to do it." They were sitting at the small conference table in the corner of Rosolyn's office.

"Naw." Vanessa pulled the financial report closer to her. "We need to get this stuff together. Texas Southern said they needed a detailed financial analysis before they could make a commitment."

"Well, Kenneth, the accountant, did a fabulous job. So I think this will do. You can review it at home."

"Okay." Vanessa slipped the papers into her Louis Vuitton tote bag. She peered out into the lobby.

"What time does Shelly get out of school?" Vanessa asked. Lately, seeing Shelly was really the only thing that brought her out of her slump.

"Oh, she won't be here today," Rosolyn excitedly said. "A couple is picking her up after school. They've been spending a lot of time with her, since they're looking at adopting someone her age. I think they really like her. This is her fifth visit with them."

Vanessa's heart sank at the news. She was happy for Shelly, but the thought of never seeing the girl again was depressing. She didn't mean to be selfish, but she felt a connection with Shelly. Maybe it was because they were both parentless children. Or maybe Shelly just helped Vanessa keep her mind off Thomas.

"I'll let you know how everything works out. But I'm keeping my fingers crossed that this is really the family for Shelly." Rosolyn narrowed her eyes when she noticed the expression on Vanessa's face. "What's wrong?"

Before Vanessa could reply, the office door swung open.

"Oh, I'm sorry. I didn't realize you'd be here," a nerdy-looking guy wearing small-framed glasses said.

"Hey, Bruce, come on in. We're just wrapping up," Rosolyn said. "Bruce, this is my other sister, Vanessa."

He smiled widely as he walked toward them, extending his hand. "Nice to meet you." His smile was infectious.

"Nice to meet you, too. I've heard a lot about you." Vanessa stood and returned his handshake.

"Good things, I hope."

Vanessa nodded. "Of course."

"That's good," Bruce said, relief evident in his voice. "Rosolyn, I brought the part to fix your computer."

Rosolyn clapped her hands together. "Great! I didn't realize how dependent I was on that computer. I haven't been able to get anything done."

"Yeah, it appears you were having trouble getting the network stable because your Linksys kept disabling your motherboard. I suspect the Soyo KT333 board was too outdated for the card, so I brought a Q6700–Intel DG33TL Vista combination, which I'll pair with a crossover cable to the USB-equipped machine."

Vanessa and Rosolyn looked at each other like they had better take some new language lessons.

"Sorry." Bruce chuckled. "I forget not everyone is as versed in computer terminology."

"Well, whatever is wrong, just fix it, please," Rosolyn said.

He set the box he was carrying down on the desk. "I'm on it. Just give me about an hour and you'll be up and running. I just need to get one more bag out of my van."

He dashed out, a man on a mission.

"Okay, Dionne was right. He is such a nerd." Vanessa laughed.

"But he's a nice nerd," Rosolyn replied.

"And he drives a van? Oh yeah, I can see Dionne really going for that."

"Well, I was hoping she could look past all of that," Rosolyn said defensively. "Shoot, she needs somebody stable and average-looking, someone who is going somewhere and not these pretty boys like Roland that she keeps messing with." She gave a slight growl. "But Dionne ain't trying to hear nothing unless it's about Roland. I wouldn't be surprised if they were off in Vegas getting married."

"Married!" Vanessa exclaimed.

"I'm just saying, you know your sister. I wouldn't put it past her." Rosolyn put a finger to her lips as Bruce walked back in.

"You know, Mrs. Frazier, I didn't get to tell you, but thank you so much for fixing me up with your sister. I really like her. Of course you know how beautiful she is, but she has a wonderful personality," he said brightly. "I never thought I'd find someone who loves to read as much as I do. Or who likes music as much as me. Or who was just so funny."

Vanessa and Rosolyn exchanged glances again.

"Sorry," Bruce said, "I got a little carried away."

"No problem," Rosolyn said. "I'm glad you two hit it off."

"She's not feeling me like I'm feeling her," Bruce announced. His smile widened again. "But don't worry, she will." He clapped his hands briskly. "Well, gotta get to work."

Vanessa bid him good-bye as she and Rosolyn left the office.

"He's confident, isn't he?"

Rosolyn stopped, glancing back toward her door. "That's just what Dionne needs. And for some reason, I have a feeling that he is going to get exactly what he wants."

Chapter 25

The bright lights lit up the night sky. Dionne had been to Las Vegas several times, but it had never looked this good.

"Are you sure you're ready to take it in?" Roland asked, taking her hand. They were leaving Caesars Palace, strolling down the sidewalk, heading back to their penthouse suite after an exhausting yet fulfilling day.

She and Roland had been back together just under three weeks and she couldn't be happier. As Roland had promised, he had given her a weekend to remember. They'd arrived on Thursday night and they had been going ever since. He'd secured front-row tickets to Toni Braxton at the Flamingo Hotel. Then it was dinner, dancing, and gambling. But the highlight of the weekend was when Roland hit it big at craps, winning more than twenty thousand dollars. This morning he'd taken Dionne on a shopping spree and let her go crazy. And she'd done just that, buying the designer stuff she'd only dreamed about ever wearing.

Dionne had been trying to get up the nerve to tell him that she was pregnant. But they were having such a good time and since she didn't know how he would react, she didn't want to ruin their weekend.

"Hello. Are you there?" Roland said, waving his hand in her face.

Dionne let out a small giggle. "I'm sorry, baby. I was lost in thought."

"Dang, I must be a boring date if you're drifting off on me," he said as he opened the hotel lobby door and motioned for her to go first.

Dionne linked her arm through his as they walked through the massive lobby. Roland looked like a male model in his black form-fitting shirt and Calvin Klein jeans that showed off his muscular physique. She was proud to be seen on his arm. "Nah, you're not boring me at all," she said. "I'm just wondering when I'm going to wake up from this dream."

Roland stopped and turned her toward him. "Dionne, I messed up. I knew that I loved you, I just didn't realize how much until you were gone. Nothing like losing the woman you love to put everything into perspective. I'm so happy that you gave me another chance."

He looked down at his cell phone, which was silent, but lighting up. It had been lighting up all evening, and Dionne had done her best to ignore it. Roland picked the phone up, looked at it, then placed it back on the clip.

"Who is that?" Dionne asked, no longer able to contain herself.

"Nobody," Roland responded.

Dionne snatched her arm away and stomped toward the elevator. "Here we go with the lying again," she snapped, pounding the Up button. "I am so stupid for believing you could change." She hated to be going off, but that dang phone had been the only thing ruining their weekend. He'd said he couldn't turn it off because his mother was sick and he didn't want to take any chances on missing her call. Still, the constant calls were getting on her nerves.

Roland caught up with her. "Babe, chill, a'ight? I didn't want to tell you who it was because we were having such a great time and I didn't want to mess it up."

Dionne spun around. "It was Tasha, wasn't it?"

Roland sighed, nodded, then motioned for her to step in the elevator, which had just opened up. Dionne glared at the little old lady who had scooted closer to the corner like they were going to mug her or something.

Dionne was too upset to pay the woman any more attention and, in fact, didn't even care that the woman was in the elevator. "So, why does she keep calling you?" Dionne asked.

"She's texting me," Roland corrected.

"Calling, texting, whatever," Dionne snapped. "Why is she still trying to contact you?"

Roland glanced at the old lady, then put his index finger to his lips. "Can we talk about this in the room?"

Dionne was just about to go off when Roland reached down, unclipped his phone, and handed it to her. Dionne scrolled through the text messages and began reading out loud. " 'Why are you doing this to me? Why won't you take my calls? Go to hell. I hope you and that trick have a car accident and die,' " she recited.

The elevator stopped on the tenth floor and the old woman scurried off. As soon as the doors closed, he said, "I told you it was over with me and Tasha. She just ain't getting it. But don't worry, I'm not taking a chance on messing things up with you again."

A smile slowly spread across Dionne's face. "I'm sorry for trippin'." She leaned in and kissed him.

"I'm sorry for makin' you trip," he replied as the elevator doors opened.

Once they got settled back in their room, Roland called Dionne out to the balcony. He took her hand and they stood outside taking in the dry desert night air.

"My friends are gonna think I'm a fool," Dionne said. All weekend they'd been talking about their future. He was completely shocking her with his confessions of love. She was so happy, she couldn't think straight.

"That's understandable," Roland replied, wrapping his arms around her waist.

Dionne looked at him in amazement. She'd expected him to respond by telling her to screw her friends.

"Your friends are worried about you, Dionne. They don't want to see you get hurt. But you did the right thing by taking me back, and they'll see that soon enough."

Dionne laid her head on her man's shoulder. *I wouldn't count on changing their minds,* she thought. But her friends didn't have to believe Roland had changed. She did, and that was enough. Roland was serious this time, finally ready to settle down.

She turned around to face him. "I guess now is as good a time as any to tell you."

"Tell me what?"

She took a deep breath, trying to gather up her nerve. "Have you noticed that I haven't been drinking today?"

"You sure haven't," he said, as if it had just dawned on him. "And I know you love you some drinks, especially the free ones. I don't know . . ." His eyes suddenly grew wide. "Oh, my God. Are you pregnant?"

She nodded, not sure of how to take his reaction. He stared at her in shock. Then he let out a scream, picked her up, and swung her around. "Yes! I'm going to be a daddy!"

Dionne giggled as he swung her around in circles. "I love you so much, girl!" he shouted.

Suddenly, the whirling stopped.

He looked at her with a bright idea. "Let's get married!" His excitement was overwhelming.

Dionne's mouth dropped open.

"I mean, I know we have to wait for my divorce to be final," he said, momentarily dejected. "But let's get engaged. We can go get a ring tomorrow. My divorce will be final soon and we can get married right away." He lovingly touched her stomach. "My baby will be born with his or her daddy's last name."

"Roland, are you serious?" Dionne asked. "I mean, you're

not just saying that, are you? You really want to marry me?" He kept on smiling for all he was worth. "I mean, you don't have to do this just because of the baby. I can do this on my own," she added, knowing full well she didn't want to be a single mother.

Roland closed the distance between them. "I want to marry you. I want you to have my baby. And I want to live with you forever. I mean that from the bottom of my heart!"

Dionne was so happy she began crying. Roland hugged her tightly and began kissing her tears away.

Dionne sank into the warmth of his embrace. Despite all the drama she'd endured lately, it seemed like she was going to meet her goal after all: she would be married before thirty.

Chapter 26

If her heart wasn't hurting so bad, Vanessa would swear she was dreaming. That was the only way she could explain why she was sitting in a courtroom about to go before one of her colleagues in her petition for a divorce. It was bad enough that she had been forced to leave her job for eight weeks, but now she had to come back to the courthouse to go before another judge. Vanessa was sure rumors were running rampant, and she really didn't want to face anyone. She'd come up the back way, and other than the new security guard working the back door, she hadn't seen anyone she knew before entering the courtroom.

Vanessa glanced over at her attorney, Melody Mason, the best divorce lawyer in the South, if not the whole country. Melody had argued—and won—many cases before Vanessa herself.

"Are you ready?" Melody quietly asked.

Vanessa nodded. She'd already had to pull some strings just to get the case heard so soon. Thomas's attorney had tried to get the case heard in Galveston, which was an hour away from Houston, claiming Vanessa had too many ties to the Houston judicial system. Vanessa was glad when the judge overruled that request.

Vanessa had smiled inwardly when she'd learned that Mabel Caviel was going to preside over her case. While Mabel was fair, Vanessa knew Mabel respected her as a colleague—and knew that Mabel had endured an ugly divorce herself.

Vanessa glanced over at Thomas and his two-dollar attorney, some bifocal-wearing, Mr. Magoo–looking short black man.

Vanessa checked around surreptitiously for Alana. She didn't know whether to be relieved or upset that she hadn't showed. Part of her didn't know how she'd react to seeing that woman again. But the other part wanted Mabel to see her, because it would definitely not be favorable.

"All rise," the bailiff announced, snapping Vanessa out of her thoughts. She lost the mournful attitude she'd been feeling about being back in the courtroom and focused on her impending victory. She couldn't help but smirk as she stood. Thomas didn't know what he was in for. He could have his concubine. He wasn't going to get anything else.

"The Honorable Judge Vernon Jarrett presiding," the bailiff continued as a tall, distinguished-looking man with graying hair walked to the judge's bench.

Vanessa's mouth fell open. She quickly looked over at Melody, who shrugged. The expression on her face told Vanessa that she had no idea what had happened.

"You may be seated," Judge Jarrett said. He skimmed over his papers for a few seconds before finally looking up. "I'm sure you all were expecting Judge Caviel to preside over this hearing, but fifteen minutes ago, the judge recused herself from the case, citing her personal relationship with the petitioner. Since I am one of the few judges here who does not have a personal relationship with Mrs. Kirk," he continued, "in the interest of justice, I will be taking over this case."

He peered over his copper-rimmed glasses at Vanessa. She tried desperately not to show the scowl she was feeling inside.

Out of all the people in the world to hear her case, she had to get Judge Jarrett. He'd just been elected two months ago and he and Vanessa had only met once. But she knew his history. The two of them were as opposite as oil and water. He was one of those religious zealots who really believed in that whole "till death do us part" crap.

Vanessa whispered to her attorney, "Object or something. This man can't stand me." She recalled their single meeting, where he'd called her on the carpet for her divorce court procedures. "This is clearly a conflict of interest."

Melody looked confused momentarily, but then recovered. "Your Honor," she said, standing up. "I respectfully request that the court allow counsel the opportunity to find another judge."

"Request denied," he said flatly. "Now, I have Mrs. Kirk's original petition for divorce, and if both parties are ready, we'll get started."

"We're ready, Your Honor," Thomas's attorney said with a small smile.

The judge turned to Melody. She shrugged at Vanessa, then gave her arm a reassuring squeeze. "We're ready, Your Honor."

Vanessa shook her head in frustration as Melody sat down. "What are you doing?"

"Let me handle this," Melody whispered. "I've encountered much worse obstacles than this."

Vanessa pushed open the door to her chambers.

"Just let me handle this," she said mockingly. "I got this. I've handled situations much worse than this." She flung her purse down on her desk with a loud clatter. She knew she should've left the courthouse, but she was so angry, she needed to come into her chambers and cool off.

Melody entered cautiously, readying herself for Vanessa's wrath. "Mediation isn't that bad. It's normal. You know the drill."

Vanessa spun around. "Yeah, I do know the drill. And I know Vernon can end this sham of my marriage with a stroke of his pen, but noooo, he wants to get all self-righteous on me."

"All he's asking is for you to go to mediation. If it doesn't work—"

Vanessa cut her off. "It won't."

"If it doesn't work," Melody continued, "you come back and he'll grant your divorce."

Vanessa shook her head like Melody just didn't get it. "Melody, I've been doing this long enough to know that when a marriage is over, it's just over. There's no sense in delaying the inevitable."

"And I've been handling divorces long enough to know that an extra thirty days won't kill you," Melody responded.

But that wasn't the end of Vanessa's complaints. "How dare he try to make me go to a spiritual retreat?" she cried. "That's against the law. He must've forgotten who he's dealing with." She folded her arms and pouted as she stared out her fifth-floor window.

"Technically, it's not against the law," Melody said. "Each judge can recommend mediators. It just so happens that all of Judge Jarrett's are spiritual advisors."

"Well, that's some bullsh—"

"Vanessa Colton-Kirk! I know you're not about to let such foul language come out of your mouth."

Vanessa looked up at her Aunt Ida standing in the doorway of her office. Ida was clad in a peach pillbox hat and matching lace dress. She had an appalled look on her face, one hand on her hip and the other clutching her Bible.

Vanessa sighed. "Not today, okay, Auntie? I'm not in the mood." She hadn't even realized that Ida was in court for the divorce hearing, but knowing her aunt, it shouldn't have come as a surprise.

"And you think I care about you not being in the mood?" She walked in. "Hey, baby, I'm Ida, Vanessa's aunt," she said to Melody.

"Hello, I'm Melody Mason, Vanessa's attorney."

"I know. I saw you at work out there. You sure are a pretty

little thing. You married? Because my grandson sure could use a pretty young thing like you, with a good job and all."

"Aunt Ida!" Vanessa snapped. As if anyone would want Bud, her worthless ex-con cousin, who didn't know the meaning of "steady job." Thankfully, he lived in Miami, where he'd moved trying to con some woman into supporting him. But no one could tell Ida anything bad about her only grandson.

"Sorry," Ida said.

Melody laughed. "No, it's okay. But to answer your question, I'm happily single."

Ida shook her head. "Umph, umph, umph. You women today, I tell you the truth. Those two words don't even belong together—happily single. God intended for men and women to be fruitful and multiply."

"You don't have to be married to do that," Melody said slyly.

Ida's eyes grew wide as she stared at Melody in shock. "Lord Jesus," she mumbled.

Vanessa finally smiled. "Melody, please don't get my aunt started."

Melody quickly made for the door. "Well, I gotta run. But Vanessa, please call one of those mediators today. Remember, the sooner you do it, the sooner we can get back in here."

Vanessa nodded. After her attorney left, she arched her neck back, stretching the muscles, took a deep breath, and readied herself for her aunt's lecture. Yet Ida didn't say a thing.

"What?" Vanessa said, as Ida stood staring at her.

"I didn't say a word," Ida replied, shaking her head.

"No, but you're about to."

"You're right," Ida said, sitting down. "This should serve as a lesson to you."

Vanessa kept her temper at bay. "What kind of lesson would that be?"

"I told you God don't like ugly. For all you know, you lost your job—"

Vanessa cut her off. "I didn't lose my job."

"Excuse me," Ida said, giving the attitude right back. "For all you know, you might have been forced to leave because you've been acting so ugly." Ida thrust an envelope toward Vanessa. "Here. This is a card from that little girl, Shelly, over at that center. She gave it to Rosolyn, and Rosolyn gave it to me to give to you. Like I work for the post office."

Vanessa's foul mood immediately evaporated as she took the envelope. She tore it open to reveal a piece of paper with a huge happy face. Underneath the brightly colored face were the words "Good luck at court today!"

"Awwwww," Vanessa said. "That is so sweet."

"You told that little girl about you going to court?" Ida asked, astonished.

"Yeah, but don't worry, I didn't get into details. She asked me to come by the center today and I told her I couldn't because I had to go to court. That's it." Vanessa held the paper to her chest. "This is so sweet."

"It is," Ida nodded. "Too bad you just using the poor child."

Vanessa was about to respond when Nicole stuck her head in the door. "Judge Colton-Kirk! Are you back?"

Vanessa suddenly remembered that she was standing in her office. She needed to leave before people started asking questions.

Vanessa fashioned a polite smile. "No, I just stopped by to handle some business."

Nicole smiled at Ida. "Hello." She turned her attention back to Vanessa. "Okay, then. You take your time. We have things covered here."

Ida stood up. "Take your time, all right. Take this time and get right with God. That's the only thing that's gon' get you right . . . if you get right with God."

Vanessa chuckled at her aunt's warning. That was what the judge thought, too, with his religious retreat. They had no idea how badly she wanted the marriage to end and no amount of praying would change that.

Chapter 27

Dionne watched her brother-in-law kick back in his recliner. Even in a relaxed setting, he looked like somebody's preacher. His shirt was unbuttoned at the top, but it was still starched; his gray slacks were just as crisp. Even though he was just over forty, his black hair was peppered with gray.

"Dionne, I'm still having a hard time believing you're getting married. But I'm truly happy for you," Henry said.

"Thank you," she said, eyeing the large clock over the mantel. They'd been back from Vegas for two weeks now and things were still going good. "I hope Roland can get his work wrapped up in time to join us for Sunday dinner."

"I'll believe that when I see it," Ida said, crossing the living room and heading into the kitchen.

Dionne ignored her aunt. "I just wish *everyone* could be happy for me."

"Well, sometimes we have to make ourselves happy, and not other people," Henry said. "I just urge you two to go through some premarital counseling. I don't marry folks in my church unless they go through it."

That's why we're not getting married in your church, Dionne thought.

"Dionne, since you didn't help us cook, you think you can come in here and set the table?" Rosolyn yelled from the kitchen.

"Bryson, don't you want to go help your mother set the table?" Dionne slyly asked her nephew, who was sitting in a corner playing his Game Boy.

"I'll do it for a dollar," he said with a big, toothy grin.

Dionne's mouth dropped open as she turned to Henry. "Y'all raising a little blackmailer."

"My son is a negotiator. If there's a way to earn a buck, he'll find it," Henry proudly said.

Dionne laughed as she stood. "Forget it. I'll set the table myself."

Bryson shrugged like it didn't bother him a bit.

Dionne walked into the kitchen just in time to see a look of shock cross her sister's face. Vanessa covered her mouth, then ran out of the kitchen.

"What's going on?" Dionne asked.

Rosolyn looked both confused and concerned as she said, "I don't know. I just told her Shelly's getting adopted."

"Who is Shelly?" Dionne asked.

"This little girl at The Mason House Vanessa has grown attached to." Rosolyn glanced toward the door where Vanessa had disappeared. "I had no idea she was that attached to her, though."

Ida stood off to the side wiping her hands on her apron. She was taken aback by Vanessa's reaction, too.

"Let me go talk to her," Rosolyn said.

"I'm coming with you," Dionne added.

They found Vanessa sitting on the edge of the bed in the guest room.

"Are you okay?" Rosolyn asked, sitting next to her sister. "I'm sorry for breaking the news to you so abruptly. I had no idea it would affect you like that."

"I had no idea either," Vanessa admitted. "I mean, I guess I didn't realize how attached I've become. I mean, I haven't been going to the center for that long. But just hearing that she's gone, and I won't be able to see her again . . ." Vanessa seemed mystified at herself. "Well, to hear that without warning kind of caught me off guard."

"I stopped getting my hopes up on this stuff a long time ago. But once they made up their mind, everything moved so fast," Rosolyn said. "The Taylors have been visiting with Shelly on a regular basis. They don't have any children and have grown very fond of Shelly."

"But you could've at least called me up so I could say good-bye."

"I'm sorry," Rosolyn said. "I didn't realize your feelings were that serious."

"Dang, Vanessa, are you feelin' this little girl or something?" Dionne asked.

Vanessa loudly exhaled. "I'm sorry. I'm overreacting." She rubbed her temple. "The stress of everything, I guess, just has me emotional."

She stood up promptly. "Let's go eat dinner. I don't know why I was getting all attached anyway. It's not like I have anything to offer the girl." Her face darkened with a scowl. "No, with the drama in my life, it's best that I don't get involved with any kids, especially emotionally needy ones like Shelly."

Vanessa flashed a fake smile at her sisters. If only she could make herself actually believe those words.

Chapter 28

Vanessa surveyed her reflection in the full-length mirror standing in the corner of her bedroom. She wanted to look conservative but cute. Thomas needed to see what a good thing he'd messed up.

"I still can't believe you're going to talk to some stranger about your business." Ida's voice snapped Vanessa back to their conversation. Vanessa had the phone nestled in between her ear and shoulder as she got dressed for her first mediation session.

"In my day, you kept family business in the family," Ida declared.

Vanessa deftly broke off a piece of thread that was sticking out of her Donna Karan suit. "I can't believe it either," she said. "Trust me, I don't want to do it, but the judge is being a jerk."

Vanessa had protested Judge Jarrett's "spiritual counseling" requirement, filing a formal conflict of religion complaint. Although the mediation recommendation hadn't been thrown out altogether, as she had hoped, Judge Jarrett had been forced to revise his order to regular mediation.

"Well, if you gotta talk to someone," Ida said, sniffing, "why don't you go talk to Pastor J. over at that fancy-schmancy church you go to—every Christmas, Mother's Day, and Easter."

"Because I don't want to talk to any pastor," Vanessa replied, ignoring her aunt's hint of sarcasm.

Ida tsked. "Umph. That's where you went wrong in the first place. You need to take your problems to God first and foremost. And then, if you just got to have more than that, take it to a man of God."

Vanessa released a long-suffering sigh. "Aunt Ida, God can't do nothing for us now. Thomas and I are through. This is all just a formality. I gotta go. Talk to you later. Love you, 'bye." Vanessa hung up the phone before her aunt could say anything else.

That was Ida's answer to everything: take it to God. Vanessa was nowhere near as religious as her aunt. She did believe in prayer because that was the way she was raised, but no amount of prayer could help her and Thomas anyway. That was why she especially didn't want to take part in some spiritual retreat.

Thirty minutes later, Vanessa was sitting in a small conference room glaring at Thomas, who sat on the other side of the long oak table. A mediator sat at the head of the table, with her chocolate brown hair tightly pulled back into a bun. Her cat-woman glasses and bland gray suit made her look like the headmistress of a boarding school.

"Welcome," the mediator began. "I'm Dr. Yvette McDowell and I'll be mediating your case. It is my hope to one, make sure this divorce is something that you both want; two, make sure that all avenues of reconciliation have been explored and exhausted; and three, try to end this as amicably as possible, if that is our only recourse."

Vanessa noticed Thomas was staring at her like he wanted to say something. She could see the pain in his eyes, but she was sure it was nothing compared to the pain she felt in her heart. For a moment she wanted him to take her in his arms and tell her this all had been some horrible nightmare. She longed for those quiet times she and Thomas had shared, times she'd taken too much for granted.

Vanessa shook off those thoughts as Dr. McDowell went on to explain her role. The more bland words she spouted, the more Vanessa found evil thoughts filling her head again. Those good times with Thomas were gone. He was dragging this out to make her look like a bad wife. She looked up when Dr. McDowell patted her hand.

"Are you with us, Mrs. Kirk?" the woman asked.

"Wha . . . ? Oh yeah, I'm following you," Vanessa said.

Dr. McDowell nodded. "Okay, then I'll begin with you. What do you think your husband deserves to take away from this marriage?"

"Please." Vanessa snorted. "He needs to leave with what he came with—nothing."

Thomas's expression changed dramatically. He now wore a cold, angry look. "If I seem to recall, neither one of us had much," he said evenly. "And I do believe that I worked just as hard as you did throughout this marriage."

"Hmph!" Vanessa spat. "Yeah, you were working hard all right, but it didn't have anything to do with building a foundation for our marriage."

"Now, Mrs. Kirk—" Dr. McDowell said.

"It's Miss Colton," Vanessa said, cutting her off. "I'm going back to my maiden name."

Thomas displayed a thin smirk. "You never left your maiden name in the first place, Mrs. *Colton-Kirk*. Like you were too good to take my name."

Vanessa cocked her head. "Oh, is that why you cheated? Because I hyphenated my name?"

Thomas sighed, shook his head, but didn't respond. He was never good at clever comebacks.

Dr. McDowell held up her hands. "Okay, now, the purpose of this meeting is not to go back and forth on whose fault the disintegration of your marriage is."

"It's his fault," Vanessa said.

"The purpose of this meeting," Dr. McDowell continued, shooting Vanessa a chastising look, "is to see if reconciliation is at all possible."

"I can answer that for you now," Vanessa said. "Absolutely not." She sat back and defiantly folded her arms across her chest.

Dr. McDowell flipped her legal pad to a new page and pulled out a pen, then looked at both of them. "Per Judge Jarrett's order, I'll be the one to make that decision." She turned to Thomas. "I'll begin with you, Mr. Kirk. Do you still love your wife?"

Thomas bit down on his bottom lip and his eyes slowly watered up. "I never stopped loving my wife. I will never stop loving my wife."

Vanessa couldn't believe her ears as the mediator turned to her. "Mrs. Kirk?"

"Colton."

Dr. McDowell inhaled. "Until your name is legally changed, I'm going to go by Mrs. Kirk. Mrs. Kirk, do you still love—"

"No," she said flatly.

"So, you just fell out of love with me just like that?" Thomas said, staring at her like he was trying to see into her soul.

That cut her deep. What did he think? "Having your husband get another woman pregnant can do that to you."

Thomas lightly chuckled as he shook his head.

"Do you think this is funny?" Vanessa leaned forward, her brow furrowing.

"What happened to for better or for worse? Till death do us part?" Thomas asked.

He was acting like this was some sort of theory. "All bets are off when a baby is brought into the picture," Vanessa said quietly, hating his calmness. When had she ever found that attractive? "Go be with your mistress and stop wasting my time."

"So there's no way you could ever forgive me?" Thomas said.

She looked at him like he was crazy. "You know better than that."

"Why did I know that would be your answer?" he said, shaking his head.

Vanessa blew out an exasperated breath. "Then why did you ask?"

"Okay, it seems we're making some progress here," Dr. McDowell said brightly. She turned back to Thomas. "Mr. Kirk, why do you think your marriage is disintegrating?"

"Disintegrated, as in past tense," Vanessa interjected.

"Mrs. Kirk, please!" Dr. McDowell admonished. "I understand that you are harboring some anger in your heart, but as an officer of the court I think you would understand all too well why order is necessary in conducting this mediation. So will you please cooperate?"

Vanessa held up her hands in surrender.

"Thank you." Dr. McDowell turned back to Thomas.

"Let me see, when did our marriage start disintegrating?" Thomas held his finger to his temple as if he were thinking. "May 31, 2003."

"What's the significance of that date?" Dr. McDowell asked as she scribbled on her notepad.

Thomas kept his eyes focused on Vanessa. "That's the day we got married."

Dr. McDowell twitched, startled by his answer. "So you think things started going downhill the day you got married?"

"Yep, pretty much," Thomas deadpanned. "My grandmother used to always say you can't change a leopard's spots.

She always said what a woman shows you before she marries you, be ready for after she marries you." He chuckled piteously. "Do you know Vanessa was late for her own wedding?" Thomas nodded as he recalled that day. "What woman do you know would be late for her own wedding?"

"I had a good reason," Vanessa responded defensively.

"You always do," Thomas shot back. "At least good to you."

"Anyone would understand why I was late. It's not like I was off somewhere sipping tea."

"Going to a rally to meet Hillary Clinton doesn't quite classify as a good reason to me," Thomas replied coldly.

"That's just it," Vanessa said, this time talking directly to Dr. McDowell. "He doesn't understand the importance of my career."

Granted, she was just a divorce court judge now, but it was all part of Vanessa's master plan. She planned to get a few years of judgeship under her belt, then run for a Texas State Senate seat on a family values platform. From there she would run for a U.S. Senate seat and who knows, maybe even seek out a seat on the Supreme Court. How was she supposed to do that now when she couldn't even keep her own family together?

"I understood, all right. But at any point did I ever come first to you? I didn't," Thomas replied, not giving her a chance to answer. "Not even on our wedding day. It's been that way ever since."

He was hitting too close to the mark. She had known for a long time that she should try harder. She said weakly, "Don't put the blame on me because you're an adulterer."

Thomas didn't press his advantage. "You're right, I'm a horrible person for what I did. If I could take it all back, I would." He looked sincerely at Vanessa. "I regret hurting you. I regret my relationship with Alana. But I can't regret this child. The child I've so desperately wanted. The child I wanted you to give to me."

Vanessa was fighting back the tears that were threatening to overtake her. His words pierced her to the heart. Thomas was actually going to be a father. She wanted kids one day, just not yet. But she *had* wanted them and she had wanted them with Thomas.

Never in a million years had Vanessa dreamed that her life would take such a wrong turn.

"Mr. Kirk," Dr. McDowell said. "What was it that you felt you got from the other woman that you didn't feel you could get from your wife?"

Vanessa's ears perked up at that question.

Thomas contemplated his answer before saying slowly, "I don't know. I mean, even though I was with her only a couple of times, Alana made me feel important, both emotionally and physically."

As soon as he said the latter part, he looked like he wished that he could take his words back.

Vanessa released a pained laugh. "So that was it? She made you feel like a stud in bed? She was your freak in the sheets?"

Thomas rubbed his forehead. "That's not what I meant at all. I just . . ."

"And what happened to 'we only slept together one time?'"

Vanessa continued. When he didn't respond, she said disgustedly, "You are such a liar."

"Vanessa, have you ever given any thought to the fact that maybe you *weren't* fulfilling your husband in bed? I mean, that is a big deal to a man," Dr. McDowell stressed.

Vanessa's eyes widened in astonishment. "What?"

"I tell all my clients the reality is that sex is important in a marriage. If Thomas was sexually frustrated, it's to be expected that he would seek fulfillment somewhere else."

Thomas's eyes brightened in agreement. "I've been trying to tell her that."

Vanessa couldn't believe they were ganging up on her. She scowled at Dr. McDowell, then realized that wouldn't get what she wanted. She kept her gaze steady as she asked Dr. McDowell, "Do you have enough?"

"Well, I really would like to talk with you all some more."

Vanessa scooted her chair back and stood. "Let me rephrase that. *You have enough.* There is nothing left to discuss or mediate. Thomas and I are over. Forever."

Vanessa shot daggers at her soon-to-be-ex-husband one last time as she hurried out the door. She expected Thomas to hurt her, but Dr. McDowell had crossed the line—both professionally and as a woman. Vanessa fought back the tears as she stomped to her car. She would add Dr. McDowell to the list of people that had better learn she wasn't a person to be messed with.

Chapter 29

Vanessa logged on to the Bank of Texas's website. She printed out the paperwork to have Thomas's name removed from the bank account and credit cards. She checked the balance on her private savings account, grateful that she had gone against Aunt Ida's advice and kept a separate account, one that Thomas knew nothing about.

Ida had said separate accounts were the devil's first tools to destroy marriages. Vanessa was glad she hadn't listened.

Since leaving the mediation yesterday, she'd been on a mission to remove Thomas from her life. Vanessa glanced at the clock and noticed the time. "Shoot," she mumbled. She was supposed to meet Rosolyn for brunch in fifteen minutes. Vanessa quickly showered, dressed, and jumped in the car.

Rosolyn shot her an evil look when she walked up to the table at The Breakfast Klub thirty-five minutes later.

"Sorry," Vanessa said, sliding into her seat. "I was handling some business and got a late start."

"Mmm-hmmm," Rosolyn said. "Well, I just ordered. I'm starving."

"That's fine," Vanessa replied. "Let me go place my order." Vanessa stood back up and walked over to the cashier to place her order. Her stomach was cramping really bad, probably because she hadn't eaten all day. "I'll take the waffles and wings and an iced tea."

"What's wrong? Why are you rubbing your stomach," Rosolyn asked as Vanessa returned to the table.

"It's hurting. I guess I need to get some food into my system."

Rosolyn shot her a concerned look, but let it pass when her cell phone rang. "This is probably the surprise I had for you." She looked at the phone, then handed it to Vanessa.

Vanessa eyed the phone suspiciously before taking it and saying, "Hello."

"Hi, Miss Vanessa. Did Mrs. Frazier tell you? I have a new mom and dad."

Vanessa smiled at the sound of Shelly's voice. "Yes, she told me," she said, her eyes showing their appreciation to Rosolyn. "I am so happy for you. But promise me you'll keep in touch?"

"Of course I will." Shelly's voice brimmed with contentment. "You know, I have my own bedroom and everything. They have a giant house, even a pool, and a dog. He's so cute.

His name is Pugly because he's a pug and Mr. Taylor—I mean, Daddy—said he's so ugly." Shelly laughed. Vanessa had never heard such a happy sound from the little girl. "They said they wanted me to make their family complete. They used to have a daughter, but she died. And so I think we'll be perfect for each other." She paused, then explained the equation she had worked out. "They lost their little girl. I lost my parents. And now, it's like we found each other." The excitement was evident in her voice.

"Mommy and Daddy said I could give you our address and phone number," Shelly said. "And when we get settled, they said you can come visit me."

"Here, I'll give you mine." Vanessa rattled off her information before bidding Shelly good-bye with the promise to keep in touch.

"You know, you are going to make a good mother when you get your own child," Rosolyn said.

"At the rate I'm going, I'll be too old to enjoy my kids," Vanessa quipped.

The two of them chatted some more until the waitress returned with their food. Vanessa immediately dug in.

"Girl . . ." Vanessa chewed slowly, swallowed, then finished her sentence. "Please tell me how you do it. I know you told me about the problems you and Henry had, but you make marriage seem so easy."

The first time Rosolyn tried to bring up Thomas a few weeks ago, Vanessa had changed the subject; she hadn't been in the mood to talk about him. But now she wanted her sister's advice. She wanted to understand where she and Thomas had gone wrong. She wasn't going to mention Dr. McDowell because she had her own plans to deal with the good doctor, and she didn't need her sister trying to talk her out of it.

"Please," Rosolyn replied, "marriage is far from easy, even for a man of God. Henry has his issues, too. You just have to decide what you will and won't deal with in a marriage. It's hard work. It demands a lot of give and take. Something I don't think you did enough of."

"I beg your pardon." Vanessa stopped chewing and narrowed her eyes at her sister. "I gave a lot in my marriage."

Rosolyn sipped her tea before responding. "What did you give? Thomas gave up his desire to have a family. He gave in to your decision to work all crazy hours. What did you give up?"

"Ummm, I gave up a lot."

"Okay, like what?"

Vanessa thought about it for a minute. The truth was, she hadn't given up much. Most of the time, what she wanted prevailed. She set her fork down and leaned back. "Okay, maybe I wasn't the best wife, but that still doesn't excuse him going out and sleeping with another woman."

"Hey, I totally agree with you," Rosolyn said. "But have you ever, even for a half a second, considered forgiving him?"

Vanessa thought about it, but Rosolyn continued before she could answer. "I mean, you do love him, don't you?"

Vanessa was silent. She loved Thomas with everything inside of her—even if she didn't act like it.

"All I'm saying is just think about forgiving him."

"And then what?" she asked, bewildered. "Just accept this baby? Have this child be a part of my life? No, I can't do that. I'm no fool."

"Neither is Henry." Rosolyn's expression turned pensive. "He just loved me enough to forgive me."

Vanessa bit down on her bottom lip. "Oh, sis, I'm sorry. I wasn't thinking. I didn't mean it like that."

"No, you meant it," Rosolyn said. She took another bite of her food. "People automatically think because you forgive somebody for something like infidelity, it makes you a fool. It doesn't. It makes you human. God forgives us for all kinds of things every single day."

"Well, I'm not God."

Rosolyn sighed. "I know that. I'm just saying that many people would say Henry is a fool. But he chose to honor his commitment to me, and so he dug deep down inside, prayed a lot, and used his faith to help him get over the pain of my betrayal." She paused, thinking of another angle. "Would you basically say I'm a good person?"

Vanessa let out a slight chuckle. "Right up there next to Mother Teresa."

"Then how do you think I could've possibly gotten pregnant by another man?"

"I think you just made a horrible mistake. You weren't trying to hurt Henry."

"Exactly," Rosolyn replied.

Vanessa smiled at her sister. She got the point. "Okay, you and your reverse psychology. But just so you know, it's not working. Thomas and I are over. And the only thing I have for him is a one-way ticket out of my life. As a matter of fact, I've already got something in the works to ensure that that happens."

"What?"

Vanessa flushed guiltily. "Don't worry about all that."

"I don't have bail money," Rosolyn said, knowing how bullheaded her sister could be.

"Naw, it's nothing like that. Let's just say I'm confident that the mediator will grant my divorce expeditiously."

Vanessa had to get down in the gutter to get the ammunition she needed to ensure her divorce, but desperate times called for desperate measures.

"I'm going to tell you like I told Dionne—I hope you know what you're doing."

Vanessa weighed her sister's words. Maybe what she had planned wasn't right. But Dr. McDowell's sex analysis and Thomas's quip about her not fulfilling him was the last straw. She was sick and tired of letting people make a fool of her. It was time she fought back.

Chapter 30

Vanessa stood impatiently in the immaculately decorated lobby. The sleek, contemporary furniture was evidence of Dr. McDowell's good taste, and the numerous awards that lined the wall were testament to her success. She might have had all of these accolades, but after the way she and Thomas ganged up on her, Vanessa felt like someone should give the doctor a lesson in tact. It had taken her a week and a lot of money, but she'd gotten what she needed.

Vanessa shot the receptionist another impatient look. The woman feigned a smile as she placed the receiver back on the hook. "Dr. McDowell will see you now."

"Thank you," Vanessa said, quickly brushing past the receptionist's desk, clutching a manila folder for dear life.

"Judge Kirk." Dr. McDowell stood and greeted Vanessa with a warm smile. "I was actually going to give you a call today. I wanted to ask you to come in for a private session."

Vanessa measured the woman, gathering up the nerve to do what she had come here to do. "Well, I wanted to talk to you, too."

"Wonderful. Get with my secretary and we'll set something up," Dr. McDowell said.

"Nah." Vanessa closed the door.

"Excuse me," Dr. McDowell said, narrowing her eyes. "I do have an appointment coming up. I really would like to talk to you a little more because I'm concerned about the hostility that you're harboring toward your husband, but we will have to schedule a time to do it."

"You ever been married, Doctor?" Vanessa asked, casually sitting in the chair in front of the desk.

"What does that have to do with anything?" Dr. McDowell asked, sitting back down.

"I'm just wondering. I know you have your degrees and all. But I'm just curious as to whether you've ever been through what I'm going through."

"Well, for your information I dealt with infidelity several years ago," she replied matter-of-factly.

"Did you stay in your marriage?"

"I stayed, and I'm proud to say that we worked through our troubles."

"Oh, you worked it out, huh?"

"Yes, my husband and I worked things out."

"How noble of you. But as I told you, there is no chance of Thomas and me working things out." Vanessa crossed her legs and tried to maintain a cool professionalism.

Dr. McDowell shook her head. "I think it's too soon to say that for sure. I'd like us to talk a bit more, get to the root of some issues. But as I said earlier, you'll have to set up an appointment. Now, I really must—"

"There is no point in us talking anymore." Vanessa cut to the chase. "I would like for you to sign the order for Judge Jarrett recommending that we be allowed to move forward with the divorce."

Dr. McDowell looked at her sternly. "I am sorry, Mrs. Kirk, but I'm going to have to disagree with you. It is still too soon to make that assumption."

Vanessa sat back and calmly said, "You're going to open that drawer and pull out the correct form. And you're going to fill out the form recommending the divorce be granted immediately."

Dr. McDowell drew back in confusion. "I'm not going to be able to do that."

Vanessa held up the manila folder that she had been holding in her lap. "I have something here that I think will make you change your mind." She tossed the folder onto Dr. McDowell's desk. Vanessa had hired a PI, and he had found out some very interesting things about the good mediator.

Dr. McDowell eyed the folder suspiciously before picking it up and opening it. Her eyes immediately grew wide. "Wh- where did you get these?"

"Now, you must know that I'm a resourceful woman. I happen to like that one right there," Vanessa said, pointing at the second picture. "It's something about that red lace that just brings out the natural hue of your skin. Oh, and that's not a bad one either." Vanessa leaned in and pointed to another picture. "But I thought your husband had black hair. This man is blond. And well"—Vanessa picked the picture up and cocked her head to the side as she studied it—"he looks like he can't be any more than twenty-five."

She set the photo back down. "Now, I know you said you and your husband worked through your issues, but I don't know how he would feel about these, especially since they're dated . . . what, last week? And my sources tell me the guy in that picture used to be a patient of yours. The last time I checked, the ethics board frowned on that sort of thing. We wouldn't want the ethics board, or your husband, to ever get wind of this, now would we?"

Vanessa hated to stoop to this level, but she was serious. She would do whatever it took to get Thomas out of her life and end Dr. McDowell's meddling as soon as possible. "I know this is a lot to digest right now, but I'll trade you," she continued. "A signed recommendation for dissolution of marriage for these." She pointed at the pictures again. "And once I have that letter, I'll forget I even know this stuff exists."

"I don't believe this," Dr. McDowell mumbled.

Vanessa's face softened. "Doctor, I'm speaking to you woman to woman. I'm sorry to do this to you. I didn't want to. But you don't understand how this man hurt me. I want out. Now."

Dr. McDowell's eyes slowly met Vanessa's. She sighed, then turned to her side desk drawer and removed a sheet of paper. She quickly filled it out, signed it, then handed it to Vanessa.

Vanessa broke out in a big grin as she took the paper. " 'Resolution to dissolve marriage,' " she read happily. " 'I, Dr. Yvette McDowell, do hereby certify that after counseling both parties, it is my recommendation that the marriage of Thomas and Vanessa Kirk be dissolved.' " Vanessa made a mock salute as she stood. "Thank you very much. Now you can rest assured that your secret is safe with me."

Vanessa ignored the look of contempt on Dr. McDowell's face as she headed out the door.

She did feel bad about blackmailing her like that, but as she glanced at the piece of paper clutched tightly in her hand, she knew it was all worth it.

Chapter 31

"So you really got back together with him?" Trina looked at Dionne like she had lost her mind. "I mean, this isn't some practical joke?"

Dionne sighed. She, Trina, Melanie, and Kyla were enjoying lunch at the Black Walnut Café. "I never set out to get back with Roland," she said. "But I guess he just broke me down."

"Mmmm-hmmm." Melanie sucked her teeth. "What about Tasha?"

Dionne knew that question was coming. "That's over. Roland called Tasha with me on the other phone, apologized for hurting her, but told her he loved me and wanted to be with me."

"Whatever." It was obvious Melanie didn't believe him. "Remember, Omero did that to me, had me all excited and stuff, thinking he really loved me. All along, though, he'd called the chick beforehand and told her he was about to call and break up with her, but for her not to believe it because he was pledging Kappa and they were making him do it."

Trina laughed. "I remember that."

Dionne rolled her eyes. "Well, that was in college and Roland isn't pledging anything. He was for real."

"That's what I thought," Melanie mumbled.

Dionne ignored their negativity. She knew they wouldn't be turning backflips over her news but she had at least hoped they'd be happy for her. "Roland said he had to finally follow his heart and his heart was with me. And I believe him."

Melanie pointed her breadstick at Dionne. "All I have to say is, you believe that if you want to."

"No, I have a really good feeling. I think actually losing me made him realize just how much he loved me." She paused as she studied her friends, trying to decide if she should tell them everything. "What?" she finally asked as Melanie cocked her head and stared.

"I'm just trying to see are you the same person that went to college with me, because to be so smart, you sure are dumb," Melanie said.

"I resent that," Dionne replied. "I mean, come on. Didn't you give Marcus another chance several times?" That shut her up. Melanie's main man had dogged her out so many times Dionne had lost count, so she was in no position to talk about anybody. "All I'm saying is I think Roland deserves another chance. I think he's learned his lesson and he's ready to do right by me."

"Okay, let's just say he has learned his lesson. Do you really want to be the rebound chick? I mean, is his divorce even final yet?" Trina threw in.

"The hearing is in two days," Dionne informed her happily. "And Roland and his wife have been separated for so long, it's not like I'd be the rebound woman."

Trina held her hand up in defeat. "Okay, it sounds like you have your mind made up. I just hope you know what you're doing."

"I do," Dionne replied. "And when you all are at my wedding next month and can see how happy I am, you'll know I'm right." She raised her glass, ignoring all of the eyes staring her down. "Can I get a toast?"

"Did you say wedding?" Melanie asked.

"Next month?" Kyla added.

Dionne nodded as she wiggled her finger at her friends. She'd been making a concerted effort to keep her hand under the table so that they wouldn't see her ring.

"Oh, snap!" Melanie said, taking her hand.

"Oh, my God," Trina said. "That has to be at least two carats."

"Two and a half," Dionne supplied. As soon as they returned from their Vegas trip, Roland had taken her straight to Robbins Brothers to pick out the beautiful princess-cut engagement ring.

"Wow. I guess he is serious," Kyla said.

"So, now can I get a toast?" Dionne asked, deciding to wait and share the news about the baby.

Everyone raised their glasses. "I'll toast," Melanie said, "but I still don't have a good feeling about this."

Dionne clinked her glass with her friends. She had a good feeling this time around, and like Roland had said, her friends would just have to see it for themselves.

Chapter 32

Vanessa strutted into Judge Jarrett's office, smug and confident. She had considered letting her attorney deliver the paper, but she wanted Vernon to see the look of satisfaction on her face.

"Vanessa," he said stonily after his secretary ushered her in.

"Vernon."

Vanessa sat down, trying to keep the smirk from creeping up on her face.

"It's my understanding you have something to show me?" he said.

"I do." Vanessa slid the paper across his large cherrywood desk. She waited for his reaction as he picked it up and read it.

"So, Dr. McDowell has recommended that the marriage be dissolved? So soon?"

Vanessa nodded confidently. "I told you there was no salvaging this marriage. I guess she was able to see that from jump."

"Was she now?" he said, removing his eyeglasses and setting them on the desk.

Something in the tone of his voice made Vanessa shift uncomfortably in her seat. He was matching her smug look, when he should be all sad and defeated.

"Vanessa," he said, "as you may know, I'm not one to play games, so I'm not going to beat around the bush here. I don't take kindly to blackmail."

Vanessa's eyes widened. As she opened her mouth to speak, Judge Jarrett held up his hand to cut her off. "Save it. Don't dig yourself a deeper hole than you're already in. Dr. McDowell has already been here. She told me everything."

Vanessa was speechless. It had never crossed her mind that Dr. McDowell might actually come clean. She'd acted so high and mighty during their first session, Vanessa was surprised that she would openly admit to the skeletons in her closet.

"I am appalled that you would stoop to such a level, especially in light of being on thin ice with the judicial commission as it is," he continued. "Dr. McDowell was very worried that you would follow through on your threat to ruin her life. I assured her that you wouldn't. Or else, Judge Kirk," he said firmly, "I will ruin yours. I know you have political aspirations, but just as you so callously tried to expose Dr. McDowell, I will make sure the *Houston Chronicle* and every TV station in town—and of course, the judicial commission—know what you tried to do. Which, need I remind you, is a criminal offense. Now, I am willing to chalk up this little blackmail scheme to you being under duress because of the strain of the divorce."

Vanessa fought back the tears. She refused to let Vernon see her cry, but as he was talking, the magnitude of what she'd done began to set in.

His expression softened. "Vanessa, I understand this is very difficult for you. I've presided over enough divorces to know it's not easy, but you have to follow the order of the court. You should know that better than anyone."

Vanessa averted her gaze to the floor, ashamed.

"I know you don't agree with my use of faith and spirituality in my courtroom, but for me there is no other way. I am of the belief that a marriage cannot survive without God at the center. If I can help one couple to see that, then I'm doing what I've been called to do."

"So you expect me to forgive Thomas, too?" she asked, all confidence gone from her voice.

"It's not what I expect," he said kindly, "it's what God expects. After all, He forgives us every day."

She shook her head, tears finally overtaking her. "I just can't do it."

He nodded knowingly as he handed her a Kleenex. "Believe it or not, I can respect that. All I'm asking is that you be sure. Look, just go to this spiritual marriage retreat for me. If, after completing that, it's still what you want, I'll grant your request. Okay?"

Vanessa eyed him doubtfully.

He sensed her apprehension because he held up his hands.

"I'm serious. Just try it and if it doesn't work, we can both say you tried."

"Okay."

"And apologize to Dr. McDowell and we'll all forget about this."

Vanessa nodded, grateful that Judge Jarrett hadn't decided to ruin her life.

Chapter 33

Dionne paced back and forth across her living room. She had wanted to go to court with Roland so bad. She wanted to be there during this emotionally trying time, but more than anything, she wanted to see his marriage come to an end with her very own eyes. That meant that she and Roland could truly move forward with building their future together. She was approaching her fifth month, and her pregnancy was becoming more and more noticeable, so they needed to let the world know they were engaged.

That was the argument she had given him as to why she should go to court with him. However, Roland had convinced her not to come: "It'll just make things worse. The judge might frown on it and my ex will go into a tizzy."

She glanced down at the clock on her cell phone and saw the red light blinking, indicating that she had a text message.

"Bruce." She sighed when she saw the text. Bruce had been pretty understanding when she'd explained that she had to focus on repairing her relationship with Roland and couldn't spend time with him anymore. That was something she knew Roland wouldn't go for.

"'Just wanted to make sure you were doing fine,'" she read. "He is so sweet."

She pushed thoughts of Bruce out her mind and checked the time. It was just after two. The hearing was at ten, so Roland should be coming home any minute. She had wanted to call him on his cell phone, but she'd discovered an hour ago that in his haste to get out the door this morning, he'd left it on the bar.

Dionne busied herself around the house for the next half hour. She was just putting another load of clothes into the washing machine when she heard the front door opening. She dropped the clothes and ran into the living room.

"Roland!" Dionne stopped in her tracks as he stormed inside and slammed the door behind him. The look on his face told her the case hadn't gone as he had hoped. "Wh-what's wrong?" she asked nervously. "Did you get the divorce finalized?"

Roland walked closer to her. The eerie look in his narrowed eyes set her heart to racing. "Roland, you're scaring me. What's wrong?"

He took his finger and wrapped a lock of her long, curly hair around it. "You're a beautiful woman, do you know that?"

"Roland, would you just tell me what happened in court today? Are you officially divorced?"

A sinister smile crossed his face. "Oh, there was no divorce granted today."

"What?" she cried. "I thought everything was taken care of. I thought there wouldn't be any problems."

He let her curl drop as he walked around her. "I thought so, too," he whispered, leaning into her ear. "But guess what? When I got to court this morning, got before the judge, confident that this nightmare that was my life was about to be over, her attorney dropped a bombshell on me." He paused dramatically and every muscle in Dionne's body tensed up.

"They produced documents," Roland continued, "proof of my so-called secret bank accounts and my dealings with Casper."

Dionne's eyes widened in shock. She'd completely forgotten about the email that she had sent Liz, Roland's wife.

Roland pumped his fists like he was trying to stay calm. "Needless to say, I was dumbfounded. I kept going, how in the world did she find out about the money? I was very careful about not letting anyone know about those accounts because I didn't want her getting her dirty claws on it. The only person who knew anything was my brother, and I knew he would never tell Liz. He can't stand her either." Roland let out a harsh chuckle. "So, I immediately thought Tasha had found out and let Liz know. Then I remembered the night Link came to my house. I know you heard everything but I didn't think anything of it because I knew I could trust you."

Roland started pacing back and forth, pounding his fist in his palm. "I stood in that courtroom telling myself, there's no way Dionne would have ever told Liz that, even if she was pissed off at me. She knows how evil my wife is. She knows I deal with some shady people. She knows I could go to jail." He gave her a mocking look. "There's no way Dionne would do something like that. I finally surmised that either my wife had hired a private investigator or Tasha had found out, and then bam!"

He slammed his palm on the table, causing Dionne to jump. "Exhibit A. Bank statements. Followed by Exhibit B. Deeds to my property on Westheimer that nobody knew about but you."

Dionne closed her eyes in utter despair. What she wouldn't give to go back to the day she sent that email. "Roland, let me explain," she began.

"Explain what?" he bellowed. "Explain how you committed the ultimate betrayal? Explain how you gave my wife the ammunition to ruin my life even more than she already has?" He let out a sinister laugh. "Needless to say, the judge didn't like the fact that I concealed the money and the property, so now I'm facing perjury charges since I lied on the stand at our last hearing. And the judge also let me know he was going to be notifying the IRS as well. All the while my wife smirked and asked for a delay so that she could get a 'true assessment of my worth.'"

Dionne trembled as he railed at her, "You helped my wife destroy me!" She'd never seen him this angry.

She held her hands up, trying to get him to calm down. "Baby, please listen. I . . . I was upset. You, I mean, you had hurt me so bad with Tasha."

He folded his arms across his chest. "So you thought you'd pay me back by giving my wife ammunition to make my life even more of a living hell than she already has, huh?"

"It's not like that. I love you," Dionne pleaded.

She gasped as he picked her up by the throat and rammed her back against the living room wall. "Don't say that. Don't ever say that again!"

Dionne grabbed his hand, which was planted firmly around her neck, yet he wouldn't release his grip. It was getting harder to breathe. "Roland . . . I . . . can't breathe. The baby . . ."

Roland glared at her, his chest heaving, anger contorting his face. He slowly let her go and she dropped to her knees, rubbing her neck and crying uncontrollably.

"I hope your revenge was worth it," he said as he shot her one last hateful look and walked out the door.

Chapter 34

Vanessa was so not in the mood to listen to the Richard Simmons look-alike as he chimed on about the sanctity of marriage. The portly, alabaster-colored man was driving her crazy already—and he'd just begun their first counseling session at the retreat. Sam, as he'd told everyone to call him, ran the marriage ministry of a local church with his wife, Lisa. They traveled the country talking to couples about their marriages, using spirituality as the basis for their counseling.

"I always tell people to seek help early," Sam said, standing at the front of the room next to his wife. She was a petite brunette with deep dimples and eyes that seemed to sing. She was a good foot and a half shorter than him, yet they looked like the all-American couple. "The average couple waits six years before seeking help for marital problems—and half of all marriages that end do so in the first seven years," Sam continued. "That means that the average couple lives with unhappiness for far too long."

Vanessa glanced over at Thomas, who nodded as he listened attentively. *He makes me sick to my stomach,* she thought. If he'd been unhappy for so long, why had he stayed?

Vanessa had refused Thomas's offer to ride to the retreat together, instead choosing to show up just one minute before it started. Even then she refused to speak to him. She just took a seat in one of the chairs set up in a circle around the room. In all, there were ten couples and Vanessa and Thomas were the only black pair, which made her even more uncomfortable about sharing their business. She just had to make it through the weekend and she'd be able to move on with her life.

"I also try to tell couples to edit themselves," Sam continued sagely. "Couples who avoid saying every angry thought when discussing touchy topics are consistently the happiest. Happy couples have high standards for each other. The most successful are those who refuse to accept hurtful behavior from each other. The lower the level of tolerance for bad behavior in the beginning of a relationship, the happier the couple is down the road."

Vanessa felt her resolve weakening as she wondered what Thomas was thinking. Was he upset with himself that he had accepted certain behaviors from her from jump? And was she really as bad as he had made her out to be?

Lisa smiled at her husband as she took over the conversation.

"In a happy marriage, couples make five times as many positive statements to each other and their relationship than negative ones. A good marriage must have a rich climate of positivity. Make deposits to your emotional bank account."

Lisa slowly scanned the circle before settling in on Vanessa. She smiled benevolently as she read the name tag. "Vanessa, what's something positive you've said to"—she leaned over and read Thomas's name tag—"your husband, Thomas, in the last six months?"

Vanessa couldn't help but scowl at the woman. Why did she assume Vanessa was with Thomas? Maybe she was with the Asian man sitting next to her.

Vanessa contemplated blowing the woman off because she really didn't want to do this silly crap. But every eye in the room was on her, so she finally said, "I told him that I hope the baby he is having with another woman is happy and healthy."

Thomas bit down on his bottom lip. Both Lisa and Sam looked shocked, as did several other people in the room. Vanessa didn't care. She wanted these people to see there was no chance of her and Thomas getting anything from these sessions.

"Oh. Okay," Lisa replied, looking to her husband for relief.

"You know, before we get to the positive reinforcement exercises, there are a few more things I wanted to say," Sam said smoothly, stepping in front of his wife. "Marriage today is very complex. In previous generations each partner knew what was expected of him or her; the roles were defined. If each partner filled those expectations, there was a reasonably good chance that the marriage would endure. Men and women cut each other a great deal of slack in other areas, so long as each played by the prescribed rules and fulfilled their socially defined roles."

Lisa stepped back into the conversation, relieved that some of the tension was dissipating. "Of course, that's the way it used to be done. Now people question what they want out of marriage. Families rely more upon hired domestic help in the form of housekeepers, caregivers, and day-care providers to fulfill many of the customary roles. Marriage began to take on a different meaning and serve a different purpose than was traditionally the case."

Vanessa was tired of listening to them. She felt like she was back in school, the way they were rambling. They began talking about the role God played in marriage and how a strong relationship with God was essential in building a strong marriage. They intertwined their hands and smiled at each other again as they talked about all that God had done for their marriage. Vanessa released an exasperated sigh. They had to be faking all this bliss. Nobody was that doggone happy.

"God realizes that since a marriage involves two sinful human beings, divorce is going to occur," Lisa said.

That caused Vanessa's ears to perk up. Now they were talking a language she could relate to.

"As Matthew 5:32 tells us, the phrase 'except for marital unfaithfulness' is the only thing in Scripture that possibly gives God's permission for divorce and remarriage," Lisa continued.

"Bingo, I'm covered," Vanessa said under her breath as she shot Thomas an evil look.

Sam stepped up the force in his voice, making Vanessa feel like he could hear her thoughts. "Sometimes lost in the debate over the exception clause is the fact that whatever 'marital unfaithfulness' means, it is an *allowance* for divorce, not a *requirement* for divorce," he said. "Even when adultery is committed, a couple can, through God's grace, learn to forgive and begin rebuilding their marriage. God has forgiven us of so much more. Surely we can follow His example and even forgive the sin of adultery."

Vanessa was sick of hearing that line, too. Yes, she was well aware that God had forgiven us for so much more. But she wasn't God, and as far as she was concerned, forgiveness simply wasn't an option.

Chapter 35

Dionne heard the doorknob jiggling and she silently cursed.

"Open the door, Dionne. You can't hide forever." Rosolyn's voice boomed through the front door. "I know you're in there!"

She contemplated ignoring her, just as she'd been ignoring her calls for the last three days. But Dionne knew her sister. Rosolyn wasn't going to go away.

She huffed, threw back the covers she had draped over her legs, and trudged over to the front door. Dionne pulled her robe around her swelling stomach and tightened her belt.

"Why are you so loud?" Dionne snapped, swinging the door open.

Rosolyn burst past her. "Why are you sitting up in this house like you lost your best friend?"

"Go away, Rosolyn," Dionne said, plopping back down on the sofa. "Can't you see I'm depressed here?"

Rosolyn made her way over to the window and flung open the curtains on the large bay window that overlooked the court-yard. "Get over it," Rosolyn said. "People break up every day. You were too good for Roland anyway. While you're sitting up here moping over that loser, there is a good man ready, willing, and able to treat you like the queen that you are."

"Rosolyn, please don't start."

"Now you know I'm not about to let you sit up in this house moping. Okay, yes, you messed up by giving his wife that informa-tion. But he messed up, too. If he hadn't ever cheated on you in the first place, this would've never happened. So he needs to accept some responsibility. And if he can't see that, then it's his loss."

"If only I could get him to see that," Dionne moaned. She was tired of crying. She'd shed so many tears that she felt like she was all cried out.

Rosolyn walked into the kitchen, grabbed an Ozarka water out of the refrigerator, and made her way back into the living room. "I'm telling you, baby sister," she said, unscrewing the cap on the water, "it's like Vanessa said, the best way to get over a man is get yourself another man. Get dressed. Bruce is on his way over."

Dionne cut her eyes, totally annoyed. "I know you did not invite him over to my place?"

"Okay, I didn't. But I should have." Rosolyn sat down next to Dionne. "I'm serious, sis. I don't like seeing you like this."

Dionne sank back into the sofa, dejected. "I should've listened to you. You told me not to do anything I might regret. I did, now I'm paying the ultimate price."

"What price? The fact that he broke up with you?" She tsked. "If you ask me, he did you a favor."

Dionne turned to Rosolyn, her eyes misting. "Ros, I'm pregnant."

Rosolyn almost choked on her drink. "Oh no, Dionne." She looked at her in pity. "How'd you let that happen? And please don't tell me you did it on purpose."

"Of course I didn't," Dionne huffed. "I just messed up. We always use protection but with the stress of everything, I just missed a couple of days with my pills."

Rosolyn paused, letting the news sink in. "How far along are you?"

"Four months, almost five. That's why I really want me and Roland to work. I don't want to become another statistic, somebody's baby mama. Not to mention the fact that I love him."

"Well, you know I'm a proponent of the family structure, but not if that family is dysfunctional."

"My friend Melanie said just because I have a baby by him doesn't mean I have to be with him. That's what I keep telling myself," Dionne deadpanned, recalling her conversation earlier that day where she'd told Melanie about the pregnancy.

"That's what's wrong with people today. We just don't care about the family structure anymore. Children need to be raised in two-parent homes," Rosolyn responded, shaking her head. "But two *stable* parents. And that other parent doesn't have to be the baby's biological father. It can be someone like Bruce."

"I'm just saying, I had a plan mapped out. The baby was supposed to come after marriage."

"You know what they say about the best-laid plans. Besides, that's your problem, all caught up in following some life plan."

Dionne exhaled in frustration. She didn't know why she was even bothering. "Look, just respect me on this please?" She'd been calling Roland, but he had yet to answer. "Let me see your cell phone." Dionne thought maybe he'd pick up if he didn't recognize the number.

"No, that's like me giving you a crack rock. I'm not contributing to your addiction to that man," Rosolyn said defiantly.

"Give me the phone," Dionne demanded.

Rosolyn groaned, but picked up her purse, pulled her phone out, and tossed it at Dionne.

Dionne took a deep breath and dialed Roland's number. He answered on the second ring.

"Roland, it's me. Can I—"

He hung up.

Dionne closed her eyes as she fought back tears. "I can't believe this," she said, slamming the flip phone shut.

Rosolyn sat with her legs crossed, shaking her head. "I can't believe you're going to sit here and let yourself be degraded like this."

Dionne wiped her eyes. She guessed she wasn't all cried out after all. "You just don't understand, Rosolyn." She sniffed.

Rosalyn stood up. "I understand that you want to sit here and have a pity party over Snoop Doggy Dogg. And if that's what you want to do, then that's your prerogative. But I want you to remember, it's his loss, and baby or no baby, you need to suck it up and get yourself together."

Dionne knew her sister was right. She had her baby to think about. And that baby was coming—with or without Roland in the picture.

Chapter 36

Vanessa couldn't believe how much she was getting into the renovations at The Mason House. She stood back and surveyed the new mural being painted by several art students from Jack Yates High School. It was phenomenal. They were creating a park scene with kids playing on swings, dancing, playing jump rope and other games. The students had done an excellent job, even making some of the kids in the mural look exactly like some of the kids from the facility.

"Isn't it beautiful?" Rosolyn said, walking up behind her. "Girl, I just don't know how to thank you."

"I should be thanking you," Vanessa replied. "With all this mess going on with me and Thomas, coming here is what's keeping me sane." She paused, then added sadly, "Although it's not the same with Shelly gone." It had only been a couple of weeks since Shelly went to live with the Taylors.

"Look at that girl in the green dress," Vanessa continued, pointing to the mural. "It looks just like Shelly."

Rosolyn's hand went to her mouth. "Oh, my goodness. I can't believe I didn't tell you this. I've been so busy. The Taylors' adoption will be finalized today."

"What?" The sinking feeling Vanessa had felt before just knowing Shelly was with the Taylors intensified at the thought of everything becoming official. She told herself, for the hundredth time, that she wanted Shelly to find a permanent home.

She nodded, still unable to say anything.

Rosolyn patted her sister's back reassuringly. "But she gave you her information. The Taylors are nice people. I'm sure they'll let you see her."

Just then Rosolyn's assistant came barreling into the room. She had a frantic look on her face. "Mrs. Frazier, we have a problem."

Rosolyn furrowed her brow. "What is it?"

Before she could answer, they heard a loud cry from the front lobby. Rosolyn took off, Vanessa and her assistant close behind her.

"Nooooo! Please don't bring me back! I promise I'll be good!" Shelly was there, crying hysterically. Her hair was parted into two ponytails, giving her a more childish look. Bright pink ribbons were wrapped around each ponytail, and she wore a pink frilly dress and pink patent leather shoes. She was hugging a tall man who was crying, too.

"I'm sorry, baby girl," he said, trying to pull her off him.

"What is going on?" Rosolyn asked sternly, stopping in front of them.

Shelly pulled away from the man, saw Vanessa standing behind Rosolyn, and raced toward her.

"They don't want me!" Shelly cried. "Why doesn't anyone want me? Why does God hate me so much?"

Vanessa had no idea what had happened, but tears filled her eyes at the sight of Shelly so hysterical.

"Mr. Taylor, do you mind telling me what is going on?" Rosolyn demanded. "What happened?"

Mr. Taylor fidgeted nervously. "It's not her. She's a wonderful child. It's just . . ." He looked down at the floor.

"Just what?" Rosolyn said.

"It's just that it's too painful for us. When we got her home and . . . and my wife . . . she just couldn't take it."

"I tried on her dress. I didn't know," Shelly cried. "I'm sorry. It was just so pretty. I just wanted to see how it would look. It was hanging in the closet. But she saw me in the dress and she lost it. She started screaming and yelling at me. I didn't know."

"Shhhh," Vanessa said, stroking the back of her head.

Several people had started to gather around and stare. Rosolyn turned to her assistant. "Please take Shelly to my office."

When the assistant tried to pull the girl away from Vanessa, she clung tighter, her wails growing louder.

Vanessa said, "I got her. I'll take her back."

Vanessa walked Shelly into the office, where they could have some privacy. It took her almost fifteen minutes, with Shelly quivering and crying into her chest, to calm the little girl down. And once she did calm down, she sank into a quiet depression.

Ten minutes after that a defeated Rosolyn walked into her office. A strained silence filled the air.

Rosolyn reached up to stroke one of Shelly's ponytails, but Shelly moved her head out of the way.

"Sweetie, it's not you . . ." Rosolyn began.

Shelly stood and brushed her hands down her skirt like she was trying to compose herself. "I shoulda known better than to get all excited. Don't nobody want me," she calmly said.

"Shelly—" Rosolyn said.

"It's cool," Shelly said, her voice quavering. "I'm used . . ." She turned and ran out the office door before finishing her sentence.

Both Rosolyn and Vanessa had tears in their eyes.

"Shouldn't you go after her?" Vanessa asked.

Rosolyn shook her head. "No. Unfortunately, Shelly has been down this road a few times. She prefers a little quiet time to herself. I'll go talk to her later."

"You mean this has happened to her before?"

"Not quite to this extreme," Rosolyn said, agonizing over Shelly, "but this is the third time she's had something promising fall through."

"What? But she's such a sweet girl."

"I know, but she's also a preteen, and everyone wants babies and young kids. But this time it wasn't about her age. The Taylors' daughter died in a car accident. She would've been Shelly's age, and when they saw her in that dress, Mr. Taylor said his wife went ballistic. It made them realize they weren't ready to replace their daughter."

"They were trying to replace their daughter?"

Rosolyn nodded sadly.

"Then it's a good thing she didn't go with them," Vanessa said with defiance.

"I know, but it's not such a good thing for Shelly. I don't know how much more heartbreak that little girl can take."

"Can I go talk to her?" Vanessa said.

"You can try, but like I said, she goes into a shell. It usually takes her a couple of hours before she comes out."

Vanessa decided to take her chances. She walked out to the back courtyard where she saw Shelly sitting up against a tree. She had her poetry book open. Vanessa eased up behind her, looked over her shoulder, and read the title. " 'The Unwanted Butterfly'? "

Shelly didn't look up at her, nor did she close the poetry book. Vanessa eased down next to Shelly. "I could write a poem like that myself," she said. "My mom and dad left me, too." Shelly looked at her like she was trying to gauge if Vanessa was being truthful.

"They died when I was a little girl. I used to always wonder why God would take my parents away from me."

"I wonder that, too," Shelly softly said. "I also wonder why He can't find me a family."

"You know, there are a lot of things we don't have answers for. We just have to trust God," Vanessa said, surprising herself with those words. She'd do well, she thought grimly, to listen to her own advice.

"I just hate it," Shelly mumbled.

"Hate what?"

"LaTonya said they might as well keep my bed empty because I'd be back. She told me nobody would want me. She said nobody over ten gets to leave The Mason House. Now, I have to go back in there and listen to the 'I told you so's.'" She pouted.

"You just tell LaTonya that God has something better in store for you."

"LaTonya don't care nothing about God," Shelly huffed. At the thought of her upcoming humiliation, she stood up. "I gotta go."

"I'll see you later, okay?" Vanessa called out after her. "I'm going to keep on coming, Shelly, do you hear?" Shelly didn't turn around as she continued inside.

Chapter 37

Dionne felt like a stalker. Who was she kidding? She *was* a stalker. She crouched down in the front seat of her Maxima, pulled the gray hood further up on her head, and adjusted her sunglasses. She'd been sitting outside of Roland's apartment for two hours now. She wanted desperately to just go up and knock on his door, but she'd tried that last week and he wouldn't answer.

Dionne's heart jumped when she saw Roland toss his duffel bag over his shoulder and head out of his front door. He was dressed in his workout clothes, and he looked better than ever. It had been three weeks since he walked out of her life and it felt like three years. He was so angry, he'd even changed his phone numbers. So Dionne had no choice but to stalk him in order to get him to talk to her.

Roland walked down the steps to his car, popped open the trunk, and tossed his duffel bag in.

Dionne started her car and waited for him to pull out. When he did, she followed, staying a safe distance behind. She caught a glimpse of herself in the rearview mirror. If anything, she thought wearily, she was probably drawing more attention to herself with the dark glasses and the hoodie. But at this point, she didn't care. All that mattered was getting her man back.

Dionne pulled into the 24 Hour Fitness parking lot and watched to see where Roland parked his Escalade. She waited until he went inside, then pulled her car into an empty spot in the same row. She settled in to wait, knowing it would be at least an hour before Roland came out.

She tried to listen to some music, but it seemed like every song they played was a love song, so she cut the radio off.

She waited patiently until she finally saw Roland making his way out of the gym about an hour and a half later. Dionne jumped out of her car and raced over to block his path. "Roland, can we talk?"

He let out a disgusted sigh and kept walking. "There ain't nothing for us to talk about. Go talk to my wife." He continued toward his car and Dionne scurried to catch up.

"Roland, you have to give me a chance to explain. I mean, you had done me so wrong. I was in pain—I was hurting and I wanted you to hurt the way I was."

"Well, now we're even. Holla." He pulled out his key and hit the button to disable the alarm on his truck.

"I forgave you."

He stopped and spun around to face her. "Then you're a fool. Because I'm only goin' to give a woman one time to stab me in the back, and babe, you plunged the knife deep." He leveled a warning finger at her. "So let me spell this out for you. Leave. Me. The. Hell. Alone. It's nothing you can say, will ever be able to say, to make me change my mind."

Dionne's lips quivered. "How can you be so cold? I thought you loved me."

He licked his lips and let out a slight chuckle. "I did. That's why I can be so cold. You know better than anyone I don't toss the word 'love' around too much. When I say it, I mean it. Now I wish I had never said it. Never felt it. Maybe then your betrayal wouldn't hurt me the way it did." He paused, inhaling deeply. "You just don't get it, Dionne. Do you want to know why I never told you I loved you before?"

Dionne stared at him, blinking back the tears. She couldn't answer him.

"It's because I did. And it scared the hell out of me, because the only other woman I ever loved was my wife and she hurt me beyond imagination. You think I cheated on my wife. Well, I did. But only after I caught her cheating on me," he said scornfully. "And I know you're wondering about Tasha. I broke it off with Tasha when I got married. I only went back to her when I found out my wife was cheating. But I wasn't in love with Tasha. She took whatever I gave her. I kept her around because she was okay with that. Or at least she made me believe she was. When she started making demands, I said, if I'm going to be committed to anyone, it's going to be the one woman who has my heart. And that woman was you, Dionne." He headed for the truck again, agitated. "I didn't want to say I love you because I didn't want to feel it. Then when I came back to you, I had decided to take another chance on love." He laughed bitterly. "So I guess that makes me the fool after all."

"Roland . . ."

"Save it, Dionne. I'm done. I'll say this as nicely as I can. You don't want me now—you thought I was a dog before? Babe, you ain't seen nothing yet." He flashed a smug look as he got into his truck.

Dionne watched as he pulled off.

She stumbled back to her car, her heart aching. She fumbled with the key trying to get the door open, then again trying to insert the key in the ignition. When the keys fell under the gas pedal, Dionne buried her head in her arms on the steering wheel and gave in to devastating sobs. Her romantic dreams were over and this time she had no one to blame but herself.

Chapter 38

Vanessa hugged the toilet as another wave of nausea rushed over her. After she threw up—for the third time today—she stood up and stumbled toward the bathroom sink. She turned on the faucet, grabbed a face towel, wet it, then wiped her face down. She could no longer keep fooling herself. She had to go to the doctor. Of course, her first thought was maybe she was pregnant. But she quickly shook that off. She couldn't be pregnant. God wouldn't be that cruel, would He?

Vanessa felt a lump form in her throat as she made her way back into the living room. Her house was eerily quiet. She found herself longing to hear that annoying humming Thomas always used to do. She grabbed the cordless phone and collapsed on the couch. She needed someone there to take care of her, call the doctor for her, fix her soup. Instead, she was all alone.

Vanessa punched in her gynecologist's office number. After explaining to the receptionist that she just had to get in today, she got an appointment for two-thirty.

Good, she thought, pushing the End button on her phone. That meant she could get a couple more hours' sleep. She quickly called Rosolyn, begged her to drive her to the doctor, and when she agreed, fell back onto the bed.

The sound of the alarm on her cell phone woke Vanessa up just after noon. She had been hoping to feel better, but she actually felt worse. Now, in addition to the nausea, she had horrible cramps, and her head was pounding again.

Vanessa sat up on the edge of her bed, then jumped up and raced to the bathroom when another wave of nausea hit her.

"Dear God, please don't let me be pregnant," she muttered after dry-heaving for about ten minutes.

Vanessa didn't know how she managed to get dressed, but when her doorbell rang at one-thirty, she was ready to go.

"Oh, my goodness," Rosolyn said, eyeing her sister. "You look horrible."

"Thanks," Vanessa said, dragging herself over to the bar to get her purse. "The bad part is, I look better than I feel. Let's go."

They arrived at the doctor's office with ten minutes to spare. Vanessa slept for most of the ride over. She fidgeted in the chair as she waited for the nurse to call her name.

"Vanessa Colton-Kirk," the nurse finally said.

Vanessa stood. "That's me."

"The doctor will see you now." Vanessa followed the nurse back, and after doing the usual weigh-in and blood pressure check, she waited on the high padded reclining examining table for her doctor.

"Well, hello, Vanessa." Dr. Roman flashed a smile as he walked into the room. Dr. Roman was a handsome George Clooney–looking type who had the personality to match his looks, which was why his appointment book stayed full.

"Hi, Doctor," Vanessa wearily responded.

"What seems to be the problem?" he asked, eyeing her chart.

"What's not the problem?" Vanessa replied. "I'm nauseous, having severe pelvic pain, and I have headaches out of this world. I think the headaches and cramping may be caused by stress, because I've been going through serious personal problems, but the nauseous feeling, I just don't know."

He nodded, continuing to read her chart. "Any chance you could be pregnant?" He didn't look up. If he had, he would have seen Vanessa flinch.

"I guess there's a chance. I mean, I'm on the patch, but I did go a week without it."

He looked up at her, shooting a look as if to say "you know better." "Let me take a quick look." He washed his hands, then slipped on a pair of gloves.

Vanessa lay back as he flicked a light at her eyes, listened to her heart, then gently pushed and prodded her abdomen. She closely watched his expression, but it revealed nothing. "Okay," he said, "let's get a blood test." He handed her a slip of paper to take to the lab. "We'll expedite this, so you come back in here after they draw your blood."

Vanessa nodded as she hopped off the edge of the examining table. "I'll see you in a bit, then."

An hour passed before Dr. Roman walked back into the examining room. Vanessa had been about to lose her mind. The waiting was driving her crazy.

"Well?" she asked before the doctor stepped all the way in the room.

"Well, I'm not sure if this is good news or bad news."

Vanessa held her breath.

"You're not pregnant."

She closed her eyes and released a heavy sigh. "Thank you, Jesus," she muttered.

"I guess that's good news," he said. "However, we can't go thanking Jesus just yet. I'm concerned because your blood pressure is very low. And during your examination I felt what I believe are fibroids. Have you ever been told you have them?"

"Fibroids?" Vanessa asked, horrified by the sound of them. "No. I don't know much about them, and I definitely didn't know I had them."

"Well, it appears you do. Usually, we don't worry about them, but yours are large enough to cause concern. I'll need to take a closer look."

"Are they cancerous?" she asked, dreading the answer.

"No, fibroids are benign, but yours appear to be the size of a grapefruit, which would explain your pelvic pain. And so we need to take a closer look."

Vanessa sighed thankfully. She wasn't pregnant and she didn't have cancer. Anything else she would deal with happily.

Chapter 39

Dionne silently cursed her blank computer screen. She could not believe that she'd opened that stupid attachment. But it had come from Melanie's email address, so she didn't think anything of it.

She should've known Melanie wouldn't send an attachment called "Life Is Beautiful."

The ringing phone caused her to put her panic on pause. She snatched up the phone when she saw Melanie's number on the caller ID.

"Melanie, did you send me an email called 'Life Is Beautiful'?" she said hurriedly.

"Huh? Calm down. What are you talking about? I've been at the mall all day. I haven't been on my computer."

"Oh, my God." Dionne groaned as she watched her computer screen flicker. "I got an email from your address with an attachment. I opened it up and now my computer is going crazy."

"Dionne, you know I don't forward that stuff. And what about your virus protection?"

"I don't have it." She groaned again. "It expired and I didn't have the money to update it."

"Dang, girl," Melanie said. "Well, what is your computer doing?"

"It flashed a message that said, 'Life is no longer beautiful,' then my screen started going crazy." She wanted to scream in frustration. "I cannot believe this. My résumé, everything is on here."

"Dionne, first unplug it," Melanie suggested.

Dionne reached down and yanked the cord out of the wall. The computer screen went black.

"Do you know somebody who can figure this out?" Melanie asked.

Bruce immediately popped into Dionne's mind. *Nothing like an IT guy at your fingertips,* she thought. "Let me call you back, Mel." She hung up before her friend could respond and quickly scrolled through her phone to find Bruce's number. They'd talked a few times since she and Roland broke up. She'd told him what happened but declined his offer for another date.

Thirty minutes later, Bruce was standing on her doorstep.

"Oh, thank goodness you're here," she said, holding the door wide open.

"Your knight has arrived." He chuckled.

"I am so happy to see you," she said, shutting the door behind him. "Please tell me you can save my computer."

"What's wrong with it?"

"I don't know. I think I have a virus. I opened an attachment called 'Life Is Beautiful,' and my computer went crazy."

The smile dropped off his face. "So I guess you didn't see on the news about that being the new super virus, and that whatever you do you shouldn't open it?"

"I don't watch the news," she huffed as she led him upstairs to her bedroom, where she kept her computer.

"Well, it's pretty serious. It wipes out everything and completely destroys your hard drive. But let me take a look and see if I can fix it."

"Please, try. My book is on there." Dionne hadn't told anyone but Bruce that she was working on a novel. She hadn't even told Roland because she didn't want anyone laughing at her. But Bruce hadn't laughed. He'd encouraged her to get it finished.

"Well, we can't have that," Bruce said. "Your book is the next great American novel, so we've got to retrieve it."

"I will be eternally grateful."

His eyes lit up. "That's a deal."

Dionne went to get a glass of milk to settle her nerves while Bruce went to work on the computer. It took him twenty minutes of tinkering with its metallic-looking innards before he walked back in the living room pointing two fingers at his chest.

"Am I the man or what?"

"You got it fixed?" she squealed. When he nodded, she jumped up and threw her arms around his neck. He felt firm and muscular, and she was surprised at the sudden sexual tension that rippled through her body. She pulled away, not knowing where that feeling was coming from. She didn't like Bruce like that.

He seemed pretty happy about it. "Yeah, the virus had pretty much destroyed everything on your system, but I was able to go in and quarantine it. I saved almost everything."

"I owe you big-time."

He hesitated a beat, before saying, "Then come with me to my fraternity's ball next weekend."

"You're in a fraternity?"

"I sure am." He threw up his sign.

Dionne chuckled. "Wow, I never would've taken you for a frat guy."

"A lot of people underestimate me," he said, his tone turning serious. "But it's all good. I like people not being able to figure me out. Thinking one thing about me"—he lightly licked his lips—"and then finding out something totally different."

"Ooooh, a man of intrigue," Dionne said. She was just about to accept his invitation when she remembered her burgeoning belly. She quirked her lips and turned away. "I'm not going to be able to go to the dance with you."

"I thought you said you were eternally grateful," he joked. "And you told me all about your breakup, so I don't have to worry about hammering anybody," he added, playfully flexing his muscles.

"I am grateful," she allowed, "and no, you wouldn't have to hammer anyone. Me and Roland are finished." She didn't add that she still hoped they'd find some way to get back together.

Dionne debated over what to say next. She finally decided

she needed to let him know about the pregnancy—it was only so much longer she could wear these big shirts. Plus, she decided, that way he wouldn't get any ideas about them being together and they could just be friends.

"Let's sit and talk for a minute," Dionne said.

Her firm voice caused an apprehensive look to cross Bruce's face. He followed her to the sofa.

"As you know, I just got out of a relationship," she said, and he nodded. "Well, the thing you don't know is . . . I-I'm pregnant."

The twinkle in Bruce's eye faded. "Pregnant?" He eyed her stomach, then caught himself and quickly tried to cover the disappointment in his voice. "I noticed you looked a little, ummm, fuller. I just thought you put on a little weight."

"Fuller, huh?" She brushed her oversize shirt down, making her pregnancy pretty evident now. "Fatter, you mean. But I'm lucky, so far, I'm all belly, so it's not as noticeable."

He finally smiled. "I was just trying to be politically correct. But, pregnant, wow. Congratulations. You seem like you'd make a good mother."

"I just wanted to tell you because, I don't know, I just want things to be on the up-and-up."

He nodded his appreciation. "Thanks." He hesitated, then said, "I like kids. Maybe you'll let me take the little fella out to the park sometimes. Or the little girl out for ice cream," he added.

"Sounds like a plan," she said, smiling. She had no doubt Bruce would hold true to his word. She just hoped Roland would step up and do the right thing.

Chapter 40

Vanessa scanned the rack looking for the 120-watt flood lightbulbs she needed. Three of the lights were out in her kitchen and she could no longer put off replacing them. Today was the first day she felt her usual self, so she had to take advantage of that and get some things done.

Vanessa silently cursed as she scanned the back of the lightbulb cartons. This was something Thomas normally did. She didn't even know what type of bulbs she needed. *Was it fluorescent or incandescent?* she wondered as she read the back of both cartons.

"Shoot, I don't know," she mumbled, tossing both into her basket. She pushed the basket down the aisle, frustrated. Vanessa hated Target. Truth be told, she hated shopping, period. She didn't have the patience for it. But she needed all kinds

of things around the house—toilet tissue, garbage bags, gro-
ceries—things Thomas used to get. Vanessa made a mental note
to hire an assistant. She didn't have time for stuff like this.

"Well, well, well. Hello, Miss Vanessa."

Vanessa stopped just short of running her basket into a pink
stroller. "What the . . . ?" Her eyes made their way from the
baby, up to a flat stomach, then to the smirk on Alana's face,
which seemed to be taunting her.

Alana relished Vanessa's shocked expression. "Oh, you didn't
know we had the baby?" She gently ran her finger over the baby's
caramel face. The baby was sleeping peacefully and looked like
a little doll, except for the pink headband around her head that
seemed to Vanessa like it was cutting off her circulation. "Her
name is Thomasina. She's three weeks old," Alana proudly said.

Vanessa looked at Alana, astonished. "And you have her
out in a germ-infested store?" Vanessa didn't know a whole lot
about kids, but she thought that you probably shouldn't bring a
newborn baby out into public like this.

Alana placed her hands on her hips. "Don't you worry about
where I got my baby. Her daddy had to work late or else he
would've been here. So, I brought her out to get some air while
I pick up a few things to cook my man dinner."

Vanessa didn't know why Alana was so spiteful. Hadn't she
caused enough problems? Now she seemed to be taking pride
in torturing her.

"Mmmm-hmmm," Alana continued. "I know all about how
you tried to make Thomas into a househusband, but I take care
of my man, the way it's supposed to be. I give him what he

needs." She reached down and rubbed her baby's head again. "And what he *wants*." She looked back up at Vanessa. "You could learn a thing or two."

Okay, forget the career. Hello, jail. Vanessa was about to clean go off on this little tramp. "Little girl, you don't know who you're messing with," she said, stepping away from her basket. "I will—"

"You will what?" Alana said, bucking up to her. "Get me fired? Try to have me arrested? Been there, done that. I know you were responsible for me losing my job." She was breathing right in Vanessa's face. "But guess what? Since I didn't have a job, Thomas had no choice but to let me and our baby move in with him in his apartment. So thank you. Your little plan only brought me and Thomas closer. And since I am so broke, I *want* you to hit me." She raised her chin. "Make it good so I can get your house and your money in addition to your man."

Vanessa was indeed about to haul off and hit her in the jaw, but something wild in Alana's eyes stopped her. This wasn't some ordinary "I got your man" type of anger. The venom in her voice was laced with an emotion much deeper. All of a sudden it occurred to her that Alana just kept popping up wherever she was. Alana, whom she had never met prior to all of this drama, seemed to get a perverse joy out of tormenting her. She had Thomas. What more could she want?

"Alana, what is your problem with me?" Vanessa calmly asked. "*You're* the other woman, remember?"

"I want your life," Alana spat.

"That's obvious."

Alana bristled at Vanessa's ironic response. "No. I want your life destroyed. I want to take away everything that ever meant anything to you. Your man, your money, your job. Everything."

Now Vanessa was really confused. "What is wrong with you? You act like I'm the one who did you wrong."

Alana released a maniacal laugh as she stepped back. "You really don't know, do you?"

Vanessa looked at her in surprise. "Know what?"

"What this is all about?"

"Really, I don't."

"Do the names Mark and Leslie Irving mean anything to you?"

Vanessa cocked her head, thinking. A vague bell went off in her head. Where had she heard those names?

"Let me refresh your memory," Alana said. "Mark and Leslie Irving are my parents."

Yes, she'd seen their names in the background check she'd had done on Alana. "And what does that have to do with me?" Vanessa asked, growing concerned. Hot tears had started streaming down Alana's cheeks, and her anger seemed to be intensifying.

Alana shot an evil look at an old man who had stopped to stare at them. He quickly scurried off as she spun back to Vanessa.

"My parents came through your divorce court in April two years ago."

Vanessa looked at Alana like she was crazy. As if she remembered everyone who came through her court.

Alana folded her arms across her chest and shook her head. "Isn't that a crying shame? You destroy lives, then don't even think twice about it."

"You know what, Alana?" Vanessa retreated behind her shopping cart. The crazed look in Alana's eyes was scaring her. "I don't have time for this. It's obvious you have some issues."

Alana jumped in front of the cart to keep her from leaving. "Oh, no, you don't! You're not gonna just run off. My father stood in your courtroom and begged you not to grant my mother her divorce. He told you that she was sick. He asked you for six months to let them try counseling. Six months!" Alana screamed, causing more people to stop in the store and stare. "But noooo, you dismissed him. Told him to shut up before you had him thrown out. Then proceeded to grant my mother the divorce, and give her the house and half his money."

Vanessa was dumbfounded by this outburst. "You've got to be kidding me. How am I responsible for your mother wanting to leave your father?" She was trying her best to stay rational because Alana was losing it. Thomasina had woken up and was staring wide-eyed at her mother, but Alana didn't seem to notice or care.

"My mother was an alcoholic who cleaned herself up long enough to come in your courtroom and put on a front," Alana continued, the venom in her voice growing stronger. "Had you bothered to listen to my father, or even given him a chance to get her to a counselor while she was in her right mind, they'd still be together. And my father . . ." She choked back her tears. "My father would still be alive today."

Vanessa's hand went to her mouth.

Alana nodded, finally wiping away her tears. "That's right, my father was so distraught that he put a bullet in his brain three weeks later. And guess what? My mother sobered up long enough to realize what she'd done. She cried to me, telling me how much she loved him and wished she could do things differently. She said my father was right, that she didn't really want the divorce. She only did it because he was trying to put her in rehab. She blamed herself for my father's death and took a bottle full of pills. Less than one week after my beautiful father, the man I adored and loved with every ounce of my soul, took his life, my mother died on my bathroom floor."

If looks could kill, Vanessa knew she would be under the ground.

"Alana, I can understand your grief," she began calmly.

"You can't understand anything!" Alana screamed.

"Excuse me, is everything all right?" Someone had gone and gotten the manager. He was standing at the end of the aisle with a security guard behind him.

Vanessa looked from the manager to Alana, whose chest was heaving up and down. She couldn't believe she was actually feeling sympathy for the girl, but Vanessa could relate to her losing her parents. "We're okay. She's a little upset. I was just leaving." She looked at Alana. "I'm really sorry," Vanessa whispered.

"No, but you will be," Alana spat as Vanessa wheeled her cart away.

Chapter 41

Vanessa pulled into Ida's driveway. She was so shaken up that she didn't want to go home. It was Sunday, so she knew her aunt had a soul food spread to die for. And a good meal was just what Vanessa needed after that horrible run-in with Alana.

Vanessa couldn't believe that Alana had purposely set out to destroy her life. That meant that she'd seduced Thomas on purpose. Vanessa shook away the sensation of fear creeping up on her. Thomas was sleeping with a woman who was emotionally unstable.

She silently cursed as she stepped out of the car. She'd been in such a hurry to get out of the store that she'd left everything she'd needed. Now she was going to have to go back.

"Forget that," Vanessa muttered as she used her key to let

herself in. She'd just have to pay Dionne to go do it because her shopping days were done.

"Hey, baby girl," Ida said as Vanessa made her way into the kitchen. Ida was leaning over the stove, stirring a big pot. She had traded in her signature lace dress for her signature duster dress. A lace apron was wrapped around her waist. Dionne was at the kitchen table, looking through an *Essence* magazine.

"Ummm, it smells good in here," Vanessa said, savoring the aroma of the candied yams. "Where's Rosolyn?"

"She had to go over to some church where Henry was preaching this afternoon." Ida elbowed Vanessa out of the way. "Can you get your nose from all up in my pot? And what's wrong with you?" she asked, eyeing Vanessa suspiciously.

Vanessa tried to look innocent. "Who said something was wrong with me?"

"That frazzled look on your face said so, that's who," Ida said, wiping her hands on the apron. "Dionne been sitting up here pouting all day. Now here you come looking all sad. Sit down and tell me all about it." She motioned toward the kitchen table.

"Aunt Ida, I said nothing's wrong."

Dionne looked up, studied Vanessa herself, then said, "Girl, don't even fight her on it. You know she's not gonna let up until you tell her what's wrong. And even I can see that something is wrong. Maybe your life is as messed up as mine."

"What's goin' on with you?" Vanessa asked.

"Uh-uh," Ida said. "I've heard her story already. What's yours?"

Vanessa removed her jacket, preferring to find out about her sister. "Where do I begin?" she asked, draping the jacket across the back of the chair. "I saw Alana at the store today," she said as she sat down. "Honestly, I think she's following me."

By the time Vanessa finished recounting what had happened, both Dionne and Ida were staring at her in shock.

"Lord Jesus. What are you gon' do about this cuckoo puff? She sounds like she's unstable."

Vanessa nervously fingered a place mat. "You know I've harbored a lot of hate toward Alana, but it seems like her hate for me is even deeper."

"That's exactly why you need to do something," Ida replied.

"You're a better person than me," Dionne said, "because she wouldn't even have gotten a chance to tell me her reasons for busting up my marriage. The minute she got up in my face, I would have—"

"We know what you would've done, Laila Ali," Ida said shortly.

"I don't know what I'm going to do," Vanessa said worriedly.

"I'll tell you what to do. Get a restraining order 'cause the girl is crazy," Ida said. "And you need to make sure you tell Thomas about it."

"I haven't talked to Thomas in almost a week."

"Well, you need to talk to him," Ida said. "You and your sister and these relationships with your menfolk," she continued, shooting Dionne a chastising look. "Y'all think I'm stupid, but somebody got something they need to be telling me. I had my fish dream again."

Vanessa looked at her aunt in bewilderment. "Fish dream?"

"Yeah, somebody's pregnant." She eyed Vanessa suspiciously.

"Don't look at me," Vanessa said, waving her hand no. "I just went to the doctor two days ago. I assure you that I'm not pregnant."

Ida turned her attention to Dionne, who quickly diverted her eyes. "Ummmm-hmmmm. I knew it. You never have been good at lying to me," Ida said. "I knew something was up when you came up in here in that big ol' shirt. Know you like skimpy little outfits."

Vanessa's mouth dropped open. "Dionne, you're pregnant?" She touched Dionne's stomach, then jumped back. "You are pregnant!"

Dionne was about to protest, but when she opened her mouth, a loud sob came out. She didn't know what overcame her, but she began crying hysterically.

Ida walked over to her. "There, there. You're gonna be all right," she said, stroking the back of Dionne's hair.

"B-but Roland won't take me back!"

"I thought you all worked that out," Vanessa said.

"We did. But I messed it up."

Neither of them asked what she did. Ida just continued to stroke her hair. "Well, you come from a line of strong women who have faced adversity head-on. You will be just fine."

Looking on, Vanessa's heart ached for her sister. It looked like neither of them would get the happiness they so desperately wanted.

A bout of silence hung in the room before Ida reached over, picked up the cordless phone, and handed it to Vanessa. "Now you. Call your husband."

"For what?" Vanessa replied, frowning up.

"To tell him about that crazy woman."

She looked at the phone hesitantly. Part of her wanted to tell him right away, but the other part wanted him to stew in his own mess.

Vanessa released a defeated sigh. No matter what Thomas had done to her, he at least needed to know about Alana, and about how the destruction of their marriage had all been carefully orchestrated.

Chapter 42

The sound of pounding on her front door caused Vanessa to bolt upright out of her sleep.

"Somebody has lost their mind," she muttered, glancing at the alarm clock, which brightly displayed 3:12 A.M.

Vanessa grabbed the butcher knife she had started keeping under her mattress since Thomas left, and cautiously headed to the front door.

"Vanessa, it's me. Open the door, please."

"Thomas?" she said through the door. She'd called to tell him about Alana, but since he hadn't answered, she hadn't bothered to leave a message. So she had no idea why he was here now at this ungodly hour.

"Yeah, please open up. I need to talk to you."

He sounded like he'd been crying, Vanessa thought, alarmed. She looked out the peephole. He *had* been crying. His eyes were red and he had on a pair of old sweats and a T-shirt, which was totally unlike Thomas, Mr. *GQ* himself.

Vanessa unlocked the dead bolt. "This had better be good," she said as she swung the door open.

Thomas stumbled inside, another unpleasant surprise. He reeked of liquor and the stench made Vanessa cover her mouth. "Ugggh, what in the world?"

"She lied, Vanessa," Thomas said, flopping down on the sofa. "I can't believe that she lied."

Vanessa kept her distance. "Who lied, Thomas?"

"Alana. She lied about the baby." He buried his face in his hands and let out a heart-wrenching sob.

Vanessa stood over him, not sure of what to do. She'd never seen him like that. "What are you talking about?"

"Thomasina is not my daughter." He looked up at her with a pitiful face. "I had a DNA test done. I got the results back today. She's not my baby."

"What?" Vanessa didn't know whether to be angry, ecstatic, or to just wring Thomas's neck. He'd destroyed everything they'd built for this child—who wasn't even his.

Anger won in the end. How dare he come to her crying about the other woman's baby? Any sympathy she was briefly feeling for him went out the window. "Well, that sounds like a personal problem. Why are you bringing this to me?"

He continued to look lost. "I don't know. I just left and started driving. This is where I ended up."

"You're drunk." She turned up her nose at the smell of the alcohol filling the room. "What are you doing behind the wheel of a car?"

He ran his hand over his head. "I am such a fool," he said, ignoring her chastisement. "I wanted a baby so bad that I let her con me."

Vanessa wasn't going to disagree there. "If you wanted a child so bad and you believed her so much, why'd you have a DNA test, Mr. Oh-no, Alana-can-do-no-wrong? I thought you knew the baby was yours. Isn't that what you said?" She knew he was hurting, and she probably shouldn't be twisting the knife even further, but right about now she could only see that he'd destroyed their marriage for nothing.

He regained some of his usual common sense. "As bad as I wanted it to be mine, I knew there was a possibility that it wasn't. When she told me she was pregnant, I was happy." He looked up quickly, not wanting her to take that the wrong way. "I didn't want to hurt you, but I told myself, I'm finally going to be a father. I'm going to be the father I never had." Darkness settled on his brow. "But I didn't want to go through life with that doubt in the back of my mind. The DNA test was just to ease my doubt. I never expected it to come back with this."

He got up and walked distractedly to the fireplace. He often had stood there while they talked after a day at work. Vanessa wondered if he noticed that all of the pictures of him were gone. If he did, he didn't say anything. He kept talking. "When I confronted her, at first she said the test was wrong. Then she admitted that she was pregnant when she met me."

Vanessa couldn't believe Thomas would be so dumb as to fall for the oldest trick in the book. "Did you do the math at all?"

"I did, but she started talking about women are actually ten months pregnant. I looked it up online and it said the same thing." Thomas took a deep breath and plopped back down on the sofa. "I don't know. I was just blinded by the fact that I was going to be a father."

At that moment Vanessa saw her husband in a different light. She saw how much being a father meant to him. Before, she always blew him off whenever he talked about children, but the anguish in his face told her just how devastated he really was. She thought about the time she'd spent with Shelly. It had brought her great joy, and Shelly wasn't even her child. She briefly imagined what happiness their own child could've brought.

Vanessa shook off the thought as she took in the distressed look on Thomas's face. She knew what she was about to say would only add to his pain, but she had to tell him. She sat on the sofa beside him. "Thomas, not only was Alana already pregnant when she met you, but her getting you into her bed was all planned."

Vanessa then spent the next twenty minutes once again telling the story of Alana's parents.

Thomas sobered up as he listened to the plan of revenge. "You mean her ruining my life was all a setup?"

Vanessa nodded somberly, surprised that she was resisting the urge to go off on him. "Yeah, she planned it all. But the fact remains, you slept with her," she couldn't help adding.

Thomas's tears turned to anger. "I can't believe she played me like this." He kicked over the coffee table, sending its magazines sliding along the floor.

Vanessa folded her arms and glared at him. "Look, I understand you're upset and all, but you need to go back to your own home if you're going to tear stuff up."

Thomas glanced down at the overturned table. "I'm sorry." He sat the table upright, then gathered up the magazines and rearranged them in piles.

They momentarily stared at each other before Thomas said, "Can I stay here tonight?"

She raised an eyebrow. "Are you high in addition to being drunk?"

"Please. I'm exhausted. I don't even know how I made it here. I'm too tired, angry, and drunk to get behind the wheel of a car. And if I see Alana again tonight . . . there's no telling what I might do," he added in a menacing growl.

Vanessa felt a chill run through her body. Her husband had never said anything like that before. "Fine, Thomas," she said evenly. "You can sleep on the sofa. But tomorrow I want you gone. You made your bed, so go lie in it."

She turned and headed back to her room, ignoring the warm feeling creeping up inside her about having Thomas back in the house.

Chapter 43

V anessa absolutely, positively could not believe what she had just done. She must have stone cold lost her mind.

She looked over at Thomas's naked body sprawled out across their bed. No, make that *her* bed. She'd kicked him out. She was about to divorce him. After everything she'd done to get Judge Jarrett to grant the divorce, he'd signed everything and they just had to wait the customary thirty days before it became official. So there was no way she wasn't going through with it.

Thomas stretched, opened his eyes, and smiled lazily when he saw her staring at him. "Good morning."

Vanessa pulled the covers over her naked body as she climbed up close to the headboard. She tried to remember what had happened. She'd gone to bed leaving Thomas on the sofa. Then, right before daylight, he had crawled in bed next to her. She remembered initially feeling tense, but as he slowly began massaging her shoulders, she'd relaxed. It had felt so good having him next to her. The next thing she knew, she was waking up naked.

Thomas laughed. "What are you doing with that?" He motioned to the bedspread she had shielding her body. "It's not like I haven't seen all of that before."

"Thomas, th-this was a mistake." Vanessa was flustered. She was usually so in control. She could not believe that she had allowed herself to succumb to a moment of weakness.

"We are technically still husband and wife." He flashed a sly smile. "We still have twenty-one days." Thomas got up and slowly walked around to Vanessa's side of the bed. He sat down and took her hand. "Do you still love me?"

She snatched her hand away. For someone who just found out he'd been lied to about his supposed child, he sure seemed in a good mood. "Don't mistake what happened last night as me still loving you."

He gave her a shrewd look. "You know what? Your mouth can say anything it wants. But your body is telling the true story. You love me." He grinned broadly.

"Whatever, Thomas." She swung her feet over to get out of the bed, still holding the cover up to her body. He grabbed her hand and pulled her back to him. "Did you forget? You came over here crying because your mistress played you. I just had a moment of temporary insanity," she said.

His expression turned sad as he recalled what happened.

"I haven't forgotten. What Alana did will always burn inside of me. But this . . . being with you again brought me a joy I haven't had in a long time. Maybe this was a sign," he finally said. "I prayed for God to find a way for us to get back together. Maybe this is it."

Vanessa wasn't going anywhere near that far. "Yeah, right, Thomas. I told you that's not gonna happen."

He looked up at her and took her hand again. "Vanessa, pray with me."

She looked at him like he was crazy. "Pray with you? What, you picked up something at that religious retreat? We haven't ever prayed together."

"Maybe that was our problem."

Vanessa was silent. She wanted to snatch her hand away, to tell him where he could go, tell him to go pray with his fake baby mama. But the words wouldn't come out.

She yanked her arm away again.

"Please, I'm begging you," he said. "You don't have to say anything. Just kneel with me and I'll pray for us both."

"Well," she said, finally giving in, "I can't very well pray naked, can I?" She grabbed her robe off the chaise longue. She took her time putting her robe on.

Thomas watched her intently. It was almost like he was trying to see inside her soul. It didn't feel creepy, though. It felt nice. Once she walked back over to him, he took her hand and gently eased her to the floor. For the first time since they'd said "I do," they prayed together.

After Thomas finished, Vanessa tried to shake off the conflicting feelings racing through her. She stood up and immediately doubled over in pain.

"Agggghhhh!" she screamed, clutching her stomach. Her eyes widened in horror as she felt something gushing down her legs.

"Vanessa! What's wrong?" His gaze drifted down to the floor where she'd been kneeling. A small puddle of blood was pooling at her feet. "Oh, my God!" Thomas exclaimed. "Wh-what's happening?"

Vanessa stood, frozen in shock as blood continued to stream down her leg.

Thomas sprang into action. He put his arm around her to guide her to the bathroom. On the way, he grabbed the cordless phone with his free hand. After sitting a stunned, very frightened Vanessa on the toilet, he dialed 911.

"Hello, we need an ambulance! Right away! My wife . . . she's bleeding really bad!"

Thomas gave the 911 operator the address and hung up. Vanessa was hyperventilating as she continued to stare at the blood. "Thomas, what's happening to me?"

"I don't know, baby," he said with none of his usual calmness. "The paramedics are on their way. They're going to—"

"Aggghhh!" Vanessa's scream cut him off. She doubled over and clutched her stomach again. "Thomas, help me," she cried weakly.

He stared in horror. Vanessa was now sweating profusely.

"It h-hurts so bad," she cried.

"Hang on, baby," he said, leaning over to hug her. "Help is on the way."

Vanessa grabbed his neck. "Please don't let me die."

"You're not gonna die," he said unconvincingly. "You're gonna be fine."

Vanessa saw his mouth moving, telling her more words of comfort, but she could no longer make out what he was saying. The next thing she knew, her entire world went black.

Chapter 44

Dionne paced back and forth across the room. She glanced over at Thomas, nervously rocking in a chair in the corner of the hospital's waiting room. Ida sat on the other side of the room, reading a passage from her Bible. Rosolyn had gone down to the chapel.

They'd been holding a vigil for the past two hours, waiting for a doctor to tell them what was wrong with Vanessa.

Thomas had called Ida from the ambulance on the way to the hospital. She, in turn, had called Dionne and Rosolyn. Now all of them were in the waiting room, trying to keep from going crazy.

"When are they going to let us know something?" Dionne snapped. She rubbed her own stomach as she felt her baby kick.

The stress must have gotten to the baby, because this was the fifth kick she'd felt since she'd gotten the news. She could no longer hide her pregnancy as her little mound had turned into a mountain.

"Just be patient, baby," Ida soothingly said. "We have to let the doctors do their job."

"Well, we've been waiting forever," she said, pacing back and forth. "This is ridiculous."

Everyone turned as a tall, handsome doctor walked into the waiting room. He glanced down at the clipboard he was holding. "Is Thomas Kirk here?"

Thomas jumped up. "That's me."

The doctor removed his glasses and wiped his brow. "I'm Dr. Roman, Vanessa's ob-gyn."

"Ob-gyn?" Thomas asked.

Dr. Roman nodded. "Yes, they called me because of the nature of Vanessa's illness."

"What's wrong?" Thomas asked. He had been wringing his hands for hours, and worry lines filled his forehead.

Dionne stepped up next to Thomas. The look on the doctor's face was scaring her. "Yeah, Doc. What's wrong with my sister?"

"Well, Mrs. Kirk has severe fibroids, two of them the size of grapefruits, and it appears that one of them has attached itself to her uterus. Also, we cannot stop her vaginal hemorrhaging."

All three of them let out collective gasps.

"I didn't know fibroids could cause all that," Rosolyn said, walking into the room.

Dr. Roman slowly nodded as he turned to her. "It's rare but they can, and it can be very dangerous."

"S-so what does this mean?" Thomas asked. "And what caused it to happen?"

"We don't know," Dr. Roman said, "and that means we have to act fast. She's already lost a lot of blood."

"So does that mean she's gonna be all right?" Ida said, finally chiming in.

"We need to perform an emergency hysterectomy or we're in danger of the blood loss proving fatal." Dr. Roman looked directly at Thomas. "The problem is, she is sedated and can't make the decision. It's going to be up to you."

"What?" he asked incredulously.

"We don't have much time," Dr. Roman continued. "We considered embolization, but there is no guarantee with that, and could lead us right back to this point. My professional opinion is that it's too risky to chance."

"Speak English, Doctor," Dionne said, her voice strained. "What does that mean?"

"It means if we don't perform the hysterectomy immediately, your sister could die."

"Then you go perform it," Ida responded forcefully.

"Wait," Thomas said. "A hysterectomy. That means she can never have children?"

Dionne, Ida, and Rosolyn all turned to stare at him.

"You got your kid, so what do you care?" Dionne snapped.

"No, it's not that," Thomas said defensively. "I just know that Vanessa really wants to have children, just not right now."

"If I may be frank, Mr. Kirk," Dr. Roman began. "If we don't do this surgery now, your wife might not live to have children."

Ida stepped over and gently touched Thomas's arm. "Baby, I know this is difficult for you, but you have to think about what's best for Vanessa."

"And stop thinking about yourself because at least you have your child," Dionne cried. "It's not like you two are gonna stay together anyway." She was getting irritated. Her sister was lying in there dying, and he was hesitating about granting permission for her lifesaving operation because he wouldn't get his precious kid.

"Dionne," Thomas said, annoyed, "Alana's daughter is not mine."

Dionne looked surprised and her expression softened.

"And just so you know," he continued, "yes, I want a child, but I want Vanessa more. I just know my wife. She's going to be furious at me for making such a decision without her input."

"Well, she can't give her input," Rosolyn interjected.

Dr. Roman cleared his throat. "Time is of the essence. We don't have any options. I assure you, if there were another way, I would do it." He handed the clipboard in his hand to Thomas. "These are the consent papers. I will give you a few minutes. But as I said, we need to act fast. I'll send the nurse back in and you can let her know what you all decide."

He hurried out of the waiting room.

Ida turned her attention back to Thomas. "We don't have a choice."

"I know," Thomas said as a tear rolled down his cheek. "I just hope she forgives me. For everything."

Chapter 45

Vanessa's eyes fluttered open as she tried to focus on where she was. Gradually, it became clear that she wasn't home. It looked like she was in a hospital.

"Well, hello there," Ida said, closing her Bible. "We were wondering when you were gonna wake up."

Vanessa tried to sit up, but a piercing pain shot through her abdomen. "Owww." She lay back against a stack of starched pillows.

Thomas jumped up, alarmed. "How are you feeling?"

"Oh, man, I'm hurting." She groaned.

"Can I get you anything?" he said.

The anger she wanted to feel toward him wouldn't form. She felt utterly exhausted, yet grateful that he had been with her when she passed out. "No, I'm fine. What happened?"

A guilty look passed over his face. "Your fibroids created some serious problems," Thomas said.

"Wow," Vanessa replied. "I didn't know they were that bad."

Ida walked around to the other side of the bed. "I wish you'd told me about them. Your mother and your grandmother had them." Ida shook her head. "But for some reason we just don't talk about our medical history. Maybe if we had, you could've been better prepared for this."

Vanessa was shocked and not because she had no idea fibroids ran in her family: she had never seen her aunt beat herself up about anything.

"How bad were they? And did they remove them?" Vanessa asked, looking around. "Can I get something to drink?" Her throat was parched and she desperately needed some water.

Ida walked over to the tray on the back wall and poured some water from the small brown pitcher. "Thomas, I'll take some coffee from the coffee shop downstairs. Can you run get me some?" she said, handing Vanessa the water.

Thomas hesitated but then nodded. "Okay, I'll be right back."

As soon as he left the room, Vanessa struggled to sit up. "Are you sure you're okay?" Ida asked, fluffing her pillow.

"Can you just please tell me what happened? Where's the doctor? And how did I end up in the hospital?"

"You passed out from the shock and pain." Ida repeated everything Dr. Roman had told her.

Vanessa sat stunned. "How could I not know how bad

things were? I mean, I was in so much pain. I should've had it checked out sooner."

"No sense talkin' about what you should've done," Ida said firmly. "The good thing is you're goin' to be fine, except . . ."

Vanessa could tell from the look on her face there was something important her aunt wasn't telling her. "Except what?"

Ida inhaled deeply. "Except they had to perform an emergency hysterectomy."

Vanessa was startled. "What are you talking about?"

Ida looked very uncomfortable. "Baby, there is no easy way to tell you this, so I'm just gonna spit it out. You were hemorrhaging and they couldn't stop it, so they had to perform the hysterectomy."

"What?"

Ida sadly nodded. "Yes, there was no other way."

The reality of what her aunt was saying slowly sank in. "You mean, they took out my uterus?"

Ida squeezed Vanessa's hand gently.

"No!" Vanessa jerked her hand away. "They can't just do that without my permission, can they?" she asked, becoming frantic.

"They had permission."

"From who?" Vanessa demanded. "The only person that could authorize something like that is me or Thomas." She stopped and stared at her aunt in disbelief. "Thomas told them they could give me a hysterectomy?"

"Sweetie, you have to understand, he didn't have a choice."

"How dare he?" Vanessa cried. "It wasn't his place to do

that!" She couldn't believe what she was hearing. Granted, she didn't want kids now, but she did want them one day. Now, hearing that she would *never* have them was a devastating blow.

"Vanessa, this was a matter of life and death," Ida pointed out. "And just so you know, me and your sisters advised Thomas to sign the papers letting the doctor give you the hysterectomy. It was either that or take a chance on you dying."

"That wasn't your choice to make!" Vanessa thundered. Then she recoiled at the pain that was shooting through her abdomen.

"Well, it was a choice that had to be made." Ida made a har-rumphing sound, like Vanessa better come to her senses. "I'm sorry, but if I had it to do all over again, I'd do the exact same thing." She folded her arms defiantly.

Vanessa turned toward the door as Thomas cautiously opened it. "One cup of nice hot coffee," he said, easing back into the room. The dire look on Vanessa's face stopped him cold. "I guess your aunt told you?"

"I guess she did," Vanessa said. Tears started running down her face. "How could you do that?"

Thomas set the coffee cup down on the rolling tray and walked over to the bed. "I'm sorry, Vanessa. You may not agree with my decision, but I stand by it. I couldn't take a chance on losing you."

"I'm not yours to lose anymore. Did you forget that?"

He ignored her sarcasm. "Even if you never talk to me again, I can take comfort in the fact that you're alive and well. And at the end of the day, that's what's most important."

Vanessa rolled her eyes, but his look was so tender, she knew he meant it.

Thomas turned to Ida. "I'll be outside if you need me."

Vanessa refused to look at him as he left. As soon as the door closed, Ida said, "Don't you ever get tired of being a mean, ornery, stubborn child?"

Vanessa blanched. "What is that supposed to mean?"

"That man has been here by your side since they wheeled you in. He's been worried sick about you. He didn't want to make the decision he made, Vanessa, but when the doctor said you might not make it otherwise, he didn't hesitate."

"I can't have kids." Vanessa said the words like the reality was still sinking in.

"Yes, you can. You can adopt. God does everything for a reason."

"Including taking away my ability to have kids? There's a reason for that?" She slumped back against the pillows in defeat. In a quiet voice she said, "I didn't want kids before, so God decided to show me and take away my ability to have them at all."

"Girl, hush. God doesn't work like that. Maybe there's a beautiful baby out there that He wants you to adopt," Ida counseled. "Maybe He wanted you to get your marriage right first."

"Yeah, right. My marriage is over. Especially now that I can't have kids," Vanessa mumbled. "Not as bad as Thomas wants kids."

"Thomas has already told me that he doesn't care if you can't have kids. He wants to repair his marriage."

"What?" Vanessa said.

"That's right. And I'm going to get him so you can talk to him yourself."

Vanessa lay back, too tired to argue. If Thomas said it didn't matter whether or not she could have kids, he was lying. After all, all of the problems they'd had stemmed from the fact that they didn't have kids. There was no way she could believe he was okay with that now.

Vanessa tried to shift in her hospital bed, but the IV stopped her from turning over and getting comfortable. She was just about to complain when she noticed a white teddy bear with a halo over its head sitting on the stand next to her bed. It looked just like one she had bought for Shelly. Curious, she picked it up and pulled out the card in its lap.

She read the words out loud. " 'I miss the way you make me smile when you walk into the room. So get better fast so you can come see me soon. Hugs and kisses, Shelly.' "

Vanessa leaned back against her pillow, her spirit slightly lifting. Once again, Shelly had been the only one who could ease her pain. She didn't want Shelly to see her like this in a hospital bed, but when she got out, she was going to visit The Mason House as soon as she could.

Chapter 46

Dionne took a deep breath and rang Roland's doorbell. Yes, he had told her countless times that it was over. But she simply couldn't take no for an answer. Yes, Bruce was a good man, but her heart was still with Roland. And his heart was with her. She knew it. All she had to do was get him to forgive her.

After seeing what Vanessa had done with her marriage, she wanted Roland to take her in his arms and let her know they could weather this storm.

He opened the door and blinked at the sight of her. "What part of 'it's over' don't you get?"

"I left something over here," she said, pushing her way inside.

"You didn't leave nothing."

Dionne turned abruptly so they were facing each other chest to chest. "I want you to feel something." She took Roland's hand and put it on her stomach. He tried to pull it away but she held his hand firmly until he felt what she was trying to get him to feel.

"Don't be trying to use the baby to get—" He stopped and a smile crept onto his face. "Oh, my God! Did the baby just move?"

Dionne nodded. She knew he would be touched if he felt the baby move. Rosolyn had told her to drink some grape juice and that would get the baby moving. So she'd done that just before ringing Roland's doorbell.

"Dang. That's wild," he said in amazement. He looked up at her face and his eyes started watering. "Why'd you have to do this to me?"

"Roland, you will never understand how sorry I am. But you can't stand here and tell me that you will not be a part of our child's life."

He sat down heavily on the living room sofa. "Well, I can be a part of his life without being a part of yours."

"You're right. And I can't do anything but respect that. I just ask that you be a part of your baby's life," Dionne pleaded.

He cut his eyes at her. "You know I'm going to be there for my kid."

Dionne wanted to jump for joy but she kept her composure. "That's all I'm asking. I love you and I want you back, but if you can't do that, I understand."

Roland was just about to respond when they were interrupted by a pounding on the door. Dionne immediately had a flashback to Tasha.

She took a deep breath, praying that it wasn't her. She was making progress with Roland right now, and she wasn't about to let Tasha mess that up.

Roland started toward the door, but Dionne grabbed his arm. "Don't get it."

Roland snatched it away. "It's probably my neighbor. I'm parked in his parking spot because somebody was parked in mine."

Dionne didn't force the issue. She readied herself for a confrontation with Tasha.

"Yo, man, sorry about that," Roland said, opening the door.

Before he could get the door open all the way, two men both weighing well over three hundred pounds, burst in. "You 'bout to be sorry, all right." The first one in launched a ferocious punch to Roland's stomach.

"Yo, yo, man," Roland panted, falling to the floor.

The taller of the two, who was sucking on a red Twizzler and wearing a black leather coat even though it was seventy-five degrees outside, immediately shut the door. Dionne recognized the man as the same one who came to Roland's place that night.

Roland struggled to get off the floor. "Come on, Link," he croaked. "You don't wanna do this."

"Oh, I don't?"

Link nudged his friend with his shoulder and took the Twizzler from his mouth. "You hear that, Red? He said I don't wanna do this."

"Nah." Red laughed. "I think you do wanna do it."

"Get up, punk," Link said, kicking Roland viciously in the side.

Roland let out a groan as he buckled over in pain. Red walked around and grabbed him by the back of his collar, and hurled him like a rag doll across the room.

Dionne was frozen in place on the sofa. They hadn't acknowledged her presence and she sure as heck didn't want to bring any attention to herself.

"What's the rule?" Link said, angrily.

Roland just groaned. Red walked over and picked him up by his neck. "Tell the man the rule," he growled.

Roland coughed but couldn't answer.

Red flung him down on the love seat. Link walked over and stood in front of him. "You seem to have forgotten the rule," Red repeated.

"I think you need to refresh the rule," Link said, taking a bite from his Twizzler.

"I think I do." Red leaned down over Roland. "Say it with me. Keep Link's name out ya mouth."

Roland mumbled incoherently. Dionne jumped when Link suddenly reached back and slapped him across the face. "Say it with *me*, then. Keep Link's name out my mouth!"

Roland winced in pain, but managed to say, "K-keep Link's n-name out my mouth."

Link smiled, but only for a moment. "That's good." He scowled as Red came up beside him. "But, Houston, we still have a problem."

"A big problem," Red echoed.

Dionne trembled as she debated whether she should go to Roland or try to make a run for it.

"You knew the rules," Link continued, "but you broke the rules. And Mama says, he who breaks the rules pays the price." He pulled out a chrome automatic. Dionne let out a small scream.

Link finally acknowledged her—by turning and pointing the gun at her head. "I'm gon' need you to shut the hell up before I blast apart that pretty little head of yours."

Roland stood woozily. "Come on, Link. She ain't even in this."

Link turned his attention back to Roland and shook his head. "You know, I'm not understanding how all of a sudden the FBI, the IRS, and my baby mama is in my business. Your insurance company has filed suit against me for falsifying claims. The FBI is investigating me for fraud. The IRS wants their money, and my baby mama claims I haven't been giving her enough money since the cops told her about all my extra income."

"Link ain't having a good day," Red said, shaking his head.

"Really, I'm not. I'm pissed," Link said sternly. "Naw, I'm 'bout two blocks past pissed." He used the pistol to scratch his head as he stared at Roland. "Help me understand how I've been running my business for nine years with no problems. But one year of foolin' with you and my entire operation falls apart."

"M-man, I don't know what happened."

Dionne gasped as Link put the gun to Roland's temple. "I do. Somebody got to running their mouth and forgot the golden rule. How did my name come up in your divorce hearing?"

Dionne's eyes bulged in horror. She prayed that Roland's nosy elderly neighbor had heard the ruckus and had called the police.

Link continued, "See, the way I see it, if the FBI and everybody else ain't got nobody to snitch, they ain't got a case."

"Come on, Link. How long have you been knowing me, man? You know I ain't gon' tell nobody nothing," Roland said, begging.

"Then how did they find out about our business deals in the first place?"

"Man, I don't know. It must be my ex-wife. She must've hired somebody to follow me or something."

"Then that means you weren't handling yo' business. You sloppy, boy, and I don't do work with sloppy folks."

He screwed a silencer on the pistol. "I also don't leave no witnesses," he added, eyeing Dionne. He pointed the gun at her. "I think I'll do this pretty young Tyra Banks–lookin' thang first."

Roland jumped up. "No! Man, this is our beef. Please don't do this to her. She's pregnant!"

"Ooooooh," Link said, eyeing Dionne's stomach. "You know what? It seems like to me that I should do little Tyra over here and let you live with the guilt that your big mouth killed your gal and your kid."

Dionne was shaking so hard, she didn't know what to do.

"Yeah, that's what I'll do," Link said, aiming the gun at her head. Cowering, she began crying even harder.

Dionne couldn't believe her quest for revenge had brought them to this. She closed her eyes and began reciting the Lord's Prayer as Link slid a round into the chamber.

The next thing Dionne knew, she heard Roland cry, "Noooo!" She opened her eyes to see him dive on top of Link and tackle him to the floor.

The two of them began wrestling, muscular arms flying. The gun went skittering across the hardwood floor. Roland grabbed a lamp and smashed Link across the head. He took Dionne's hand and screamed, "Run!"

Dionne took off toward the front door. She had just swung it open when gunshots rang out. She spun around; Red had pulled his own gun and fired several times into Roland's back.

Dionne screamed in horror as Roland stiffened and toppled to the floor. When she looked up, she saw Red pointing the gun at her.

"Freeze!" Several cops appeared in the doorway. "Drop the gun! Now!"

Red hesitated, then cursed as he slowly lowered his gun.

As the two police officers headed toward him, Dionne dropped to Roland's side. She vaguely noticed the cops placing both Red and Link under arrest, and heard one of them say an ambulance was on its way, but after that she saw only the whites of Roland's eyes and the pool of blood spreading underneath him.

"Baby, baby!" she cried. "Hang on, help is on the way. I'm so sorry."

Roland struggled to breathe. "I'm s-sorry, too. D-don't feel bad. This isn't your fault."

The pool of blood was growing larger by the second. "Shhhh. Don't talk." She looked up at the cops. "Please help him," she begged.

"The paramedics are here now," the cop responded, motioning toward the two men running toward them.

"Please help him," Dionne frantically repeated as the paramedics immediately went to work on Roland.

"Tell my son I love him," Roland whispered, wincing in pain.

"Oh, so you just know it's a boy, huh?" Dionne tried to joke. She gently rubbed his face. "Well, I'm not gonna tell your son anything. You're gonna tell him," Dionne said, squeezing his hand tighter. "When you get better, we're gonna make everything right and you're gonna tell him."

Roland didn't respond as he closed his eyes. Dionne closed hers as well, saying a prayer that God would indeed make everything all right.

Chapter 47

Dionne couldn't stop crying. She was at Memorial Hermann Hospital inside a cold, antiseptic-smelling hospital room. Roland was barely holding on. He'd suffered two gunshot wounds to the back, and the doctors told her it wasn't looking good. He'd just returned from a grueling four-hour surgery and had yet to wake up.

"Roland, please wake up. We need you. I'm so sorry." Dionne gripped his hand tightly. She couldn't believe that this was happening to her. Roland was lying in a hospital, fighting for his life, all because of her.

"Come on, baby," Ida said, gently placing her hands on Dionne's shoulders. Dionne didn't even remember how she'd managed to call her family and tell them what had happened.

But somehow she must have gotten in touch with them in the ambulance ride over because Rosolyn and Ida had arrived just minutes after they wheeled Roland into surgery. Rosolyn had gone home about an hour ago, but Ida had been in the waiting room all evening. She'd been the one to call Roland's parents, who were returning from vacation in Florida.

"You've been here all night. You need to go home and get some rest," Ida gently said.

Dionne pulled away. "I'm not going anywhere." She was about to protest some more when the hospital door swung open.

"Oh, my God," a woman said, her hand going to her mouth.

She was a creamy caramel color, with brown, bone-straight hair hanging down past her shoulders. She was slender and dressed in expensive-looking clothes.

"Roland?" the woman said, racing to his bedside.

She paused when she noticed Dionne. "Who are you?" she asked accusingly.

"I'm Dionne. Who are you?" She was exhausted, and worried sick, so really, it didn't matter who the woman was.

"I'm Liz. Roland's *wife*." Liz's eyes made their way down to Dionne's protruding stomach. She raised her eyebrow and cocked her head.

Dionne closed her eyes and took a deep breath. *Please, Lord, not this. Not now,* she thought.

"Well, well, well. We finally meet. The trick who has my man's nose wide open."

Dionne couldn't deal with the wife from hell right now. "I just want to be here for Roland," Dionne said, pulling his hand up toward her heart. "Can we do this another time?"

Liz folded her arms. "You and all these other heifers Roland messed with think y'all slick."

Ida cleared her throat and stepped forward. "Miss, I really don't think this is the time or place for this."

Liz curled her lip. "Number one, who the hell are you? And number two, don't nobody care what you think." She clicked her teeth.

Ida stepped closer to her. She was clenching her Bible tighter and Dionne could see the little vein starting to protrude from her forehead. "I'm about to be your worst nightmare, little girl."

Dionne jumped up and grabbed her aunt's arm. "Aunt Ida, no."

Ida caught herself, then shook her head. "These young girls today done straight lost their minds. In my day and age, we would've never talked to our elders like that."

"Well, this ain't your day and age, old lady," Liz snapped.

Before Dionne could respond, Ida had swung and hit Liz upside the head with her Bible.

"Aunt Ida!" Dionne admonished.

"I don't know who she thinks she's talking to!"

"Owww!" Liz screamed. "Are you crazy?"

"I'm about two seconds from crazy!" Ida shouted.

The commotion caused the nurse to come running into the room. "What in the world is going on here?" she asked, a horrified expression on her face.

"That woman attacked me!" Liz yelled, rubbing the side of her head.

"No, I didn't, but I'm about to!" Ida said, leaning in to try and hit Liz again. Dionne once again jumped in between them.

"Stop it! Stop it right now!" the nurse exclaimed. "And what are all of you doing in here anyway? There is only supposed to be one visitor in here at a time. Two of you need to leave."

Liz crossed her arms defiantly across her chest. "I ain't going nowhere."

Dionne looked at the nurse in anticipation. "Neither am I. I mean, I've been here since he arrived."

"Well, all of you can't stay in here." The nurse shot them a stern look.

"I'm his wife, so if anybody should be in here, it's me." Liz grinned wickedly.

Dionne looked at her, astonished. "You're his wife in name only. You're getting a divorce."

"Getting. Not got. So I'm staying with my husband." Liz walked over and began stroking Roland's cheek.

"But . . ." Dionne looked to the nurse for assistance.

"But nothing. See ya," Liz said airily.

The nurse motioned toward the door. "I'm sorry. I'm going to have to ask the two of you to leave."

Dionne began crying. "No. That's the father of my child. I can't leave him."

Liz let out a snort. "So you say. A DNA test will have to prove that. In the meantime, it's a fact that I'm his wife, so I ain't goin' nowhere."

"Liz, please don't do this. I mean, I'm the one who gave you the information to help your divorce."

Liz snarled at her. "Thanks. Now beat it."

Ida gently grabbed Dionne's arm and led her to the door. "Come on, baby. Let's go wait in the lobby before they put us out the hospital altogether."

"But they can't stand each other. She's just doing this to be vindictive," Dionne cried. "Roland would want me here, not her!"

Liz smiled as she waved at Dionne. "Buh-bye."

Dionne sobbed uncontrollably as Ida led her into the waiting room.

Dionne couldn't believe she'd ever helped that woman. She'd let her quest for revenge blind her so badly that it had led to this—Roland laid up in a hospital, his estranged wife sitting vigil.

She'd give anything if she could just turn back the hands of time.

Chapter 48

Thomas swung the door open and helped Vanessa inside the house. She'd spent four days in the hospital and although she was nowhere near her usual self, she was feeling much better.

"I'm not an invalid," Vanessa complained, though not too hard.

Thomas smiled, but still didn't move his arm from her waist. "I know you're not. But I would feel much better if you'd just let me help you, how about that?"

Vanessa chuckled and eased down onto the sofa. Just as quickly as it came, the smile left her face. "Whatever, Thomas."

She still ached over the thought that she would never have children, but over the last few days she'd come to realize that Thomas had done the only thing possible. He didn't want to take a chance with her life, and the more she thought about it, the more she knew he was right. At the same time, she knew her inability to have children now ruined any chance they had of ever working things out.

Ever since he'd told her Alana's baby wasn't his, Vanessa had to admit, a small part of her wanted to believe that because of that, they might possibly stand a chance. But now, with this new situation, Vanessa didn't ever see them being able to work things out.

Thomas got Vanessa situated on the sofa, helping her remove her shoes and get comfortable. "Let me guess: you want it on TNT so you can see more reruns of *Law and Order*."

Vanessa smiled. "You know me so well."

He paused, his expression serious. "I do." He sat down next to her. "Which is why I know that we need to talk about what happened, I mean, with the surgery and all."

Vanessa took the remote from him and pushed the button to turn the TV on. "What's there to talk about?" Since going off on him in the hospital, she'd refused to speak about her feelings regarding the surgery.

She began taking the array of pills she'd been given out of her bag. There was a course of iron tablets, as the blood loss had left her anemic. There were also anti-inflammatory tablets and painkillers, which she knew she would use up. She also was going to have to have hormone replacement therapy to control the symptoms of menopause.

"For starters, let's talk about us," he said earnestly. "I don't want a divorce."

"Thomas, let's be real. You wanted a baby so bad that you were willing to destroy everything we had. Now you want me to believe that that just changed?"

"I still want a baby, but the part that you never got is I didn't just want a kid for the sake of having a kid. I wanted a family. I wanted a family with you. I *want* a family with you. Yes, I would love to have my own child. But if that's not God's will, then it's just not. There is some beautiful child out there just waiting for us so we can complete our family."

Her mind immediately turned to Shelly. As Aunt Ida would say, maybe this was God's will all along.

Vanessa didn't realize she was crying until he reached up and wiped her cheeks. She had been visualizing what it would be like to have Shelly in her life on a permanent basis, but she didn't see how she could do it alone. But to hear Thomas say he would like to adopt made her so happy.

"Vanessa, baby. I am sorry," Thomas continued. "The spiritual retreat helped me see that first and foremost, we need to take it back to God."

Vanessa looked at him. Maybe Aunt Ida was right. Since they'd gotten married, they'd rarely gone to church as a couple. "Thomas . . ." Vanessa didn't know what to say.

"I'm not kidding. I love you and I want this to work."

"Thomas, I'm tired," Vanessa said, her mind racing back to the reason they were heading for a divorce in the first place. She didn't want to get so caught up in the idea of adopting Shelly that she turned a blind eye to everything they'd gone through.

"Okay, I'm going to let you get some rest." He fluffed the pillow behind her back and helped her put her feet on the sofa.

The whole trip home and the conversation with Thomas was draining. Vanessa closed her eyes as she felt Thomas get up from the sofa. He returned a moment later with an afghan, which he threw over her. The last thing Vanessa remembered was Thomas leaning in and kissing her on the forehead and saying, "Sleep well, baby. I'll be right here when you wake up."

Vanessa fell asleep with visions of her, Shelly, and Thomas as one big happy family dancing in her head.

Chapter 49

Dionne pulled the black, wide-brimmed hat down farther to cover her face. She couldn't believe that she was having to go incognito to her boyfriend's funeral. But Liz had threatened to have her jumped if she showed her "big-bellied ass" at the funeral.

Even still, Dionne decided she was going to have to take her chances. There was no way she was not going to pay her last respects to the father of her unborn child. Both Bruce and Rosolyn had urged her to let them come with her, if she insisted on going. But Dionne had felt like this was something she needed to do on her own. Roland had died less than thirty minutes after Liz kicked her out of his hospital room. She was devastated that she hadn't been with him then. She had to be here now.

Dionne was seated in the next to the last pew. The pastor, Rev. Terrance Ellis, had just finished reading the obituary when Roland's mother let out a piercing scream.

"Noooooo! Lord, Jesus, noooo. Take me." She flung herself across her son's coffin.

Dionne caught Liz rolling her eyes in disgust as she took her place at the podium. She also had on a big black hat, but hers was complete with a veil. She wore dark sunglasses and an inappropriately short black suit.

Not only had Liz kicked her out of the hospital room, but she'd even tried to forgo formal services and simply have Roland cremated. Luckily, his mother wasn't even trying to hear that.

"My darling husband would be so honored to see all of you gathered here today," Liz told the congregation, a small smile crossing her face. "As many of you know, we had our issues. But we were working through them. We were on the path to rebuilding, so his death is simply devastating to me."

Dionne struggled to contain her anger. This skank was sitting up in church, lying like a dog.

"I don't understand God's will . . . but . . ." Liz covered her mouth as she struggled to keep from bursting out crying. Dionne felt like giving her a standing ovation, because the acting job she was giving was worthy of an Oscar. Her stomach turned as Liz continued to play the grieving widow role. Dionne had noticed Tasha, who also seemed truly broken up. At one point during the service, their eyes met and they seemed to bond through their pain.

As the minister wrapped up the eulogy, Dionne read the obituary again. "Roland leaves to mourn his devoted wife." There was no mention of her or their unborn child. Not that she expected anything, not with Liz behind the planning. But she felt that the woman should have some sympathy, knowing that she and Roland were divorcing and he had a child on the way. She didn't love him. She was just an evil, conniving woman.

Dionne stood as the pallbearers began wheeling Roland's body out. She felt her knees go weak and she wished she'd taken Rosolyn or Bruce up on their offer to come with her. But Dionne wanted to do this alone. She had to do it alone.

She held onto the bench in front of her to steady herself. The lady standing next to her must have sensed how difficult this was for her, because she gently patted Dionne's hand. "It's gonna be okay. He's in a better place," the woman said.

Dionne just glared at her through tear-filled eyes. Why did people say that? It's not like it made a grieving person feel any better. Yes, he was in a better place, but she wanted him here with her.

Dionne didn't know how she managed to walk past Roland for the final viewing, but the next thing she knew she was standing in the back at the cemetery, lost in her own world. Liz's shrill scream knocked her out of her daze.

"How dare you show your face here?" she shouted. "Isn't it bad enough that I had to deal with my husband's death? And now you have the audacity to show your face here!"

Liz was being held up by Roland's brother. Roland's mother was behind them and she quickly came to Liz's side. "Baby, what's going on?"

Liz pointed her finger at Dionne. "Her. That's the woman who broke up my marriage!"

Dionne's mouth fell open. Several people gasped as they turned to stare at her. Roland's mother looked at Dionne in disgust.

Liz sobbed and grabbed Roland's mother's arm. "Mother Lewis, she took him from me in life. Why can't she let me have him in death?"

Dionne continued to watch in disbelief as Liz sobbed.

"Please, please, someone get her out of here. I can't take it," she cried, turning to Roland's brother. "She robbed me of my final moments of joy. She's the reason Roland and I broke up, and she's the reason he's dead!"

Roland's mother stormed over to Dionne and wagged her finger in Dionne's face. "I don't know who you are, but you are obviously bringing more stress to my daughter-in-law. So I'm asking you to leave."

"But—"

"But nothing," his brother said, appearing next to his mother. "Leave. Now!"

Dionne's hands were trembling, but she couldn't move. Suddenly, she felt someone wrap an arm around her waist. She looked up to see Bruce by her side, his eyes full of concern.

"Come on, Dionne. Let me take you home," he said.

Dionne seemed in a daze. *Where had he come from?*

"I'm sorry, I couldn't let you go through this alone," he whispered.

Liz let out another loud sob, startling Dionne.

"Get her out of here!" Roland's brother snapped again.

Bruce nodded apologetically as he led Dionne out of the cemetery.

"Let me take you home. We'll come back and get your car later," he said, getting her settled in his van.

"Please, don't be mad," he said as he climbed in on the other side. "But I knew this would be painful for you, and I just couldn't let you go through this by yourself."

She didn't respond as she stared out the window through tear-filled eyes. She wasn't mad. In fact, she was grateful. She didn't know what she would've done if Bruce hadn't shown up at her side.

Chapter 50

Vanessa placed the phone in its cradle. Rosolyn had just finished filling her in on the fiasco at Roland's funeral.

"I can't believe she went to the funeral," Vanessa said to Thomas, who was sitting on the sofa massaging her feet. "Someone called Aunt Ida before Roland was in the ground good and said his family just outright acted a fool toward Dionne."

"I hate to hear that," Thomas replied. "Do you want to go over there?"

Vanessa thought about it. "Rosolyn said Aunt Ida is over there. Let me call." Thomas handed her the phone and Vanessa punched in her sister's number. Ida answered on the second ring.

"Hey, Auntie. How's Dionne?"

"She's a little shaken up, but she's fine. I knew I should've went and sat with her to make sure she didn't go to that funeral."

"I can't believe what they did. Do I need to come over there?"

"Naw, I'm about to leave myself." She lowered her voice. "Some strange-looking fella is over here. His name is Bruce. I tried to tell him I got her, but he gave me this look like he wasn't going nowhere. Almost made me tell him off, but it was something about him that I liked. He was doting on her and treating her like she needs to be treated. And when I saw him in her bedroom saying a prayer for her, well, you know . . ."

"You were ready to get her married off to him," Vanessa laughed.

Ida chuckled. "You know it. That's the kind of man she needs in her life," she declared before sighing wearily. "But don't worry, your sister is gonna be fine. What about you? How you feeling?"

"Better. I go back to work tomorrow. I'm ready to get out of the house."

Someone knocked at the door. "Auntie, let me call you back." Thomas removed her feet from his lap and went to the door.

"Hey, Rosolyn," Vanessa said as her sister walked in. "I didn't know you were so close."

"Yeah, I was just down the street when I called you. How are you?"

"I'm okay," Vanessa said. "Worried about Dionne."

"Well, Aunt Ida said she'll be fine." She glanced behind her. "Say, I have someone who wants to see you."

Vanessa's heart warmed when Shelly bounced in.

The girl's eyes lit up at the sight of Vanessa. She raced over and threw her arms around her neck. "Miss Vanessa, I've been so worried about you."

Vanessa hugged her tightly. The little girl felt so good in her arms. "Don't worry about me, baby. I just had a little medical scare, but I'm fine."

"You have to be careful," Rosolyn told Shelly, easing her back.

"She's fine," Vanessa said. She looked up at Thomas, who was watching them in admiration. "Thomas, this is Shelly, the little girl I was telling you about."

Thomas politely waved. "Hello, Shelly. You're every bit as pretty as my wife said you were."

Shelly blushed.

"I know you aren't really up for visitors," Rosolyn said. "But I swear, I thought I was going to have to commit this child if I didn't bring her to see you."

Vanessa squeezed Shelly's hand. "I'm glad you brought her." She turned to Shelly. "As you can see, I'm fine."

"Are you sure?" Shelly asked, her nose scrunching up. "I mean, I know you think I'm just a little kid, but I can handle it if it's some bad news."

Vanessa rubbed her cheek, wanting to wipe the too-sober look off her face. "There is no bad news. I just had some stomach troubles."

"My stomach hurts, too, sometimes, but I never have to go to the hospital," Shelly said.

"Let's hope it stays that way," Vanessa said.

Rosolyn turned to Thomas and extended her hand. "Brother-in-law, it's so wonderful to see you. Why don't you come in the kitchen with me so we can catch up. Shelly has something she wants to give Vanessa."

Thomas smiled again at his wife and Shelly before following Rosolyn into the kitchen.

"Ooooh, what do you have for me?" Vanessa asked as soon as they were gone.

"It's nothing major," Shelly shyly said. "Just a little something from me to you." She pulled out a folded piece of paper and began reciting a poem.

"That is wonderful. You are so talented," Vanessa said when she was done, pulling her into a bear hug. The hug felt so natural that Vanessa knew, without a shadow of a doubt, in her arms was where Shelly belonged.

Chapter 51

Vanessa slipped into her black Tahari suit jacket and grabbed her purse.

"Are you sure you need to be going back to work so soon?" Thomas asked.

Vanessa smiled. It actually felt good to have Thomas dote on her. As he had promised, he hadn't left her side. As much as she tried to act annoyed, she loved his determination to be there for her, especially considering the fact that she wasn't making things easy for him. Alana had been blowing up Thomas's phone, but after he'd changed his cell number they hadn't had any more trouble from her. Luckily, she didn't have their home address—at least Vanessa didn't think so. Thomas had been parking in the garage just in case.

"Thomas, I'm fine. And it's not so soon. My leave is up. Plus, I took two extra weeks medical leave—ten weeks is plenty of time."

"I'm not talking about your leave. I'm talking about your health," he said with such concern that it made Vanessa smile.

"I told you to stop babying me. It's been two weeks and I feel fine." She did. At least physically. In fact, she felt better than ever. She still was a little sore first thing in the morning, but for the most part, her cramping was gone. The pain in her heart about not being able to have children was still there, but she was working through it.

"Okay, but I still don't think it's a good idea," Thomas said.

"Duly noted." Vanessa paused, remembering how she always quickly disregarded his feelings. They hadn't officially decided they were going to work things out—they'd just fallen back into a natural rhythm. "But really, I'm going to be fine," she reassured him. "I need to get back to work. You've gone back."

"I know, but . . . I mean, I'm working from here. So I can keep an eye on you. But . . . fine." He released a defeated sigh before leaning in to kiss her on the cheek. "Promise me you'll call me if you have any problems."

"Done," she replied, heading to the door.

Vanessa couldn't help but smile as she made her way to the courthouse. She would've never thought that she and Thomas would be back together. Over the past two weeks she'd remembered why she fell in love with him in the first place. He'd made it a point that they pray every single day. And she'd actually taken up some of the pointers she'd learned in the retreat, including trying to be more positive and keeping God at the center of their relationship. Vanessa felt better than she had about them in a long time. Ida knew Thomas was there taking care of her, but Vanessa hadn't told anyone that she was considering giving her marriage another try because even though her heart wanted to, her head wasn't sure it was the right thing to do. She had agreed to let Thomas ask Judge Jarrett to put the divorce on hold until they figured out what they were going to do.

Vanessa pulled into her reserved parking spot in the back of the courthouse and made her way inside. Despite what she'd told Thomas, she was still a bit sore, so she moved gingerly.

"Good morning, Judge Colton-Kirk," the cheery sheriff's deputy greeted her. "Glad to see you back."

"Good morning, Clarence. Glad to be back," Vanessa responded, for once not worried what anyone was thinking or saying about her.

She walked down the long hallway to the elevator to take her to her third-floor courtroom. She had just pushed the Up button when she spotted Alana.

"So, I guess you think you've won?" Alana sneered, slowly marching toward her. She definitely no longer looked like a model. Dressed in a long khaki trench coat, some sweatpants, and Timberland boots, she looked like a crazy woman.

"Alana." Vanessa stepped back, looking around nervously. No one else was in sight.

"In the flesh," Alana said snidely. She had a wild look in her eyes and it sent Vanessa's heart racing. "You killed my parents and now you're trying to steal my man!"

"Alana, I don't know what you're talking about," Vanessa said, slowly moving backward. She had to get back to the main lobby, to Clarence.

Alana slammed her hand against the wall. "Don't play dumb! I know Thomas is staying at your house!"

Vanessa tried to reason with her. "You're the one who lied to Thomas about the baby."

"So?" she screamed. "He wanted it to be his kid. He would've accepted Thomasina as his if you hadn't been around."

"Alana," Vanessa pointed out, "you don't even want him. You just took him to hurt me, remember?"

"I did love him!" she spat. "No, I didn't at first, but I fell in love with him and he loved me! We had plans to be together and you ruined that!"

"You're delusional," Vanessa said. "I had nothing to do with Thomas leaving you."

Alana stepped forward and pushed Vanessa so hard that she fell against the wall. She was already sore, so pain shot through her body. "I'll show you delusional!" Alana yelled.

Despite how much she was hurting, Vanessa's first instinct was to fight; but Alana pounced before she could get her bearings. Vanessa screamed and was thankful when she saw Clarence come running toward her, shouting, "Judge Colton-Kirk!"

"Help! Get her off me!"

Alana had a handful of Vanessa's hair and was trying to pound her head into the floor. "I hate you! I hate you!" Alana screamed as she pulled at Vanessa's hair. "You've ruined my life!"

Clarence jumped behind Alana and pulled her off. "Whoa, little lady. Calm down!" he said, pinning her arms behind her.

Alana's eyes were red with rage. "I'm going to kill you!" she said, kicking at Vanessa.

Three other sheriff's deputies had arrived on the scene. Two were struggling to help Clarence contain Alana while the other helped Vanessa up off the floor.

"I won't rest until you're dead!" Alana spat.

Clarence had his cuffs out. "Ma'am, stop fighting me. You're not going anywhere!"

"Let me go!" Alana screamed. "I want to make her pay!"

"Are you okay, Judge?" a female deputy asked.

Vanessa brushed her hair down, feeling her heart fluttering madly. Her whole body ached but her pelvic area, in particular, was throbbing. "I'm okay."

"She won't be when I get finished with her!" Alana shouted.

"Get her out of here!" Clarence admonished, pushing Alana toward the female deputy. He stepped toward Vanessa. "Are you sure you're okay? I can call for an ambulance."

"No," Vanessa said, though she was still shaken up. She had regained her feet and was leaning on the wall. She was about to say something to Clarence when Judge Vernon Jarrett appeared.

He stopped dead at Vanessa's disheveled appearance and the commotion as the officers led a still-shouting Alana away. "Wh-what's going on?"

"Judge Colton-Kirk was attacked by that woman," Clarence said.

Vanessa slipped her foot back in her pump and picked up her purse. "Hi, Vernon. It's a long story. If you don't mind, I'll call you and tell you all about it. And if it's okay with you, I'm going to take a couple more weeks of leave. I-I'm not ready to come back to work."

More than anything, Vanessa wanted to get back home, surprisingly, to the comfort of Thomas's arms.

"No, of course. You take however long you need," he said, looking at Clarence for answers. The uniformed officer shrugged as if to say he didn't really know what was going on either. "I'll let Robert know," Judge Jarrett assured her, since Judge Malveaux was the one in charge of Vanessa's disciplinary action.

"Thank you." Vanessa turned to Clarence. "And thank you. That woman's name is Alana Irving. She's obviously a very disturbed person and if you hadn't come when you did, there's no telling what she would've done."

"No problem, Judge," Clarence replied warmly. "Do you need some help out?"

Vanessa was touched by his concern. "No, I just want to get home." She looked at Judge Jarrett, gratitude filling her eyes. "Home to my husband."

Judge Jarrett's eyes lit up, and although he didn't say a word, Vanessa could see the happiness written all over his face.

"God is good," she heard him mumble as she slowly made her way out of the courthouse.

Chapter 52

Dionne leaned against the brick wall, the small photo clutched in her hand. She took a deep breath and once again looked at the picture of her baby. The 3D ultrasound image was so clear. She smiled to herself. Roland had been right. They were having a boy. She stroked his picture. Her baby was sucking his thumb as he pulled his knees up to his chest.

This was the first time she'd gotten an up close and personal picture of her baby and it warmed her heart.

"Hey, are you all right?" Rosolyn's voice snapped her out of her thoughts.

Dionne stood up, hiding the picture in her hand. "I'm all right."

"You got done early," Rosolyn said. "I just ran into Marshall's, thinking you'd be awhile."

"I know. They got me in and out."

"What's that?" Rosolyn motioned toward the photo.

Dionne took a deep breath and handed the picture to her sister. "Your nephew."

Rosolyn took the picture. "Awwwww. A boy! Look at his little toes." She fingered the photo. "Wow, this is amazing."

"It's a 3D ultrasound." Dionne grinned. "That's my baby."

Rosolyn smiled as she handed the picture back to her sister. "You do know you're going to make a good mother?"

"You think so?" Dionne replied hesitantly.

"I do."

Dionne put the picture in her purse. "I just wish Roland was here to help me."

Rosolyn draped her arm through her sister's. "I know you do. But everything happens for a reason. God has given you a little boy, and you owe it to that little boy to be the best mom that you can be."

Dionne took a deep breath as they walked toward Rosolyn's car. She knew her sister was right. She'd been in a serious depression for the past two weeks. She couldn't stop blaming herself for causing Roland's death. Melanie and Trina had been by her house every day, trying to get her to snap out of it. Between them and Vanessa, Rosolyn, and Aunt Ida, Dionne had been ready to go into seclusion. The only reason she'd come out today was because she was scheduled for her 3D ultrasound.

Both Link and Red had been charged with murder and were jailed with no bond. But that was little consolation for Dionne. They could rot in jail for eternity and it still wouldn't bring Roland back.

"So, have you given any thought to what we were talking about on the way here?" Rosolyn asked once they were in the car and pulling out of the parking lot.

Dionne stared out the window. On the way to her doctor's appointment, Rosolyn had tried to convince her that she needed to tell Roland's mother about the baby. Dionne didn't think she was ready for that, especially not after the way Mrs. Lewis had acted toward her at the funeral. The other part of her didn't want to share this baby because it was all she had left of Roland. "I know I'm going to have to tell her eventually."

"Right, because she deserves to know; and didn't you say she didn't have any grandkids? She may see this as a blessing."

"I know." Dionne eased the photo out of her purse again and glanced down at it. "I'm just not ready right now. I'll do it before the baby is born, okay?"

"Well, I'm going to get with Melanie so we can plan your shower," Rosolyn said, changing the subject. "Anything in particular you want?"

Dionne shrugged, grateful her sister let the issue drop. "It doesn't matter." At least, that was the way she felt before seeing her baby's picture. Now she felt a glimmer of excitement about preparing for her son. So far she hadn't bought so much as a bib, but the thought of filling her home with baby stuff was bringing on a happiness she hadn't felt in weeks.

"I want you to know I'm praying for you."

Dionne forced a smile. "Thanks, sis."

"I know you're not strong enough to pray for yourself right now, but it's coming. You need to forgive yourself and focus on that little one." Rosolyn reached over and squeezed her hand. "It really is going to be okay, Dionne."

Dionne felt a peace engulf her as she rubbed her stomach. It felt as if Roland was telling her that he forgave her. She shook off the eerie feeling and squeezed her sister's hand back and flashed a genuine smile. "You know what, Big Sis? I finally believe that." She jumped at the vibrating feeling coming from her hip.

"What's wrong?" Rosolyn asked.

Dionne laughed. "Oh, it's my cell phone. It was going off," she said, removing the phone from the clip on her waist. "I guarantee you this isn't anyone but Bruce. He's been a godsend since the funeral. He wanted to come with me to the doctor today, but I just don't want him to feel obligated to do stuff for me."

Rosolyn was about to respond when Dionne held up her hand, cutting her off. "Hey, Bruce," she said, answering her phone.

"So is it a boy?" he excitedly asked. *You would've thought this was his child*, she thought.

"It is," she said with a smile.

"I knew it!" he exclaimed. "Now, you go home and put your feet up. I'm going to bring you a celebratory dinner." He hesitated when she didn't respond. "I mean, if you'd like. I don't want to be pushy."

"You're not being pushy," Dionne finally responded. "It's just that you're a really good friend, Bruce."

His voice dropped an octave. "Give me the chance and I

could be a whole lot more. To you and the baby," he softly added. "Just think about it. I know it's too soon for you to be thinking about getting involved with another man, but just let me be there for you and the baby. No pressure, just as your friend."

Dionne glanced over at her sister, who was straining hard to hear their conversation. She pushed her sister's shoulder and said, "You know what, Bruce, I'd like that. I'd like that very much."

Chapter 53

Vanessa was amazed at the peace that had overcome her. It was strange. Aunt Ida had a picture hanging in her living room that said, "No prayer, no peace. Know prayer. Know peace." Vanessa had never really comprehended that, until now.

They'd just finished hearing a wonderful sermon by the minister of Zion Hill Missionary Church, Rev. Lester Adams. Ida was friends with Lester's grandmother, who had invited them all out to church today. Today's sermon had actually been encouraging, with the exception of Shelly's constant squirming at her side. Vanessa and Thomas had begun the paperwork to make Shelly a permanent part of their lives. But they hadn't shared the news with the little girl. After all the disappointments she'd had in her life, they didn't want to risk anything happening.

Rosolyn had all but assured them that there wouldn't be any problems, but still Vanessa didn't want to take any chances.

"Well, well, well. If this isn't a sight for sore eyes."

Vanessa smiled at her aunt, who had caught the three of them as they made their way out the church doors.

"Somebody slap me and tell me I'm not dreaming," Ida said with a wicked grin.

"Hello, Aunt Ida." Vanessa realized she was holding Thomas's hand and she immediately dropped it.

Ida crossed her arms across her chest and chuckled. "You don't have to act like you weren't holding this boy's hand. Besides, I know he done moved back in, so I know y'all doing a lot more than holding hands."

"Auntie!" Vanessa exclaimed, covering Shelly's ears.

"And you must be Shelly?" Ida said, leaning down toward the little girl. "I've heard so much about you."

"Hello," Shelly shyly responded.

Ida reached in her purse and pulled out a dollar. "Why don't you run over to that ice cream truck and get some ice cream?" she said, pointing to the white truck parked in front of the church.

Shelly looked to Vanessa for permission. "Go ahead," Vanessa said.

"Thank you, ma'am," Shelly said, grabbing the dollar and sprinting to the truck.

They watched Shelly approach the truck before Thomas stepped over and kissed Ida on the cheek. "How are you doing, Aunt Ida?"

"I'm doing just fine," she replied. "I see you're doing fine, too."

He laughed as he looked at Vanessa. "I'm definitely blessed."

"Aunt Ida . . . this . . . this isn't what it seems," Vanessa stammered. She didn't want any pressure from her aunt.

"It seems like to me what it ought to seem like. What God meant for it to be like. It's what he meant when he talked about for better or for worse."

Vanessa rolled her eyes, knowing a lecture was coming on.

"It's what God wants you to focus on when you're sitting up there in that divorce court dismantling the bonds of marriage," she continued.

"Okay, here we go with this," Vanessa mumbled.

"I'm gonna say my piece. The Bible says that God's plan is that marriage be a lifetime commitment. So they are no longer two but one. Therefore what God has joined together, let man not separate." She wagged her finger as she preached. "The Bible makes it abundantly clear that God hates divorce and that reconciliation and forgiveness should be the marks of a believer's life."

Vanessa groaned. She was not in the mood for another sermon, especially one that had her feeling like she was the biggest heathen this side of the Mississippi.

"Now, that's not to say that if your man does stuff he ain't got no business doing, you can't cut him," Ida continued, looking over her glasses at Thomas.

"Ummmm, where does it say that in the Bible?" he playfully asked.

"That's in the revised King Solomon International New Beginnings version. I don't think it's on the market yet." She winked.

"Oh, okay." Thomas laughed. "If Vanessa gives me another chance, she won't ever have to worry about utilizing that verse." He saw Shelly standing back as other kids pushed their way in front of her at the ice cream truck. "Let me go help her or they'll run all over her."

Ida watched Thomas walk away before turning back toward her niece. "I'm real proud of you, Vanessa. Marriage ain't easy, but at the end of the day, you got to take care of your man. What Thomas did wasn't right, and biblically speaking he did commit adultery, so you got every right to walk out that door. But just because you *can* doesn't mean you *should*. Sometimes a man, or a woman, is worth forgiving. And besides, I just want you to remember the burden that you bear in this."

"Oh, here we go. You're saying I'm responsible?"

"I'm not saying you're responsible. But I want you to just recognize the role that you played. The devil is always hard at work. He is sitting in hell in his oversize recliner, feet kicked up, got a forty ounce in one hand and a cigarette in the other, just laughing. Laughing at all the destruction he's causing, because he's destroying God's work."

Vanessa couldn't help but smile. Her aunt always was dramatic. But she did have a point.

"You almost let the devil win, but I'm here to tell you, the devil is a lie!" Ida paused as they watched Dionne and Bruce walk toward them. "Your sister almost let the devil destroy her, but God gave her something precious worth fighting for," Ida continued, lowering her voice.

"Hey, Auntie, why you out here getting all worked up?" Dionne asked.

"I'm just trying to tell your sister the Word. I was telling her how happy I am to see her give her marriage another chance." Her eyes made their way down to Bruce's hand, which was resting gently in the small of Dionne's back. "'Bout as happy as I am to see this here."

"Oh, no," Dionne protested. "Bruce and I are just good friends."

Ida fanned her away. "Go tell that nonsense to someone else," she said. "That ain't no friendship I see in that boy's eyes."

"Hello, Miss Ida," Bruce said, his cheeks turning red.

Ida nodded in satisfaction. "Mmmm-hmmm, I got your friends," she mumbled to Dionne.

Dionne shook her head as she took Bruce's hand and led him away.

"'Bye, Auntie. 'Bye, Vanessa. I'll be by later for dinner. I'm bringing Bruce."

Bruce waved as he followed Dionne off.

Ida tucked her Bible under her arm. "Hmph. I ain't never seen her at church with Roland. That dog ain't never made it to Sunday dinner."

"Aunt Ida, can you not speak bad about the dead?"

"He was still a dog, God rest his soul. But that Bruce, I like him. He's gonna make a good baby's daddy."

"I really do think they are just friends," Vanessa reiterated.

"Every relationship works best if the couple is friends first." Ida stared after them. "Dionne better not let that boy get away. He's a little funny-looking, but he looks like he loves the Lord. And her."

"You got all that from two meetings, huh?" Vanessa asked.

"Yep, my third eye knows things," Ida replied. "Like the fact that your marriage is something worth fighting for. So you need to tell the devil that he can't have your marriage." Ida's expression turned vigilant. "What happened to the cuckoo bird?"

"Alana? She's in a psychiatric facility. Her family says she hasn't been right since her parents' deaths. They actually had been trying to get her some help. But after she left her job and moved, they lost contact with her."

"And that baby?"

"Thomasina is apparently with her real father. Alana's ex, who didn't even know she was pregnant."

"Mmmm-hmmm, well, I hope he changes that poor child's name. Don't no child deserve to bear that kind of cross all her life."

Vanessa hugged her aunt. "Thank you, Aunt Ida."

"For what, baby?"

"Believing when I didn't."

"Child, you ain't said nothing. I've been through too much not to believe that God can work anything out. Do you hear what I'm saying?" Ida continued, flashing a smile at Shelly as she came bouncing back toward them. "I'm a witness that you can weather any storm with God at the center of your relationship." She nodded toward Thomas. "You've got a second chance, girl. With your husband and with a child. Claim the love God meant for you to have."

Vanessa watched as Thomas made his way across the lawn and back over to them. She watched his stride, the way he smiled when he looked at her, and the love that was evident all over his face. Aunt Ida was right, she'd been given a second chance. And this time, she was determined not to mess it up.

Reading Group Guide for

Can I Get a Witness?

by ReShonda Tate Billingsley

Description

Can I Get a Witness? opens with Judge Vanessa Colton-Kirk presiding over yet another divorce in one of Houston's most notorious divorce courts. Vanessa is quick to end the couple's marriage, as she's done with countless others, but when she chooses to work late on the night of her five-year wedding anniversary, Vanessa's husband, Thomas, lets her know he's had enough. Thinking he's overreacting, she visits him at his hotel the next night and discovers him with his mistress, Alana. Thomas then drops the bombshell that Alana is pregnant and he's leaving to be with her.

Before the couple can divorce, their judge (and Vanessa's colleague, whom she's clashed with more than once) orders Vanessa and Thomas to attend a spiritual retreat together. In Vanessa's mind, time and counseling can do nothing to save this marriage. But when loneliness and bitterness attempt to get the best of her, she must look to God to find peace in her life.

Questions for Discussion

1. Discuss the role of forgiveness in the novel. How do Vanessa and Dionne deal with the rough times in their romantic relationships, when they must learn to forgive their men? How do Roland, Henry, and Thomas deal with forgiveness when the tables are turned?

2. In one of the many sermons Aunt Ida delivers to her girls, she tells Dionne that "a man's only gonna do what you allow him to do, and you allowed him to play you . . ." (26) How was Dionne "played" by Roland? Do you agree with Aunt Ida that she allowed this to happen? Why or why not?

3. Rosolyn takes a turn at preaching when she comments to Dionne, "I don't know why we women do that. . . . We get mad at our man cheating and want to jump the woman."

(91) Why do you think Dionne and Vanessa feel anger toward Tasha and Alana instead of directing it at their men? Do you think that Rosolyn's assessment holds true in the real world?

4. Discuss Aunt Ida's advice to Vanessa and Dionne. What does she mean when she tells Vanessa to "get right with God"? (168) Is she right when she says, "Seeking revenge only deepens the hole in your heart"? (106)

5. Do you agree with Aunt Ida that everything good happens in God's time? What does the book seem to say about this belief?

6. "Get to know Dionne. Fall in love with Dionne. Then maybe you won't have a problem getting someone else to love you as well." (85) Rosolyn gives this advice to Dionne. Do you think that Dionne follows it? If so, how?

7. Dionne's friends and family make it clear throughout the novel that they don't like Roland. Do you think they are justified in their dislike? Do you agree with Dionne that Roland really loved her, or do you agree with her friends and family that he didn't?

8. Was Dionne right to seek revenge using her knowledge of Roland's business dealings? Would you have done the same

thing in her shoes? How do you feel about the illegal actions Vanessa took to ensure the speedy finalization of her divorce?

9. Did your opinion of Rosolyn change after you learned the truth about her marriage? Did you gain or lose respect for Henry after his secret was revealed?

10. Throughout the book, Vanessa denies that she has contributed to the deterioration of her marriage. What do you think keeps her from acknowledging her role in the breakup? Has she realized her mistakes by the book's end or does she still hold Thomas accountable for their problems?

11. From the moment they meet, Vanessa is captivated by Shelly and the poems that the girl writes. What qualities about Shelly attract Vanessa to her?

12. Were you expecting the book to end like it did? Do you agree with Vanessa's and Thomas's final decisions? What do you think Dionne's future holds?

A Conversation with ReShonda Tate Billingsley

Aunt Ida and Rosolyn have very strong ideas about God and have no problems bestowing their advice on others. Are their characters based on anyone you have known in real life?

They are a combination of the matriarchs in my life—my mother, grandmother, and aunts, who could care less about "getting in somebody's business." If they think you're doing wrong, they'll call you on it and they don't hesitate to let you know you "ain't right with God." I also draw upon people like my best friend, Jaimi, who is quick to tell me, "Your blacks don't match" and "I know you're not going out of the house in that outfit!"

How much, if any, of Aunt Ida's advice do you follow in your day-to-day life?

Oh, wow. That's a hard one. I *try* to follow a lot of her advice, but I still struggle in my walk with God from time to time, so I know there are some things that need improvement in my own life. But I'm a work in progress . . . God ain't through with me yet.

Do you think that we should sympathize with and forgive Roland for cheating on Dionne?

Another hard one. I think people are so quick to judge, giving their opinion on what someone in that situation should do. But I think how you deal with a cheating mate is something you have to look at on an individual basis. I think that's a decision only you can make. One of my favorite lines from the book is in the chapter where the spiritual counselors tell Vanessa and Thomas that just because God says it's okay to divorce an adulterer doesn't mean you should. I think in this day and age, particularly, we are so quick to throw in the towel and sometimes God wants us to really look at the "for better or for worse" part. Now that I've gotten the "What would Jesus do?" answer out of the way . . . personally, I'd have to pray long and hard if I were in either Dionne's or Vanessa's position. I'm just not that understanding. Hey, I told you God is still working on me!

Have you ever dated a man who was like Roland, Henry, or Thomas?

I plead the Fifth.

How does Vanessa compare to main characters in your other books? Are there any personality traits that they share?

Vanessa reminds me of Raedella from *I Know I've Been Changed*. She's so busy pursuing her career, but at what cost? As with Raedella, it takes Vanessa awhile and a lot of heartache to realize her own shortcomings.

Vanessa has a difficult time balancing the demands of her career with her personal life. As a wife and mother of three with an extremely busy writing and touring schedule, what advice would you offer to Vanessa if you could?

Yes, following your dreams is important, but at the end of the day, there is nothing more important than family. No matter what dream you're chasing, you have to make time for your family.

Do you still teach writing?

Not formally, although I'd love to get back in the classroom. I do, however, mentor a lot of writers. I feel like I've been so blessed in my literary career and it's my responsibility to reach back and take someone else along for the ride.

You've commented on your MySpace blog that it upsets you when people criticize your books for not being Christian enough. What do you have to say to these critics?

It took me awhile to get to the point where I could say, "God is pleased and that's good enough for me." I've always been the type of person who wants to please everyone, but I've learned in this writing game that you're not going to please everyone. I write reality, which often includes some ugly truths. There are critics that say, "Well, so-and-so should've prayed really hard and been delivered from his homosexuality." Well, I know God is capable of anything, but in everyday life, you just don't see people being delivered from homosexuality. My writing reflects the world we live in and there are some who believe if you're writing Christian or inspirational fiction, you shouldn't address those ugly truths. But to me, God is pleased because my books are reaching saints and sinners, many of whom would not be inspired if they didn't see themselves in the pages.

You have an extremely strong fan base, which only continues to grow. You've also mentioned that meeting your readers is the best part about being a writer. How do your fans influence you and your writing? Do you ever draw inspiration for your books from them?

My fans make everything I do worthwhile. I absolutely love meeting readers. I love hearing people passionately discuss my characters to the point that I have to remind them: "These people aren't real!" I also love hearing what works and what doesn't work from readers. It helps make me a stronger writer. And I'm a people watcher. I can watch a person, their dress, their mannerisms, and so on, and create a character from there. My favorite thing to do is to go to Starbucks and write. I take in the ambience and get a lot of my character inspiration from people making their way in for a cup of coffee.

Your list of fiction titles just keeps growing. How did you manage to write eleven books in under three years? What's next?

When you love what you do, you do what you love. I absolutely love writing and so I make time for my passion. I have been blessed with a gift, and I love sharing it with the world and that's my motivation to keep churning out the books. As long as readers keep reading, this writer will keep writing! I'm really excited about my next book, which will be different from anything I've done in the past. It's about a woman who wins the lottery and just as she's about to collect her winnings, her estranged ex-husband shows up with the woman he left her for, to announce their divorce was never finalized and he wants his half of the winnings. I'm having so much fun writing this and I'm hoping the readers will enjoy it just as much. I am also excited about *Let the Church Say Amen* the movie! Which is in production now and coming to a theater near you soon!

Activities to Enhance Your Book Club

1. Log onto ReShonda Tate Billingsley's MySpace page, http://www.myspace.com/reshonda_tate_billingsley, where you can read her blog and find current articles about her. You may even be able to use MySpace to connect with one of the many book clubs across the nation that are also reading *Can I Get a Witness?*

2. In the spirit of Vanessa, Dionne, and Rosolyn, share a traumatic romantic experience from your past. You may be surprised with what you find out about your friends.

3. For your next book club selection, read a book by one of ReShonda Tate Billingsley's favorite authors: Jacquelin Thomas, Victoria Christopher Murray, Kimberla Lawson Roby, Jihad, or Eric Jerome Dickey. Or check out one of her favorite new and upcoming authors: Tiffany L. Warren, Latrese N. Carter, or Mikasenoja.